A New Crowning Begins

Dee Verhagen

MELBOURNE, VICTORIA

Dee Verhagen C/- Intertype
Unit 45, 125 Highbury Road
BURWOOD VIC 3125
www.intertype.com.au

Ordering Information:
Quantity sales. Special discounts are available on quantity purchases by corporations, associations, and others. For details, contact the "Special Sales Department" at the address above.

A New Crowning Begins/ Dee Verhagen. —1st ed.
ISBN 978-0-6450876-7-3

The only limits you have are the limits you believe

...WAYNE DYER

CHAPTER 1

"I can't believe how much fun we are having," said Rorien as the group headed to the top of the mountain.

"Well, I have had enough fun for todia. You lot can continue. I am heading to the chalet," said Elentari.

"Suit yourself. See you later," replied Rorien, kissing her before continuing with the males.

"Wait up, Elentari. I'm coming with you," said Jahan. "It's beginning to get cold out here."

"That roaring fire will have the chalet all toasty warm. Come on," said Elentari nodding her head to Jahan to follow.

The dia had been fun enough with tobogganing, snowball fights, snowmen and snow fort building. It was mid after high sun when Elentari entered the stone chalet with Jahan to drink hot chocolate. The warmth of the chalet hit them instantly as they entered, sending a shiver through Jahan's body. The smell of cedar wood mixed with pine from the wood fire and hot chocolate filled their senses. They found Princess Thea, Princess Torvi, Sarina and Awnrie warming themselves by one of the open fires in the large meeting room. The room walls were lined with wooden seats and hooks to hang jackets and the tables, chairs and couches to sit on filled the rest of the room. A being had placed mugs of hot chocolate and warm food on the large counter bench near the kitchen for every being to share.

"It is so cold out there. I don't know how any being can stand it," said Awnrie, pulling the blanket higher up her lap as she sat on the couch beside Sarina.

"It is not that bad. I've been quite warm all dia," answered Elentari taking a seat on the couch opposite them.

"It's alright for those who yield fire. You can keep warm. Us others are freezing," said Awnrie.

"You should stay close to Lorcan. He can keep you warm. Why do you think Fendton and Rorien stayed near me?" said Elentari taking a mug of hot chocolate from Jahan as he sat beside her. The rich fragrant smell of chocolate filled her nostrils and her mouth began to water.

"So, your fire was why those two kept so close," said Jahan nodding his head, "I wondered why they kept defending you from the snowballs."

"Just gave them a little heat, and they defended me. All's fair in love and war," grinned Elentari, taking a sip of her hot chocolate.

"Remind me to stay on your side next time there is any competition. Seems like you will do anything to win," said Jahan.

"Yes, I like to win," replied Elentari.

Suddenly there was a loud, rumbling sound, the roar echoing around the mountain peaks, getting louder and louder, so loud was the noise that no being would hear a thunderbolt over it. The sound was deafening to the ears. Vibrations rippled through the earth, causing the chalet to creak and crack as if it was about to split open. Through the door could be seen white power exploding into the air like blizzard clouds, as a white tsunami came quickly towards them, impacting before they could move.

The noise rushed down the mountain, becoming quiet, and the ground stopped shaking. Snow spilled out onto the floor inside the door. Groans from those who had fallen began to fill the silence, and beings began to move towards the snow, trying to make sense of it, unsure and confused.

"Avalanche!" some being yelled. Beings began to scream and panic set in as they raced to the door, trying to claw their way out.

Elentari had pulled on the oaths, trying to find her guards. They were all alive and near, but she was unable to pinpoint where they were. Rorien contacted her on their link.

'Help me, I can't move, I can't see. I have broken almost every bone in my body, and there is no light. It is cold, so cold, and I can't get out,

can't move. Help me, Elentari, help me quickly.' Rorien clung to their link

'I am coming as quick as I can. Hold on. I love you.' Elentari said as she clung to their link, holding him.

Elentari sprang into action.

"Calm down, every being, calm down. I am Princess Elentari, and this is Prince Jahan," Elentari said as she stood on a table and beings turned towards her. "Please move away from the door, except those with firepower. I need all Fire yielders to melt the snow."

Beings stepped towards the door and began to melt the snow.

"All those with water, come over here, those with air, over there. Every other being, to the rear please," said Elentari. She moved her arms in the direction for each to go. "We will work together to get every being free. Movement yielders, find your link now and get them back here and any others you see. Stay calm and listen to instruction. It will be alright."

'You too. Please be quick. I can hardly breathe,' said Rorien on their link.

'I will. Getting every being free first,' replied Elentari on their link.

Those with firepower quickly cleared the door and made a ramp out of the snow.

"Fire yielders use a movement yielder to find your link and then CAREFULLY move down the mountain. Use your fire to melt the snow. We have two Princes to find and many others," said Elentari.

Elentari grabbed a fire yielder who was more advanced than the others to take charge. "You are in charge until I find Lorcan. Take an earth yielder to create trenches for the water to flow down. We don't want a landslide to happen. Go," said Elentari.

The fire yielders moved out quickly.

"Air yielders, grab a movement yielder and find your link before CAREFULLY heading to the top of the mountain and gently move the snow far away. You," said Elentari grabbing an air yield," you are in charge to organise every air yielder, spread them out and shift the snow to as far away as possible. Can you do it?"

"Yes," answered the yielder.

Movement yielders were appearing with their links and others and handing them over to the healers.

"Air yielders go. Rescue your linked first and listen to him," said Elentari grabbing an air yielder.

The air yielders either vanished with a movement yielder or moved quickly through the door and out onto the snow, carefully making their way towards the mountain top.

"Water yielders, head straight out and move snow, take the lead from him," said Elentari grabbing a yielder.

"No, please let him be in charge," answered the yielder grabbing another yielder.

"Ok. Listen to this yielder. Now go. Any movement yielders, help them find their link and get them to safety," said Elentari.

'I am coming as quick as I can. Just organising rescue crews. I love you,' said Elentari on their link.

'And I you. Hurry and be careful. I am so cold. I can't feel my legs,' said Rorien on their link.

"Any Movement yielders, please spread yourselves out amongst each power and as yielders uncover beings, transport them back here. Healers find warm blankets and clothes, strip their wet clothes off and give them something dry. Keep the fire roaring and have lots of warm drinks on hand for them. Sarina is in charge," Elentari said as she pointed to Sarina. "Earth yielders, help the healers. I need someone to account for every being, keep track of who is here and who is missing?"

"I will do that," answered a being stepping towards Elentari.

"Good, shift yielders help. Sight yielders spread out and search for any noise, point out any life to the yielders. Where is Prince Jahan?" she asked as she scanned the room. Heads were shaking all around as eyes searched the room. "Great. It is bad enough we have two Princes trapped in the snow to find. Now we have three. Get to work. I shall be back after checking everything outside."

'I am coming. Hold on. I love you.' Elentari pulled on their link and vanished to find Rorien.

'Quickly, please, I can't hold out much longer. I am frozen and can't breathe,' said Rorien on their link.

Elentari was oblivious to those around her, oblivious to buried beings using their firepower, waterpower or earth power to free themselves. Elentari focused her mind on Rorien. Nothing else mattered. She kept moving, slowly following the link. Each time she moved, she sunk into the soft snow, unable to step forward. She was glad to yield movement instead of struggling through the snow, falling and scrambling to keep moving and not advancing very far.

'Hurry,' said Rorien on their link. His voice was getting weaker. It was so soft and slow, barely audible.

Their link began to pull her downwards. Elentari was above him. She began melting the snow using her firepower and digging furiously with her hands to get to Rorien. Tears were welling in her eyes as she fought the snow to find him.

'I'm here. I'm here,' Elentari kept repeating on their link, but she heard no response.

"Rorien, I'm here," Elentari began yelling at the snow as she dug harder, melting it, trying to find him. Still no response. She could see colour in the snow, giving her hope and kept going, digging and melting as quickly as she could.

"I can see you, Rorien. I can see you. Please answer me, oh, please answer," said Elentari as tears were streaming down her face. Their link was fragile, and she could hardly feel him anymore.

"No, no, no. Rorien, please speak to ME," said Elentari. She grabbed Rorien's exposed leg, and yielding heat began to warm him. She kept melting the snow around him. Still, there was no answer on their link.

"Please speak," Elentari said, her voice barely a whisper. She had melted all the snow around Rorien, and she had increased his body temperature, but he was still not moving. Wrapping her arms around him, she transported them to the chalet.

"SARINA!" Elentari yelled.

The room went silent and still. Sarina looked up and raced to her, taking Rorien from her arms.

"Go. Help find the Prince. I will take care of him. Help find others. Jasper is out with the water yielders. He was found quickly, just outside the door. Now go," demanded Sarina. Elentari obeyed, heading out to find Jasper.

The snowfield was humming with activity. The top of the mountain looked like a one-sided snow fight as a flurry of snow was being flung high and far away in the air. Water yielders were in the centre, launching snow sections across the mountain, a reasonable distance away from them. At the top were the air yielders causing a snowstorm to spread far across the mountain tops. The fire yielders were melting the snow further down the mountain, causing little rivers to flow. Sight yielders were standing around scouring at the snow, looking for any sign of life, and pointing yielders in the direction of life. Movement yielders were disappearing and reappearing, waiting for the next to be uncovered and take them to safety. Up and down the mountain, patches of exposed ground, you could see where yielders had removed the snow and freed trapped beings.

"All good, Jasper?" asked Elentari as she placed a hand on his arm.

"Yes, I have it under control. Did you find Rorien?" Jasper asked as he put his hand on hers.

"Yes, but he is not moving or speaking. Our link is fragile, almost gone," said Elentari. She hung her head, trying to hold back the flood gate of tears, as her hand dropped to her side.

"Have you checked on the other yielders? Did they find Jahan?" asked Jasper.

"Oh, no, Jahan," said Elentari as she lifted her head and looked to the chalet before disappearing.

"Has Prince Jahan been found?" Elentari asked the first being she saw in the chalet.

"No, Princess," the being answered as she shook her head.

"Does anyone know what power Prince Jahan yields?" yelled Elentari to the room as she stood on her tippy toes, craning her neck to look around the room.

"He yields air, and Prince Theonry yields sight." Came a voice from the rear of the room.

"Thanks," Elentari disappeared and reappeared where the fire yielders were.

"Is Prince Jahan here, and who is in charge?" Elentari asked, grabbing the nearest being.

"No, the Prince is not. The being in charge is over there," the being replied.

Elentari saw he was pointing to Lorcan and moved to him.

"Lorcan, you're ok. Got everything under control? Need Anything?" Elentari asked as she hugged him tightly.

"We're good. Everything is going accordingly," Lorcan said as he wrapped his arms around her. "Fendton is down helping direct water away. He was down here and found quickly. Where's Rorien and the Princes?"

"Rorien is at the chalet. He is extremely frail, and our link is fading fast. It's almost gone," said Elentari. Her head dropped on his shoulder as she began to sob.

"He will be fine. The Princes?" Lorcan asked, hoping Rorien would pull through.

"Jahan has gone missing," Elentari said, raising her head to look at Lorcan's face. "I'm looking for him to get him to safety. Theonry hasn't been found yet. Talk soon." She kissed his cheek and disappeared, reappearing with the air yielders.

"Is Prince Jahan here, and who is in charge?" Elentari asked the nearest being.

"Prince is over there," he replied, pointing to the Jahan who was talking with the being she put in charge. Relief filled her, and she moved to him.

"Prince Jahan, we need to get out of here," Elentari said, taking his arm. "We can't have you in danger." She turned to the one in charge. "Are you ok? Is there anything you need?"

"All good, just get him to safety," he replied, pointing his thumb at the Prince.

Elentari grabbed the Prince and disappeared, reappearing in the chalet. "Where is the one who is accounting for every being?" Elentari asked.

"I'm here, Princess," he said, making his way towards her as he raised his hand.

"Good. Work with Prince Jahan, and let's get every being down the mountain to the villade. Find them rooms if they haven't got one. It is going to get dark soon, and I want every being out of here. Start with groups who are all accounted for and have no being missing. Jahan, grab one of the movement beings and get them to gather half of the movement yielders to help evacuate every being. Any questions?" asked Elentari.

"What if they can't afford a room?" asked the one accounting.

"All rooms will be taken care of by me," replied Elentari.

"And me," said Jahan.

"Where are the princesses, Thea and Torvi?" asked Elentari, scanning the room.

"In the kitchen, taking care of drinks and food," said the one accounting.

"Good. Get to work evacuating every being, make sure you get every beings detail for me," said Elentari as she headed to Rorien.

"How are you doing? You look exhausted. Why don't you rest and let others take over? You can't wear yourself out," Elentari said to Sarina as she placed a hand on her shoulder.

"I am getting tired, but he needs healing," Sarina said, looking up at Elentari.

"Have you stopped the blood flow?" asked Elentari. Her eyes were scanning the room to see how many were injured.

"Yes, I'm working on his broken bones," Sarina said as she turned back to Rorien.

"Stop and go get some food. I will heal him while you go," said Elentari as she pushed Sarina's shoulder to move her on. "Keep organising the healers, rotate them around and give them a break. They need to have a break. Otherwise, we will end up stuck here longer."

"Ok, I will get food and start rotating every healer. Thanks," said Sarina as she stood and hugged Elentari before heading off.

'Rorien, come back to me. I need you. I need you beside me helping me to get through this. I love you,' she said on their link, kissing his lips. Their link was so weak, and she was still clinging to it, not wanting to let go. She gently lay her head on his heart, warming him more as he was feeling cold. Her hands wandered over his body, looking for broken bones and chose to mend his cracked ribs. She kept talking to him on their link, urging him to come back to her, until Sarina returned.

"Time for you to get back to organising. I will keep him safe," said Sarina as she gently nudged Elentari.

"Ok," replied Elentari, lifting her head from Rorien's chest. "Hopefully, they will find the Prince soon," she said as she rose and went to find Jahan and the being accounting for all.

"How many are missing?" Elentari asked Jahan as her eyes scanned the parchment in his hands.

"We have another thirteen to find, including the Prince," said the being accounting for all. "Plus, we have three who are unknown and asleep." He dropped his voice. "Those who are coming in now are not going to survive. Those found in the first few moments are the only ones who are ok. It is not looking good for the Prince."

"Thank you. It is what I feared," Elentari replied quietly before raising her voice to normal. "Have Sarina roster two healers to each of the unknown beings. Let's get them awake and accounted. Hopefully, they are together and haven't lost another."

"We've started evacuating whole groups and making sure they are looked after. The villade is helping and finding every being somewhere to stay. Food and drink are at the parestala for every being," said Jahan.

"Good. I will check progress and be back soon," said Elentari, disappearing to appear beside Lorcan.

"How are we doing? Are you making sure every being is taking a break if they need it?" asked Elentari.

"We are making our way through, and yes, we are breaking. Elentari, it is going to start getting dark soon. How much longer?" asked Lorcan.

"When the Prince is found, I will decide what to do. We still have thirteen to find," said Elentari.

"How is he?" asked Lorcan.

"Still extremely weak and not responding. Gotta go," Elentari said as she disappeared, not wanting to continue the conversation. She appeared beside Fendton, grabbing him and hugging him tightly.

"You ok? Everything going to plan?" asked Elentari.

"Yes," Fendton replied as he held her tight.

"How did you survive?" Elentari asked, leaning back to view Fendton's face while keeping her arms around him.

"I saw the snow coming and blocked myself in earth blocks, hoping the height would be enough. There were others down here who followed my lead and others who raced towards us. We had very little time and got out ok," said Fendton.

"Excellent. Rorien is extremely weak. He was struck hard and is just hanging on. His vital signs haven't changed, and many of his bones are broken. I am ok but have to keep going," Elentari said, breaking away from him and kissing his cheek before disappearing to the air yielders, avoiding the questions to come about Rorien.

"I've found him!" A voice further down the mountain yelled as Elentari appeared amongst the air yielders. Every being started running towards the voice.

"Stop, stay where you are!" yelled Elentari. "There are still thirteen others who need to be found. Keep searching. Updates will be coming soon, and advice on when we can stop. Until then, keep searching," said Elentari.

Yielders began to reform, and clearing continued as Elentari moved towards the voice. She could see a wide, deep hole in the snow. Prince Theonry was partially buried with his torso and left side exposed.

"Let me take him back. He needs to be with his family and secluded for the moment," said Elentari as she touched the Prince. He felt like ice. She yielded fire to remove the rest of the snow and warm Theonry, knowing it would not help, before transporting them both to the kitchen and away from every being but with his linked. She knew what was to come.

"Thea, they found him," said Elentari quietly as she lay Theonry on the kitchen floor. "But he is…"

Thea put her hand up and cut Elentari off.

"I know," said Thea, dropping her hand and walking towards the Prince. "We said our 'goodbyes' ages ago, and our link faded and snapped. I know he has been dead for a while," she said, kneeling beside him and stroking his face. "That is why I have been in here, away from every being. I can't face them." Tears were streaming down Thea's face as the emotions began to surface.

"You don't have to face them until you are ready. Torvi, can you call Jahan please." Torvi nodded, and within a few moments, Jahan entered the kitchen.

"Jahan, he has been found. We shall leave you three alone with him," Elentari said as she motioned to those in the kitchen to leave. "I will spread the news. Find me when you are ready, and we shall take you all home, all of you." Elentari touched Jahan's arm.

"It has only been a few mesiks since you and Rorien linked. I hope he pulls through," said Jahan as he put a hand on her back.

"Thanks," Elentari said and headed to the main hall dreading having to announce the news. She straightened herself up and stood up on a chair.

"Please can I have your attention…Quiet, please," shouted Elentari as she waved her hands to quieten every being. The room went silent. She dropped her hands as every eye was on her. "The Prince has been found. He did not survive and is no longer with us. We still have twelve others to find."

"Princess, only nine now," replied the being accounting for all.

"Thank you for the update. We have nine to find, and it is starting to get dark. We need a decision on whether to continue or not to continue. Any being we find will not be alive as they have been in the snow for too long. Is there any who wish to continue?" Elentari waited, watching the room and checking faces.

"It seems no one wants to continue. We shall stop looking and continue evacuating. I shall inform those outside of our decision. Please listen to instructions," said Elentari grabbing the being accounting for all. "He will guide you in evacuating. Be patient, and we will get you all out of here."

Elentari disappeared, heading straight for Lorcan, relaying the news and evacuation plan. Heads dropped, and feet began to shuffle back to the chalet. Sorrow filled their hearts at the loss of the Prince. She went to Fendton next, the air yielders, and finally to Jasper. Entering the chalet now proved difficult as she elbowed her way through the beings spilling out the door and headed for Rorien, with Jasper following close behind. Sarina was healing him, and his condition hadn't changed.

"Take a break, go with Jasper and get some food. Check on Jahan. He is in the kitchen with the Theonry and the Princess'. Fendton and Lorcan will be here soon. I will be fine," said Elentari.

Sarina nodded and headed with Jasper to the kitchen as Lorcan came into view.

"Hey, good job todia. I have chosen my guards well, stepping up and taking the lead. Well done." Elentari said as Lorcan put his arm around her shoulders.

"Thanks. How is he? Any change?" asked Lorcan.

"No, his bones are taking ages to heal. I don't know what else to do other than let him rest and hope." She sighed, trying hard not to cry but couldn't. Lorcan held her as she sobbed into his chest, her hands clinging to his shirt, holding him tightly. She felt Fendton behind her as he put his hand on her back, which straightened her up.

"I need to stay strong, strong for all here, and keep things moving. Both of you, help me to stay strong," Elentari whispered as she clasped their hands.

"We are here for you, always here," said Fendton as he kissed her cheek and wrapped his arms around her.

"Ok, brave face. Stay with him and talk to him. I will be back," said Elentari. She made her way through the crowd.

"How is it going?" Elentari asked the accounting one. It had only been just over an hori since the avalanche, yet it felt like horis.

"We are moving full groups first. Those who have had a loss are in the back room with their lost one. We will start with them once clear here. We should finish in two-three horis," replied the accounting one.

"Make sure you rest any yielders. Did you gather more yielders from the villade?" asked Elentari.

"Yes. They are mainly doing the evacuations as they are fresher," replied the accounting one.

"Good, keep it up. Yell if you need anything," said Elentari. She weaved her way through, checking on every being as she passed, thanking them for their help and patience, making her way back to Rorien. Sarina and Jasper were with Fendton and Lorcan, talking to each other and Rorien. Rorien still hadn't moved.

"Here, we got you some food and hot chocolate, I haven't seen you eat anything or rest, and here you are telling every being to stop. Time for you to stop," said Sarina holding out a mug of hot chocolate and a plate of fruit for her.

"Thanks, I need this. Next time we are in a major crisis, please make sure I am feed. My mind has been focused on others and not me. I am sure I will forget to eat. There were too many others to think of," Elentari said. She sipped her hot chocolate, her hand rubbing Rorien's leg and mending his bones.

"If I were back home, on Earth, he would have proper medical attention. Maybe, I can open a door and take him," said Elentari.

"What happens if it takes longer than seven dias to heal him?" asked Jasper, afraid she may be genuinely thinking of doing it.

"I know I can't take him back. There would be too many questions asked. No idea what would happen, but it's not going to happen. Now, any ideas on how to wake him up?" said Elentari.

No one spoke. Instead, they just stared at Rorien as if waiting for an answer to appear. They sat in silence, glad to be together and waiting for all to be evacuated.

"You should have gone to him first," said Fendton quietly, breaking the silence. He was slumped forward with his elbows on his knees and head in his hands.

"Don't you think I wanted to? Don't you realise I have responsibilities?" Elentari replied through gritted teeth, her eyes wide and mouth tight. "I certainly did not want to take charge and put every other first before him, but I had to. I am the Princess, future Queen of all the Lands and had to act as such," she glared at Fendton. "HE. IS. MY. LIFE," she said, trying not to shout at him.

"Princess, every being has been evacuated to the villade, only the dead, the Princes and Princess are here. Shall I have them transported back to their casa?" asked the male who was accounting for every being as he approached with Awnrie.

"You have the details of every being?" asked Elentari.

"Yes," he said, handing her parchments listing all the details, including where they were staying. Elentari took them and scanned them.

"Perfect. Well done. You have shown great skill during this crisis. What is it you do?" Elentari asked, looking up at him.

"I am in the Kings army," he replied, straightening up and standing tall.

"If you were not part of his army, I would be recruiting you. You have the attributes of a General, able to step up and take the lead without too much direction. You have completed your task perfectly. Please organise the Princes and Princess' to be taken home and head home yourself. Relax and take time for yourself. Thank-you," said Elentari.

"Thank you, Princess. It is most kind of you. I hope Prince Rorien is ok and wakes soon," he said, bowing and left.

"Princess? It is time to go," said a movement yielder with two others beside her.

"I didn't want to move him yet, but I guess we have too. Awnrie, take Lorcan and organise our room for him. Yielders, take them first and come back for us, please," replied Elentari.

The yielders vanished with the others, and Elentari sat alone with Rorien, speaking to him, begging him to come back to her as tears fell. A hand touched her shoulder, and she jolted, spinning around to see who it was.

"Princess, it just you two left. We need to go," said a male yielder quietly.

"Yes. Ok. Take him, and please be gentle," Elentari said, kissing Rorien's lips. "I shall meet you in our rooms."

Elentari departed and reappeared in their room. Sarina was making their bed, checking everything was ready for Rorien as the yielder appeared with him and placed him carefully on the bed.

"Princess, is there anything else I can do?" the yielder asked, bowing.

"You have helped enough. Thank you, you may go. Be with your family," Elentari said.

"Jasper and Fendton have gone to find food and drink. We thought Rorien would need something when he wakes," said Sarina. "Lorcan and Awnrie are finding more bedding for us to take turns staying here with you."

"Thanks, you are all so amazing. I'm not sure I could do this without you all," Elentari said as she began to fuss over Rorien, making him comfortable and warm and softly talking to him. When Elentari was satisfied, she sat on the bed, rubbing his feet, keeping them warm with her fire as Sarina continued to heal him, strengthening his bones.

Lorcan and Awnrie returned with more pillows and blankets as Jasper and Fendton returned with food. They spent the evening quietly watching and waiting for him to wake until Elentari yawned. Sarina shuffled every being out before helping Elentari to the bed beside Rorien and taking the first shift. Sarina stayed with her until Jasper arrived for his shift, watching her struggle to sleep and taking brief moments to continue to heal Rorien.

"Rorien!" Elentari screamed, sitting upright in bed, shaking and sobbing.

"Elentari, it's ok. It was just a dream. He is still here," soothed Jasper, coming over to hold her. "He is safe with us, see?" Jasper sat on the bed, gently running his hand over her head.

"Jasper, it was horrible," Elentari said through tears as she hugged him.

"It was only a dream. Rorien is here with us. No need to relive it, see," said Jasper, his hand pointing beside her to Rorien, and Elentari turned to look at Rorien.

Elentari checked Rorien before laying back down and placing her hand on his heart, using her fire to warm him. "I love you. Stay with me," she whispered to him as she fell asleep. Elentari woke with a start and sat up. The room was dark, and she could see flame shadows dancing across the ceiling and saw Lorcan leaning against the fireplace, watching the fire.

"Hey," Elentari said, getting out of bed and heading to the fireplace.

"Hey, you ok?" Lorcan asked, concerned.

"Yes, just can't sleep properly. I'm afraid of hurting him," sighed Elentari standing beside Lorcan near the fire. "Any change?"

"Nothing other than more wood for the fire," Lorcan grinned, attempting to make her smile.

"I think, in the morning, I will get Awnrie to get the Master of heal and sight. Maybe they can do something. What do you think?" asked Elentari.

"Good idea. The Masters may know something we don't. Can you search his mind?" replied Lorcan.

"No, there is nothing there, just space. It is like he has moved on," said Elentari.

"He is still breathing, so he is still with us. He hasn't moved on," said Lorcan.

"Have you had some sleep?" asked Elentari.

"As much as you. I think we are all sleeping a little uneasy tonight. Go back to bed and be with him. Having you with him maybe what will help him awake," replied Lorcan.

Elentari nodded and climbed back into bed and again put her hand on Rorien's heart, giving him her warmth.

Elentari woke to quiet voices and sat up to see Fendton and Sarina huddled together discussing something. "Morning," Elentari said.

"Hey, we didn't want to wake you. Lorcan told Awnrie the plan, and she has gone home to get the masters. Jasper is finding some breakfast and tea for you. There is warm water by the fire to wash," said Sarina.

"Thanks, a wash sounds good, and tea sounds even better. Fendton, can you step out while I change?" asked Elentari.

Fendton nodded, heading out the door while Sarina helped Elentari change.

"I need to wear something to greet every being after breakfast, still have princess duties to perform. Hopefully, it won't take long." Elentari sighed.

"It must be hard to constantly be changing faces, Princess in public and friend behind doors," said Sarina.

"Yesterdia, it certainly was. The princess face trying to be strong when all I want to do was be with him. Most times, it is easy." Elentari sighed, shaking her head, her body language showing she was struggling to cope.

Sarina opened the door to allow Fendton in, followed by Jasper and Lorcan.

"Tea, I do need a cup of tea. Thanks, Jasper," Elentari said as she took a cup from the tray.

"Anything to help you. Hopefully, the masters will arrive soon and will have answers for you," Jasper said, putting the tray on the table, handing her some toast and jam.

They ate in silence, waiting for the Master's arrival. She drained her tea as the Master of air, sight, heal, and movement appeared with Awnrie.

"Princess," the Masters said, bowing.

"Masters. I assume Awnrie filled you in. His vitals have not changed since I found him. Please see what you can do. I shall leave you, as I do need to make my appearance in the hall," Elentari said, heading out the door with the others following her, leaving the masters behind to complete their work.

Elentari was in the hall speaking to those from the avalanche. Lorcan, Jasper and Fendton beside her. Elentari felt a snap and froze midsentence. All blood drained from her face, her eyes grew wide, and her mouth hung open.

"Rorien!" Elentari yelled before racing out of the room.

Elentari heard footsteps behind her, and she knew her friends were chasing after her. She didn't care. All she cared about was in their room, and he was no longer with them. Their link had snapped, and Rorien was gone.

CHAPTER 2

"I can't believe we are finally linked," said Rorien, kissing Elentari's shoulder as his hands gently rubbed her naked body. She rolled towards Rorien, encouraging him to explore her body and pleasure her as she explored him, enjoying her first morning as his linked.

"Good morning Prince. Yes, we are finally linked," Elentari said as they lay there waiting for their breath to ease.

"Prince?! That sounds weird," Rorien said.

"It's not like you didn't know it would happen. You knew once we were linked, you would-be Prince. Not like me, who met the King and discovered I was his daughter within a hori," said Elentari rolling over onto her arm.

"True. It still sounds weird," said Rorien turning his head to look at her.

"Get used to it, Prince. So, Prince, am I always going to be woken up that way?" Elentari asked with a smirk as she lay her head on the pillow.

"Is it not a good way to wake up? I enjoyed it," grinned Rorien stroking her hair.

"I was curious if this was going to be the norm. I can certainly get used to it," Elentari said as she reached up to kiss him.

"Then I shall continue to wake you this way," Rorien replied, kissing her and rolling partially onto her.

"As much as I would prefer to spend the dia in bed with you, we need to get organised. We have guests for the next few dias, and I believe we may have a trip to take very soon," she said as she gently shoved him off and got out of bed to head to the shower.

"What trip? It's our mesmoon, and we have nothing planned, for a whole mesik we have no duties. So, what trip?" Rorien asked, getting out of bed and leaning against the wall, watching her fill the shower with water.

"You can wait and find out later. It is not for me to say, and I am not completely sure yet," Elentari said, removing the stopper and stepping under the water.

"Am I always going to have to work out your riddles? Can you not just tell me?" Rorien's eyes were watching Elentari as she showered, enjoying the way the water trickled over her body, wanting to take her again.

"No, not always. You only have to work out the riddles which are not mine to say," replied Elentari. She loved her stone shower that she and Fendton had designed and enjoyed the water cascading down her body as it ran dry. "Guess you don't get to shower. I used all the water," she smirked as she grabbed her towel.

"So, this is how it's going to be? You use all the water on me. You know I can fill it myself?" Rorien said smugly.

"Yes, I know you can, but bucketing is so much harder than yielding," Elentari said, yielding water and filling the shower for him. "See easy." She smiled.

Rorien stepped in the shower, removed the stopper, and cold water hit him, "No fair," he yelled as he jumped out, replacing the stopper and glared at her. "Nasty! This the way it's going to be?"

Elentari laughed and yielded fire to heat the water for him. "It is warm now," she said as she walked into the closet to dress. "Enjoy."

Elentari and Rorien found most were up and sharing breakfast outside. Their linking dia was only yesterdia, and it had continued well into the night. The newly linked had continuously moved between parestalas, greeting and thanking every being. It felt like every being within the cuedel had hugged and congratulated them and asked them to dance. It was a long, enjoyable but tiresome dia, ending with them collapsing into bed well into the night.

"Good morning, Dear," said her mother as Elentari and Rorien approached. Her adopted parents were sitting, facing the sun with a cuppa in their hands, enjoying the visit to their daughter's native land.

"Elentari, Rorien, you're awake!" yelled Rewa, racing across the grass to hug them. "Mummy said you would be sleeping all dia."

Elentari reached down and lifted Rewa high into the air before hugging her tight. "Good morning, beautiful. You were such a big help yesterdia and behaved perfectly. Did you sleep well?"

"I did. Daddy carried me to bed. I fell asleep outside," replied Rewa squirming in Elentari's arms, reaching out for Rorien. He took her from Elentari.

"Morning, little sister," Rorien said, kissing her.

"Morning, big brother," Rewa said, wrapping her arms tight around Rorien's neck. He squeezed her back before putting her down, and she raced off to play.

Grabbing a plate of food, Elentari and Rorien joined the group, catching up on all the happenings of the dia and the night before, only Lorcan, Awnrie and Fendton were missing. Todia, they would be saying goodbye to the Kings and helping to clean up the parestalas. For now, she was glad to rest. Elentari finished her tea as she spotted Lorcan and Awnrie walking towards them, both beaming and looking ecstatic. She placed her cup on the table and headed to them, greeting them away from the group and out of ear reach.

"You've been for a quick trip this morning? Did it go well?" she asked, stopping in front of them and blocking their path.

"What do you mean?" asked a puzzled Lorcan displaying a wide grin.

"You know this," said Elentari as she placed her hand on his chest, touching the oath. "I know when you are not nearby, and this morning you were very far away. Plus, I know Awnrie yields movement."

"How did you know, and when did you know? We haven't said anything to you," said a shocked Awnrie

"When we left Rhunduin, you were not quite out of my sight when you disappeared, and I felt Lorcan far away. I guessed Awnrie yielded movement, and you just confirmed it. So, did it go well?" replied Elentari.

"Yes, it did," said Awnrie beaming.

"Sensational. Come inform us all of your news," said Elentari.

"Will I ever be able to keep anything from you?" sighed Lorcan shaking his head.

"Yes and no, depends on what it is. I've summoned Fendton," replied Elentari smiling. She summoned Fendton and grabbed herself another cup of tea. Sitting beside Rorien, Elentari watched as Lorcan and Awnrie said good morning to all.

'*What was that about?*' Rorien questioned on their link.

'*Patience, you will find out soon enough,*' replied Elentari on their link.

'*Has this something to do with a trip?*' asked Rorien on their link.

'*Wait and see,*' replied Elentari on their link.

'*You are infuriating at times,*' said Rorien on their link.

The group continued to enjoy the sun, chatting about the two worlds' differences and the linking dia. Elentari and Rorien sat watching them as the warm morning sun caressed their face. They sat talking to themselves on their link, watching their two worlds coming together as Fendton came rushing towards them, looking untidy and scruffy with his clothes dishevelled.

"You had a good night then?" winked Jasper at him, slapping him on the back.

"Think so, can't remember much. I woke up in the south parestala, no thanks to Elentari. What do you want?" Fendton grumbled as he slumped into a chair, trying to shade his eyes from the sun.

"It's breakfast time, and I wanted to make sure you were alive," replied Elentari.

"Since we're all here, there is something I would like to say," Lorcan said as he grabbed Awnrie around her waist, pulling her close to him. "We have set a linking dia, it will be in Rhunduin in two dias time, and you're all invited."

Cheers and congratulations erupted as Lorcan and Awnrie were smothered in hugs and handshakes.

'*How did you know?*' asked Rorien on their link, watching the scene unfold before them.

'I didn't know, but I knew Lorcan left the cuedel this morning for an hori and guessed. They confirmed when I approached them,' said Elentari.

"Dear, where is Rhunduin?" asked Beth.

"It is a town in the East, Mum, and takes about 5 hours to get there. We will head off on the morrow and will be back before the door appears for you," answered Elentari.

"How do we travel there?" asked Beth.

"Last time we went, we travelled by foot and took our time getting there. This time we will travel by camel with Roswen and Havid," said Elentari.

"How exciting, a trip to the country by camel," said Beth.

"We're doing what now?" asked Donna.

"Travelling by camel to Rhunduin, Dear," answered Beth.

"Awesome," replied Donna as she looked towards Elentari.

"Road trip," said both girls in unison, hands doing circles in the air before bursting into laughter and falling into each other.

"Hope you have music for the road trip," said Elentari untangling herself.

"On it," replied Donna, "how long's the trip?"

"About five hours. It has been a while since our last trip, and this will be our first in my new world, most exciting," said Elentari.

"First and last," groaned Donna. "I miss you and all the crazy things we do. How am I to find another like you?"

"This won't be your last adventure together. Donna can visit Elentari anytime and vice versa. The Master's found a way," said Rorien from his seat, watching the girl's excitement.

"You're telling me this is not the last time I can come here?" Donna asked, turning towards Rorien. Excitement showing in her words and on her face.

"Yes. You can visit any time," Rorien smiled, nodding his head.

"Awesome! More adventures we can have, and this is going to be so much easier to organise than back on Earth," said Donna giving Elentari a high five.

"Let's see how I go with organising my first adventure before we decide on any more. I may be hopeless at organising everything here. After all, I don't have the internet, travel agent or Google to help me, and you may decide this world is no good."

"I shall make my decision on the dia of the doors return. Until then, fetch me a drink," Donna answered smugly.

"Gofa, please get Donna a drink," said Elentari grinning at Fendton.

"Get it yourself," grumbled a seedy Fendton, half asleep.

"Guess you have to get it yourself, tables over there," said Elentari with a half-smile as she pointed towards the table.

After breakfast was complete, the group headed to the north parestala to clean up, losing Fendton as they passed by his door. The parestala was already busy with beings removing decorations, clearing tables, stacking chairs, and carting away plates and cups. The males helped take down decorations and cart off chairs, while the females helped clear tables and pick-up items that had fallen onto the ground. The group set off to the East parestala to help clean up and found it was clean, as were the other parestalas, and everything was back too normal. Elentari was amazed at how quickly her cuedel could come together and complete a job as she had expected to be cleaning and clearing all dia. It wasn't long before the other kings arrived to say goodbye.

It was nearing lunch when they returned to the north and decided to head to the royal hall to lunch with the King. After lunch, the King took Francis and Beth on a tour of the royal area while Roswen and Havid headed back to the casa for Rewa to nap. Lorcan and Awnrie headed off to Rhunduin with Jasper and Sarina to begin preparations for their dia. Simultaneously, Rorien, Elentari and Donna organised the trip East, which didn't take them long. With the camel train booked and convincing the fire and movement Masters to officiate Lorcan and Awnrie's linking dia, it left them plenty of time to catch up and relax before supper and an early night.

"When do we leave, and where are the camels?" asked her dad on the morning of their trip east.

"As soon as every being has finished breakfast, we will head off. The camels are at the stables on the east side and are ready for us," Elentari replied. "Do you need a small bag, Mum?"

"No, Dear, I have already packed. Do we need to take anything specific?" asked Beth.

"No, Mum. Just take your clothes and what you need personally. I will take care of the rest," answered Elentari.

Finishing breakfast, the group headed off to find the camels and begin the journey east. The Cameleer had the train ready for them when they arrived, with three Bactrian camels and three Dromedary camels were all lying down, ready to be mounted. The Cameleer tied the bags to the wooden poles on the saddles of the Dromedary camels. The saddles of colourful blankets, embroidered with either floral or animal motifs, sat over a grass-filled pad with stirrups hanging down one side. Tassels hung below the belly of the camel at the bottom of the blankets. Elentari's saddle was purple with vine of red roses weaving over it and red tassels. Two saddles sat on the Bactrian camels, one between the humps and the other behind, and a single saddle on the Dromedary camels sat on the camel's shoulder, forward of the hump.

"Please stand beside the saddle of your camel," said the Cameleer.

Havid, Rorien and Fendton stood beside the Dromedary camels while Francis and Beth, Roswin and Rewa and Elentari and Donna stood beside their Bactrian camels.

"Hold the handle and swing your leg over. Use the stirrup to help you mount. I will come past and check you are alright," said the Cameleer.

Each climbed into their saddle with the Cameleer helping Rewa on and harnessed her in for extra safety. He continued along the train, checking straps were tight, and all were seated before taking hold of the lead camel.

"The camels stand rear legs first, lean right back as far as you can in your saddle and keep hold of the handle. Move forward as the front legs stand," said the Cameleer, "ready?"

The Cameleer commanded the camels to stand and began to move out. It felt odd, leaning far back in the saddle, waiting for the camel to rise. Elentari felt like she was falling forward as his back legs stood and clung tighter to the handle. It was like she was about to slide forward out of the saddle and straight onto Donna, and it made sense why she had to lean back. As the camel began to move his front legs, she leaned forward to seat herself straight and ready for riding. The Cameleer moved the train slowly, allowing them all to get used to the camel's movement, before urging the lead camel into a run and racing at speed towards Rhunduin.

The movement of the camel's walk was odd, jerky and irregular, with its body swinging back and forth. At first, Elentari felt a little unstable but shifting her body, she found the right spot and relaxed, swaying with the camel's movement and enjoying the ride.

Rorien's camel was behind Francis and Beth's. As they slowed to a walk, he spent his time pointing out things to Francis and Beth, explaining his world to them. He explained how they farmed and their harvesting as they passed through farmland. Elentari had the Cameleer stop the train at one of the farms to enable every being to stretch their legs and give their backsides a rest. Elentari and Rorien greeted the farmers. Lunch was in a small villade café off the main path, where they changed camels, and the last stop before Rhunduin was near the clearing.

"Mum, Dad. We are going to go for a walk into the woods to a clearing to meet our friends. They are different from us and may seem threatening. They are not. Please be open to meeting them and their differences," said Elentari with pleading eyes.

"Yes, Love, we will be open. How different are they?" asked Francis.

"Very. We do not have this kind in our world. Duggit and Rhen are lovely, and we have enjoyed their company. Hoofington is terrifying in size, but he is harmless," relied Elentari. She turned to Rewa. "Peana is your age, and she is as much fun as you. You will like her."

"Does she like to skip?" asked Rewa skipping as she took Elentari's hand.

"Yes, she does, and she likes to run and jump too," said Elentari smiling as she led them towards the woods clearing, leaving the Cameleer to attend to the camels.

"Elentari!" screamed Peana as she came crashing through the woods towards them.

Elentari's parents, Roswen, Havid and Donna, all stopped still at the sight of a faun. Elentari continued to Peana.

"Peana, it is lovely to see you. Where is your mother?" asked Elentari, hugging her.

"She is coming. Who's that?" asked Peana, pointing to Rewa.

Rewa was hiding behind Elentari, feeling unsure and scared. Her face was peering out from behind Elentari and holding Elentari's skirt to her face to hide.

"This is Rewa. She is the same age as you. Rewa, come met Peana," said Elentari as she twisted around to move Rewa in front of her, bending down to her level.

"Hello, Rewa. Do you like to skip?" asked Peana.

"Yes, I do," answered Rewa quietly, her face partly hidden in Elentari's chest.

"Come skip with me," said Peana holding out her hand to Rewa and skipping in a circle.

Rewa slowly moved to glance at Elentari, making sure it was ok. Elentari nodded and stood up. Rewa hesitantly took Peana's hand, her eyes darting between Peana and Elentari. Peana took Rewa's hand and began to skip, pulling Rewa along. Rewa began to relax, and the two girls skipped off to play, smiles wide on their faces.

"Elentari, your back, and you've brought company," said Rhen as she came into view from the woods.

"Rhen, it is lovely to see you. Yes, we have extras," said Elentari hugging Rhen. "These are my other world parents, Francis and Beth and our friends from Rhunduin Havid and Roswen and my long-time friend Donna."

General pleasantries were exchanged, but every being kept their distance. Havid and Roswen were standoffish and uncertain, and her parents were curious and cautious, yet unsure whether to approach or keep their distance.

"You're a faun? Are there many fauns here?" asked Donna, wide-eyed and excited, rushing over to Rhen.

"Yes, I am, and yes, there are many fauns here and in other lands," answered Rhen putting her hands out towards Donna in greeting.

"Where I come from, there are no fauns. It is amazing to meet you," said Donna taking Rhen's hands in hers.

"It is wonderful to meet you all. Hoofington is on his way, as are others. They want to wish you well after hearing your news that you and Rorien are linked. We celebrated here in song and dance for you. It was a wonderful night." Rhen's eyes darted around the group, looking at each of them. She sensed the others were unsure and stayed with Elentari and Donna.

"We missed the celebrations?" asked Rorien standing beside Francis and Beth.

"Yes, we know we were unable to attend and decided to celebrate our friends dia anyway," said Rhen, watching the group.

"Maybe we can have a delayed linking celebration together," said Elentari taking Rhen's hand.

"Yes, that would be most wonderful," said Rhen doing a little happy dance.

"What would be most wonderful?" boomed Hoofington as he stepped out from behind a tree. Elentari heard her parents take in a big breath and turned to them. Beth held tightly to Francis' arm, her knuckles white, fear dancing across their faces as they slowly edged backwards towards the path, keeping their eyes on Hoofington.

"It is ok, Mum, Dad. Hoofington is a friend. He won't hurt us," said Elentari in a soothing voice as Rorien stepped towards them to reassure them. "He is very frightening at first, but he is gentle and protects the fauns, keeping the peace within the woods. Hoofington," she said, turning back to him, "these are my parents from my other world." Elentari noticed Havid and Roswen had also backed away, and Fendton had stepped beside them, reassuring them it was ok.

'*Thank you for helping them,*' said Elentari to Rorien on their link.

"Hoofington, we were discussing having a delayed linking celebration with Elentari and Rorien here at a later date. Do you think we could do it?" begged Rhen with her hands clasped together in front of her chest.

'*That's what I'm here for,*' Rorien replied on their link.

"If all agree, then yes, we can. It is nice to meet the parents who raised Elentari," Hoofington turned and bowed to her parents.

"Th...the...thank...you," stammered Francis, his eyes wide watching Hoofington, unsure of what to do. Beth was clinging to him, not eager to move away from behind Francis, her frightened eyes on Elentari searching for reassurance.

Elentari moved part way towards her parents. "Mum, it is ok. He will not hurt me or those who are with me, if he does, it will mean war, and he is not willing to start a war. It is ok." Her demeanour was soft and inviting.

'*Can you help them while I stay with Hoofington,*' she asked on their link.

'*Yes, go,*' Rorien replied on their link.

Elentari saw Fendton with Havid and Roswen, helping them relax and explain what led them to become friends. Donna and Rhen were deep in conversation, discussing their worlds and getting to know each other, which was no surprise that Donna was calm and interested. They always opened up to the locals wherever they went, making it easier to understand their culture and get a little bit more information on hidden treasures only the locals knew. She took Hoofington's arm and led him to a log.

"Hoofington, sit with me," Elentari said as she sat down on a log at the edge of the woods still in sight, "My parents need to settle as they are most frightened of you as you are quite large and can look quite mean. We do not have minotaur's in our world." She patted the log beside her, "Come and sit quietly with me until they are ready. Watch and wait."

Hoofington nodded and sat quietly, observing them all. Fauns began appearing and talking to Donna and Elentari while cautiously watching the others. Peana and Rewa came rushing back with more little fauns in tow. Rewa grabbed her parents and began talking excitedly. Havid and Roswen started to relax and smile at Rewa's excitement. Rewa introduced them to the kids, and her parents couldn't help but laugh with the little fauns, enjoying their excitement and eventually moved over to meet Rhen. Rhen introduced them to the other fauns and finally to Hoofington.

Elentari's parents were still very unsure but made an effort to meet the fauns with Rorien supporting her mother. Fendton also stood by them to protect and shield them, offering his services as needed. Hoofington and Elentari sat silently together, answering any question directed to them, watching and waiting. When her mother removed her arm from Rorien, she called him, and he came and sat beside her.

"Hoofington, I have a question which has plagued me since we first met. You mentioned you fought for the fauns freedom. How old are you?" asked Elentari.

"I am actually in my 500's, and we live till the age of 1500. I am Hoofington the third. My great, great, add in a few more, grandfather Hoofington the second who fought for them. Saying it was me was trying to intimidate you and making you feel you couldn't take me on. Guess I was wrong. You weren't backing down," he smirked, turning his head to look at her.

"Try living with her. She always gets her way," said Rorien shaking his head. Elentari smiled and nudged him playfully.

"One question answered," Elentari said. She went silent, trying to find the right words to ask the next question.

"What is it that is on your mind?" asked Hoofington.

"About three and a half anoks ago, on the path from Rhunduin to the north, a couple who were heavily pregnant was attacked, the male killed and the female ended up dying from her wounds. Do you know about the incident?" Elentari asked quietly gently, placing a hand on Rorien's knee. He moved his hand over hers and laced his fingers between hers, and squeezed.

"Yes, that was very tragic. To this dia, I still feel sorrow and anger that I was too caught up in this fight not to do anything." Hoofington sighed and paused, his eyes staring out beyond the woods before continuing. "The sentinels saw and heard a cart coming along the path. A couple were pleading with the other being, but he kept hitting them, telling them to shut up. It was not normal, and the sentinels quickly spread the word to find safety. Fauns moved quickly and quietly into the woods and hid from sight, close to the minotaurs for safety. One sentinel kept watch, following them, waiting to see what they would do, and I met up with him. Eventually, the mean being had the male stop the cart and forced him off. The female was pleading to let her stay on the cart, he hit her, and she fell from the cart. Lucky the male caught her. The mean one threw a net at the male and threw bags at the female. They were begging for him to let them go, but the mean one just kept hitting, kicking and punching them. He was most horrible, and I could see the female was struggling with her pregnancy, maybe in labour. The mean one forced them to move into the woods to catch fauns. They begged and pleaded, not wanting to help him, but the mean one wouldn't listen. He was making the couple help him." He paused.

"After a while, the mean one got tired of hunting and took it out on the male. He fought back, but the mean one seemed to enjoy torturing them. He kept saying something like 'the mistress will be most angry at you for not catching slaves for her, and you will be punished', or it could have been princess, not sure which, seemed he said both. The mean one was fighting with a knife and whip and was enjoying the agony the male was showing. He was horrible, and I should have stepped in, but I didn't want to risk him knowing we were there, didn't want him to come back for us." Hoofington shook his hung head, and tears welled in his eyes, pausing before continuing.

"When the male slumped to the ground, the mean one laughed and began moving around him, kicking him and telling him to get up and fight. The female could hardly stand up by herself, hunched over and leaning against the tree, holding her belly and screaming, reaching out for her linked, tears rolling down her face. She was in pain, so much pain and agony stressed and frightened. The mean one turned to her and laughed before he strode over and slashed her. She couldn't move or defend herself. The mean being left thinking she was dead and took off in the cart back the way they came. I stood there, frozen to the spot, shocked that some being could be that cruel. I snapped out of it when I heard others approach. They comforted the female before removing her babe, and she died. It was horrible." Hoofington sat there in silence, tears running down his cheeks as his head slumped forward.

Elentari had tears in her eyes as she placed a hand on his arm to comfort him, knowing it was not enough to stop the regret he felt at not helping them. Her other hand was clasped between both Rorien's hands. "The babe was Rewa. She survived because of Havid and Roswen," said Elentari softly.

"The babe survived? Rewa was the babe?" Hoofington was shocked. He raised his head to look at her. He never expected the babe would survive, or he would ever meet her. He smiled as his eyes moved to find Rewa, glad the child survived, and he watched her playing.

"Yes, and the couple were my parents," replied Rorien quietly. His eyes were watching his feet shifting about in the dirt.

Elentari patted their hands and left them to continue their conversation. She walked to her parents to relieve Fendton of his duties, taking her mother's arm. Donna was happily chatting and getting along with the fauns, enjoying their company and learning about their ways, as was Havid and Roswen. Rhen was happily chatting away to Beth, who was still being very cautious. Francis had relaxed and was merrily chatting with Duggit. Of course, both had a drink in their hands.

"Anza, this is awesome, and the fauns are so intriguing and fun. Thanks for bringing me here," said Donna as she hugged her.

"Anza?" questioned Rhen.

"Yes, Donza and Anza are our nicknames, special names for each other," answered Elentari.

"I guess your name should change now you are Elentari…mmm…maybe Elza, no, Tarza," said Donna.

"No, it is Anza and will be Anza. We've had our names since we were six, and I don't want that to change," said Elentari, her hands on her hips.

"Ok, Anza, it stays," said Donna shaking her head.

"Does every being have a special name?" asked Rhen.

"No, close friends tend to find a unique name for each other. Often, it is just a shortened version of their names like Don or El," answered Donna.

"Rhen, we need to head off. It is getting late, and we have another hori to travel." Elentari said, gathering every being to say goodbye and heading back to the camel train.

On the outskirts of Rhunduin, they said goodbye to the Cameleer and left the stables. The group headed off to find Lorcan and Awnrie. Elentari thought it was strange there were no beings setting up or decorations to be seen in the parestalas as Lorcan and Awnrie were to be linked on the morrow.

"Where are you two having your linking dia vows?" asked Elentari as she met up with them at Awnrie's parents' casa.

"Here in the garden," answered Awnrie.

"You do not want to have a big celebration?" Elentari asked as she took a seat at the table. Rorien stood behind her with his hands on the back of her chair.

"No, we can't afford to have a big celebration. We are happy with a simple ceremony here."

"Forget about money and humour me. Let's say you have enough to have the dia you want. What is it you truly want? Remember, no expense spared," said Elentari with a hand on her chin and her head leaning sideways.

"It would be nice to…" Awnrie began, but Elentari cut her off.

"No, what do you want. Not 'it would be nice', what do YOU want?" said Elentari shifting forward in her seat and placing both hands on the table in front of her.

"To have our dia in the parestala with every being we know," replied Awnrie, her eyes downcast.

"Then consider it done, leave the costs to me. Which means we had better get moving. We have a parestala to set up," said Elentari standing up and heading for the door.

"Wait. We can't. It's not," said Awnrie chasing after her, grabbing her arm as she reached the door.

"Lorcan is my guard," said Elentari with her hand on the door, facing it with her eyes raised to the ceiling, "a guard to the princess of all the lands. If his link wants a large celebration for their linking dia, then it is done." She turned to Awnrie, "Do not question me and accept this as my gift to you. Now let's begin preparations," she said, continuing out the door.

Awnrie's mother and Elentari organised the catering and personally invited every being while Awnrie managed her female friends to help set up. The parestala was coming together quickly. Beings had decorated with red flowers falling from the top, and tables were being set up with black table cloths to line them, and large red bows placed on the chairs. There were red napkins to be folded into candles and place settings to complete.

It was midmorning the following dia when the fire and movement Masters arrived, ready to perform the ceremony. Beings were milling around, waiting for the Masters to arrive and for the ceremony to begin. Elentari walked the length of the parestala and took her seat at the front. The Masters followed behind and stood at their spot at the table. Lorcan and Anwrie arrived, ready to begin their walk down the parestala with Lorcan dressed in red robes and Awnrie wearing her black robes representing her power. Their whole linking items were a combination of red and black. Their candle symbolises leaving their separate lives and becoming one, the binding cords signifying the linking of their spirits together, cup of sharing both bitter and sweet experiences as one and sand jar.

As the Movement Master sealed the sand jar, Elentari stepped forward wearing her linking dress. The design was to become her ceremonial outfit with a slight change, the long ribbons crossing over her back and becoming the belt around her waist.

"Left arms please," said Elentari.

Lorcan moved behind Awnrie and presented their arms to her.

"These bands are to show all that you have completed your linking and are committed to each other," Elentari placed a silver band around Awnrie's wrist and a matching band on Lorcan's. "The bands have been specially made to represent you both. Set around the band are black onyx representing Awnrie's power. Etched into the band are symbols of fire to represent Lorcan's power. The fire symbols surrounding the gems and flowing through them." She yielded her firepower and sealed the bands.

Elentari held their wrists up, and the parestala exploded in accolades. Lorcan kissed Awnrie before moving to the completing casa, and celebrations began. It was just before midnight when the last of the guests left, and Elentari crawled into bed beside Rorien. She was exhausted, todia was her first official certified order as the princess, and she was pleased her first official act was for a friend.

The following morning, Elentari was glad they were heading back quickly to Thoroneath, giving her time to spend time with her parents before they left. It had been a whirlwind few dias, and she had spent little time with them. On the morrow, they were due to leave.

"If you have every power, why do you not just use movement and get us home quickly?" asked Donna as they sat upon their camel.

"You know the trip there is part of the destination. If I used movement, then you would not have met Rhen. Plus, I can only transport one at a time and not far. It would take me a while to transport every being home and would exhaust me," said Elentari.

"Fair enough. I did like meeting Rhen, and when I come back, can we return?" asked Donna.

"Totally, and we will go by movement," said Elentari.

"Awesome," said Donna nodding her head with a slight grin.

"When we get back, Rorien has organised a pack for you which has a potion and code for you to return. Have you any idea when you want to come back?" asked Elentari.

"Your birthday. I want to be here for your birthday to help you celebrate your first birthday here, and it is your 21st, after all. Party time in a new world, Woohoo!" replied Donna.

"Wow, I am nearly 21. Never thought I would be linked or married by 21, a Princess and responsibilities of the whole world. I have come a long way," said Elentari as she gazed off into the distance.

"A whole world away is how far you've come," laughed Donna shaking her head.

Elentari smiled, thinking that a whole world away seemed like something out of a movie, and here she was living a world away and not in a film. She snapped back to reality.

"Now remember dates are different here than back on Earth, and my birth date is different here than on Earth. I will work out which date it falls on your calendar when we get back. It's not far now, see in front is the mountain where Thoroneath is," said Elentari pointing towards Thoroneath.

CHAPTER 3

After saying goodbye to her parents and Donna and watching them step through the door, they began preparations to head west to Rorien's family home for the rest of their mesmoon. Rorien's bag was hidden amongst Elentari's many bags she had packed. After all, they were going to be gone for nearly 30 dia. Clothes, shoes and even her stuffed dragon, Drachenstein, was bundled into her four large bags and loaded into the camel cart. It was just after high sun when Elentari added a basket of food complete with her favourite tea set into the cart before setting out. They set off with the hope of reaching Chelista by supper. Passing through farmland and villades, they knew the trip would take longer than the typical five horis without stopping.

It had been three horis since they left Thoroneath and still had three to go when they stopped for tea in a clearing on the side of the path. An extra hori added to greet the farmers and the dwellers in one of the villades. Rorien removed the food basket from the cart and began to make a fire while Elentari yielded water for the teapot and heated it with her firepower. She sat sipping her tea, watching him build a fire, smiling to herself, waiting.

"What!? How did you? Oh yeah, you yield all. Why did you not say something?" asked Rorien, frowning at her with his hands on his hips.

"It was fun to watch you make a fire and being so manly, and I needed a drink to watch you. So, I made myself one." Elentari smirked, taking another sip.

"Do I get one?" asked Rorien.

"Yes, here you go," Elentari answered handing him a cup as he sat beside her. She rested her head on him. He wrapped an arm around her as they sat watching the fire, nibbling on biscuits and sipping tea. She heard a loud crashing in the woods, a fair distance behind them and coming towards them.

'*Open your senses. Something is coming,*' Elentari said on their link.

'*What?*' questioned Rorien on their link.

There is something in the woods heading our way. Open your senses and keep your guard up' Elentari rolled her eyes at him before moving herself to the other side of the fire. She stood there with her teacup in her hands, facing the woods and waiting. Rorien raced to the cart to grab his sword and stood between her and the woods, watching and waiting.

Elentari could see the tops of the birch trees moving as if some being was pushing them aside, swaying out and back. She could hear footsteps crashing through the growth, could hear branches snapping and could feel vibrations through the ground. Whatever was coming towards them was large and heavy. Her heart beat faster. A fleeting moment of panic flowed through her body as she shuffled her feet, unsure of whether to flee or stay. She could feel Rorien's heart race and turned to him, looking for reassurance. His face was terse, and he was fixed and ready to fight.

The ground's vibrations were getting stronger and heavier when she spotted movement amongst the trees and turned her focus towards it. She could make out a large shape pushing its way between the trees and pushing over small saplings. Closer and closer, it edged and larger and larger it became. She saw a giant 20-foot-tall being quickly crashing his way through the woods towards them. His humongous frame towered amongst the treetops, making her feel very tiny and insignificant, and he was still a distance from them.

'*I don't think a sword is going to help us this time,*' Rorien said on their link.

'*I thought giants were in the south,*' said a puzzled Elentari on their link.

"Get out my way," said the giant as he smashed out of the woods and raised his hand to push Elentari away. Rorien quickly yielded his air power and placed him on his backside, protecting her.

"That is not a nice way to speak to beings," said Elentari, her finger wagging angrily at him.

'*Help me to fight with air to keep him down,*' Elentari said on their link.

"You hurt Vosco. Vosco bottom hurts," said the giant angrily as he began to stand.

'*Why is it you are always finding ways to make me protect you?*' asked Rorien on their link.

"If you had been polite to me, Rorien wouldn't have put you on your backside and hurt you. Kindness brings kindness," said Elentari.

'*You are my big, strong male and I but a poor hapless female,*' she said on their link.

"You in my way" grumbled the giant as he went to push Elentari away again.

'*Hapless female my foot. You hold all powers. Maybe I should hide behind you this time, and you fight your own battle,*' said Rorien on their link.

This time Elentari yielded air and pushed the giant to his bottom. "If you ask kindly, I shall move, and if you do not try to hurt me, I will not hurt you. Where are you going?" asked Elentari changing her tone and softening her stance.

'*Well done,*' said Rorien on their link.

'*Thanks, I learnt from the best,*' Elentari said on their link.

"Vosco going home but is lost." The giant hung his head as he stayed on the ground. His height was 10 foot while sitting. Even with him sitting down, she felt very trivial as she just reached the height of his chest, and he was almost twice her size.

'*Thanks, I am pretty good,*' said Rorien on their link, rubbing his fingers on his chest.

"What is your name? My name is Elentari, and this is Rorien, my linked," said Elentari pointing her hand to Rorien.

'*Not you. I learnt from the Master,*' she ribbed on their link.

"Me Vosco. Hello Elentari and Rorien," replied the giant.

"Where do you live, Vosco?" asked Rorien.

"In mountain by the river," answered Vosco.

"You are a long way from home, Vosco," said Rorien. "Your mountain is about 2, 3 hori in that direction. How did you end up here?" Rorien was pointing towards the south.

'*Do you know how to get to his home from here?*' asked Elentari on their link.

"Vosco follow pretty birdy. He fly quick, and Vosco run fast. Birdy go away, and Vosco run home but no find." Vosco hung his head.

'*Yes, but I am not liking where you are heading with this,*' said Rorien on their link.

"Do you think you can find your way home from here if we tell you how?" asked Elentari.

'*What if we travel an hori with him towards his home?*' asked Elentari on their link.

"No. Vocso scared. No want to go alone. Vosco lost." The giant began to sob softly.

'*A HORI and NO more,*' said Rorien on their link, shaking his fist at her.

"What if we travel with you for a little bit? Would you be happy?" asked Elentari.

"Ooo, yes, please. Vosco very happy" The ground shook as he jumped up and down with excitement on his bottom.

Elentari lost her balance and fell but did not hit the ground as Vosco reached out and caught her. Her heart was racing. She was unsure and scared of what he would do.

"Vosco sorry make Elentari fall. Vosco big, bad giant." He helped her stand up, his face full of sadness for almost hurting her.

'*You realise we won't get to Chelista till well after supper,*' said Rorien on their link.

"It is ok, Vosco, you didn't mean it. You are a good giant to be kind enough to save me." She gently touched his large, rough, calloused hands. His plump fingers had dirt lining the creases of his knuckles and under his chipped nails. His hand width was longer than the length of a 30cm ruler, and the length, almost half her height. His hands could crush her easily.

'*Yes, but we have a friend to help first. He may come in handy one dia,*' said Elentari on their link.

"Can we go now? Vosco hungry and tired," said Vosco.

"Yes, we can go. Would you like an apple?" Elentari handed him an apple, and he took it eagerly. "Ut, where are your manners?" she asked as she went to take the apple back, not that she could. His hand was out of her grasp.

"Thank-you," said Vosco.

"Much better. When you use manners, you make friends and may even receive a little more." She threw another apple to him, and he ate both whole as if they were grapes.

The journey south was uneventful. Elentari spent her time talking to Vosco and getting to know him. She asked about the giants and where he lived. Vosco was a young giant at 73 and spent his leisure time watching birds. He wanted to fly like them. He was one of the youngest giants out of the 33 giants who lived at his villade, which was only large enough to hold 40 giants. They kept to themselves, not venturing away from the mountains, and ignored all wars. His species were earth giants who were reclusive, quiet and dim-witted and lived for 400 anoks. After an hori of travelling together, they spotted a soft outline of the mountain range in the distance.

"Vosco, your home is over there. Will you be ok to get home by yourself?" asked Rorien

"You are old enough and smart enough to find your way. You can do it." Encouraged Elentari

"You think me can?" asked Vosco, turning to Elentari looking for reassurance.

"Yes, it is not far, and you can see the mountains. Keep looking for your mountain, and you will be fine," Elentari answered.

"Ok. Vosco go alone. Thank you, Elentari," Vosco said and bounded off towards the mountains, waving to them.

"Bye, Vosco," said Rorien and Elentari as Rorien turned the camel around, heading back the way they came.

It was getting dark when they arrived at Rorien's childhood casa. They quickly emptied the cart, and Rorien took it to the stables as Elentari prepared them a late supper and unpacked their things. Elentari entered the wooden casa and began to explore it. It was simple with two bedrooms, a washroom and an underground storage cellar. One bedroom was set up, ready for a babe with a crib and a double bed. A washbasin sat on a set of drawers, and nappies were piled on the change bench beside a cupboard. The other room was Rorien's old room, furnished with a double bed and wardrobe. The lounge area had a couch against the wall facing the fire, a large mat on the floor and little other furnishings. A bench and table seating four were all there was in the kitchen and reminded Elentari of Rorien's casa in Thoroneath, minimal and basic. She was searching for sheets to change the bed in Rorien's old room when Rorien returned. He helped her change the bedding before they sat down to a late supper and finally collapsed into bed, sleeping till late morning.

On the morning, they headed out to the parestala to find a café for breakfast before Rorien showed her around his childhood cuedel. He took her past where he and his father would go fishing, where his friends hung out and where he learnt to yield and had lessons. During the first vika of their stay, many of his parents' friends and neighbours approached him to offer their condolences. Rorien explain what he knew of his parent's tragic death and his sister Rewa. It was almost two vikas before one discovered she was the Princess, and news of their linking dia and mesmoon spread fast with every being in the cuedel wanting to meet them. Their hopes of a quiet mesmoon dashed, and she donned her princess façade.

When they weren't lazing at the beach or wandering through the woods, Elentari found furnishings to refurnish the casa. It would give them a place to get away for a few nights every once in a while, and somewhere Havid and Roswen could come with Rewa. In anoks to come, if it were her desire, it would be Rewa's casa. Rorien kept a few items of sentimental value, and the rest donated. They replaced the bare basic furnishings with new elegantly carved furniture with bright coloured fabrics, blankets and rugs and pictures for the walls. The casa was homely and inviting.

Their mesmoon was coming to an end, and an extra basket of goodies found its way onto the cart. A new tea she liked found its way into the extra goodie basket as well as gifts for their friends. The trip home was uneventful, compared to coming to Chelista, and completed without stopping. Not even a stop for a cup of tea. Instead, Elentari made tea on the cart using her powers to fill and heat the teapot. Once home and unpacked, Rorien headed off to find Fendton and Jasper while Elentari met with the King.

"Princess, you have returned from your trip west. Was it good?" asked the King as she entered the hall.

"Yes, my King, we have returned, and it was good. I did encounter an issue, a big issue. You could say a gigantic issue on the way there," she said, curtsying.

"Is this a private discussion we need to have?" The King sighed as his shoulders sagged, wondering what mess she got herself into this time. Even Trad's stance changed.

"Possibly as you may very well not like what I have to say," she said as she stepped up to kiss her father.

"I already don't like what you are about to say," sighed the King as he stood, holding out his arm for Elentari to take. He led her to his private chamber, where Elentari filled the King in on meeting Vosco.

"Is this going to be a common occurrence? Every trip you take, you manage to find danger?" he asked, his hand stroking his chin in thought.

"I also manage to get out of danger, Papa. This new friend could be beneficial in the future," said Elentari. "You never know who is useful or when. Plus, as I said, I want the rifts between kinds to be mended."

"Yes, you did," answered the King. "But, if you continue to find danger, I will have to confine you to the Thoroneath North area," he said jokingly, shaking his fist at her.

"I'd like to see you try," she grinned. "Come have supper with us tonight, and let us fill you in on the rest of our trip."

"I shall be there." He kissed her forehead, re-entered the royal hall, and Elentari headed back to her casa.

"You are back! It is wonderful to see you again. I missed you," said Sarina as she hugged Elentari. "Lorcan and Awnrie arrived back a few dias ago and settled in Awnrie. I'm sure they would like to sup with us too."

"I have summoned them, and I missed you too. I have brought you a gift," said Elentari, handing her a package as Lorcan and Awnrie burst through the door.

Lots of excitement and chatter began as they all caught up. Lorcan and Awnrie filled them in on their mesmoon, which was spent in the East, relaxing, fishing and exploring the area. Lorcan even took Awnrie to meet the fauns. Jasper and Sarina filled them in on the happenings in the cuedel, which was very little, and Fendton said little.

"Trad, I notice you are linked, is she still with us?" asked Elentari as the King and Trad arrived for supper. It was not unusual for beings to keep wearing their link ring after their link had passed. The King had kept wearing his as once you are linked, you cannot link again.

"Yes, she is. She works late as do I, which works for us both," Trad answered.

"Would she be able to join us for supper tonight? It would be lovely to meet her," said Elentari.

Trad went silent before saying, "she finished early and is almost here."

"Wonderful," Elentari said as she clapped her hands in delight.

"She is here, Elentari," said Trad as he opened the door and Asvik entered. "May I introduce my link, who you already know."

"Asvik! This is most awesome," said Elentari, hugging her.

"Thank you, Princess," replied Asvik.

"Elentari. You are in my casa, and here I am Elentari. Here formalities are left at the door. Now leave yours at the door and be a friend," said Elentari with her hands on her hips.

"I shall, Elentari," said Asvik.

"This explains why you are always fussing over me and telling me little things about my mother. You two were close?"

"Yes. Before your mother passed, I was her assistant and friend, like your father and Trad are. It was most distressing when you were taken for both your parents and us," said Asvik shaking her head. "We had been there through the pregnancy, and I was there for your birth."

"Please tell me more about her," said Elentari, taking Asvik's hand and leading her inside.

"Please, can you tell us about your trip instead, Elentari?" asked Fendton. "I want to know everything that happened."

"I will tell you more another time, Elentari. Tonight, tell us about your trip," said Asvik, gently tapping her hand.

"It was uneventful, took a camel cart, refurnished the casa and came home," said Elentari, shrugging her shoulders.

"Elentari! You know more happened on the journey there, now explain your meeting with Vosco," growled the King.

"Fine. We met Vosco the giant and helped him home," she said.

"What is it with you and finding danger everywhere? Hoofington and now Vosco, who else are you going to get into danger to meet?" sighed Jasper.

"What was he like? Were you scared? Was he big? Why was he in the West?" questioned Fendton.

"Come, sit, and I shall explain," Rorien said as he sat at the table rolling his eyes at Elentari.

Rorien explained their meeting with Vosco, how Vosco came crashing through the woods, lost and scared and how Elentari dragged him into escorting Vosco home. He continued to explain their time in Chelista and how their quiet time away changed to being busy and exhausting when a being discovered the Princess was there. It was late when he finished answering all the questions Fendton asked.

"It is late, and on the morrow, duties begin. Time to leave," said Elentari ushering every being out the door.

"Do we have to go?" asked Fendton.

"Breakfast here first?" asked Jasper.

"Yes, breakfast here. Good night all," said Rorien closing the door and leading Elentari into bed for the last night of their mes-moon.

CHAPTER 4

It was the last vika of the seventh month. Elentari and Jasper were in the royal hall with the King when a messenger arrived with an urgent memorandum from Prince Theonry in the North. King Adtarian unfurled and read the message. His face changed from indifference to shock as he read and reread the letter. He raised his head and his eyes and stared out at nothing, looking as if he was attempting to solve an issue before his shoulders slumped forward. He reread the message as if the news would change. Sorrow filled his face as he read and reread the note while the messenger stood waiting for instructions. Trad had shifted his feet, adjusting his stance from on guard to concern for a friend. Elentari shifted in her chair, moving to face the King. Something was wrong, but what?

"My King, what is it?" asked Elentari softly, her hand gently touching his arm.

The King handed her the message without speaking, his eyes staring at the floor. She took the note and read it before reading it aloud.

To the King of all the lands.
My King,
It is with great sorrow I send word to you. Tragedy has befallen our family with the death of King Heinrich. He had not lived through the night and was found on the morning of the 37th by his guard. As to the cause of his death, the healers believe his heart gave in during the night.
Your presence to perform the burial ritual and resolve the next to sit on the throne is requested. King Heinrich's burial is planned for the 5th and the crowning to take place on the 8th.
Prince Theonry

"Papa, that was yesterdia when he died. We will need to make plans to head off. Trad, what do we need to do?" asked Elentari as Trad had placed his hand on the Kings shoulder to comfort him as sorrow filled his face.

"Everything will be ready and organised when we arrive. The King is required to perform the final ritual at the burning of the body. There is nothing we need to take with us," answered Trad, sorrow filling his voice.

"Travelling there, how do we go about that?" asked Elentari.

"The King can be transported by the Movement Master. We do not need to travel by boat," answered Trad.

"How many can the Master transport at once?" asked Elentari.

"He can transport twelve at a time, including himself. What do you have in mind?" asked Trad.

"Papa, let Trad take you to your rooms to pack and organise you to head North todia. It will give you time with your friends before the burial. I can continue here with royal duties and meet you on the dia," said Elentari, placing her hands on the Kings arm to offer him comfort.

The King looked towards her, nodded.

"Trad, organise for Asvik to go with you both," said Elentari.

The King stood, and Trad helped him to his feet and led him out. Elentari quickly wrote a reply and dismissed the messenger before summoning the scholars. She needed to understand burial rituals and the crowning of a king. She sent the King to the North to mourn with his friends while she took care of business, completing royal duties as well as organising the trip North with her guards and their linked.

As Elentari had never been North, she could not yield movement to a place she'd never been and required the Master to take them all. With his yielding of transporting twelve at a time, he could transport her and her entourage together. Elentari did wonder if they could portal through the lands instead of yielding movement. She knew by using movement instead of portal, yielders were able to offer their services as trade. The group left after breakfast and arrived in the central courtyard. The Movement Master took them to the royal hall.

The North royal casa was made of stone and looked like a single-story castle. The high outer walls were thick stone with turrets at each corner surrounding the bailey and main entrance to the royal area. Tall slit windows overlooked the bailey from the rooms. The main entrance and a few smaller doors were the only accesses into the royal site. Large vases of flowers lined the path through the main entrance to the court-yard within. The courtyard was the centre of the casa, with every access flowing out to it.

Elentari entered the double wooden doors to the royal hall, which were etched similar to her royal hall, and found little space to move. The scent of flowers was strong as she moved through the hall. The hall design was the same as hers, with four doors on the left and two along the right wall. The ceiling and walls inside the hall were exploding with geometric decoration in dazzling colours. Sharply defined outlined ge-ometric motifs and curvilinear forms in bold colours covered the Art Deco style walls. Where ever the eye looked, daring, stunning colour and themes filled the view.

Vases of flowers on pedestals lined the walls, and the hall was al-most overflowing with beings. Upon her tippy toes, as she glanced across the sea of heads, finding the crowns of the kings and princes. She could recognise all the Kings and Princes by the look of their crowns, each individual and distinct. Searching, she found her father's crown with King Reagan and Prince Baldric.

Wearing crowns in a crowd has its advantages, she thought as she weaved her way to her father, losing all but Rorien along the way.

"Papa, how are you? My Lords, it is good to see you again," Elentari said, curtsying.

"Princess, how lovely to see you. Prince Rorien," replied King Reagan bowing.

"Your majesty, you are looking well. Prince Rorien," said Prince Baldric bowing.

"King Reagan. Prince Baldric," said Rorien bowing.

"Elentari, you are here. Come, let us show our respects to King Heinrich and condolences to Prince Leopold," said the King as he took her arm and led her to the burial chamber.

The chamber was through one of the doors on the left wall. In the centre of the room was a square stone table upon which King Heinrich sat on his throne. Bunches of flowers leaned against the stone base, and beings had place jars filled with scented oil amongst the flowers. A fragrant oil lamp burned above his head. Beside his feet was a bowl, and on the floor below his feet was a large basket with food. Each dia, the flowers were removed and placed in large vases to line the hall and path around the courtyard. The jars of oil placed in storage, with one selected to fill the oil lamp above his head and the food sent to the kitchen.

King Adtarian and Princess Elentari placed eight different jars of scented oils amongst the flowers, and into the large basket, she put their food offering. From the pocket in her bag, she took out pieces of papyrus as gifts for the afterlife. The small circular pieces with coin pictures she placed into the bowl beside his feet. The larger papyrus pieces with images of camels, furniture, clothes, jewels, and other items she placed on the stone slab.

She stood in front of him, curtsying she said, "Travel safely, King Heinrich," before heading out.

"Travel safely, King Heinrich," said Rorien. He followed Elentari back into the hall.

Elentari and Rorien said their condolences to Prince Leopold and Prince Theonry. She spotted Lannis with Sven and Emmett.

"Papa, how long till the procession begins?" asked Elentari.

"Just before the high sun, the bell will toll, and the procession will begin. Go catch up with the Princes. They asked after you," the King said as he kissed her and moved her on.

"Thanks, Papa," she said as she headed off with Rorien to catch up with the Princes.

"Princess, you made it. Prince," said Prince Sven.

"Princess. Prince," said Prince Emmett.

"Princes," said Rorien

"Princess. Prince," said Prince Lannis.

"Yes, we have arrived. I have been and paid my dues, and now I can relax for a bit. How are you all?" asked Elentari.

"Good and you?" asked Sven.

"I'm well. Is this your first funeral?" asked Elentari.

"I have been to a few minor burials where the teachers perform them. No important beings for Professors or Masters to perform," said Sven.

"None of us have been to a King burial. This is the first," said Emmett.

"Don't say it like that. Makes it sound like many more are to come," said Elentari.

"There are a few before us, Elentari," said Sven

"Yes, but you say it as if they will be soon," said Elentari.

"I hope not. I'm not ready for the throne," said Lannis, taking a big breath in and exhaling loudly.

"Who here is?" asked Sven, raising his arms and shoulders in question.

"I haven't even been here a whole anok, give me a break. Sitting on the throne is a distance event, very far into the future event," replied Elentari.

"No one has been under the age of 200 before they sat on the throne. You have time," said Emmett

"I won't need to worry," said Rorien.

"You will be sitting with Elentari. Why don't you have to worry?" asked Lannis, puzzled by the statement.

"Most likely won't be sitting with her. She has other ideas," answered Rorien.

"What do you mean? Every King and Queen has always chosen their link. Who would you choose?" asked Emmett, turning to face Elentari fully.

"I have an idea but am not saying until the time to choose. If I am to govern these lands, I want kings I can trust to sit with me, kings who are happy to work with me and keep the lands peaceful. I realise there is an area which needs attention and having another to sit with me will allow me to have them in that area," said Elentari, staring across the room to avoid eye contact.

"Where are you talking?" asked Lannis.

"Are you all heading back after?" asked Elentari, changing the subject, avoiding Emmett's eyes which she could feel boring into her.

"I'm staying to head to the snow," answered Lannis.

"E, can we stay and go to the snow too?" asked Fendton as he came up behind her.

"Fen, not this time. I will organise for when we come back, won't promise anything," said Elentari as she turned to face Fen and opening a space for him.

"E? Fen?" asked Emmett.

"After our linking dia, Donna was calling me Anza, which is a nickname. Fen came up with E, and I started calling him Fen. Nicknames can be a shortened version of your name or a humorous one relating to something," said Elentari.

"Oh," said Emmett as the bell sounded.

"Best go. Catch up later?" asked Elentari.

The princes nodded as Elentari moved to the burial chamber and beside her father. Inside the room, four males were placing poles under the throne through the sides to carry him through the streets to the cremation ground. Prince Leopold stood in the door with his linked and Prince Theonry and his linked behind them. The males lifted King Heinrich off the stone. Prince Leopold led the procession out to the cremation ground, with King Adtarian, Princess Elentari and Prince Rorien falling behind King Heinrich and the other kings behind them.

The procession headed through the streets of the cuedel. Beings lined the pathway bowing to the King as he passed, showing their King respect before joining the long line. A large stack of wood was in the centre of the cremation ground. The pole bearers placed King Heinrich and his throne on top of the platform over the wood. Prince Leopold straightened the King's crown and placed his crowning items in his hands and papyrus pieces at his feet. The Master of Earth, King Heinrich's power, stood in front of the King, waiting for the procession to finish as beings surrounded the ceremonial mount, standing head bowed, waiting for the cremation to begin.

King Adtarian performed the eulogy speaking highly of King Heinrich's rule and as a minor king of his lands. The Earth Master spoke the ancient text, sending King Heinrich into the afterlife as Prince Leopold and Prince Theonry lit the ceremonial mount from either side, the wood catching alight quickly and flames engulfing the King and leaping high into the air. Prince Leopold moved to face the King and bowed, saying his goodbye before walking through the street and back to the royal palace. Prince Theonry followed, bowing to the King before leaving, as King Adtarian took Princess Elentari's arm, guiding her to say their goodbyes before walking the streets.

They walked the long way back through the streets, with Rorien and their guards following, stopping to speak to the beings who lined the path. Beings offered their condolences and handed them flowers and gifts. The walk was long and slow as they exchanged pleasantries with all. Elentari was glad for the dia to end. She met many beings on the streets and listened to their stories about their King, and hugged those who needed it, offering her condolences. It was such a long, emotional dia, and she had little time to meet with the Princes. When the Master said he was ready to bring them home, she was glad.

"Wonderful send off for your grandfather Theonry," said Elentari.

"Thank you, Princess. He would be proud," replied Theonry.

"We are about to head home. When we return, we will stay a bit longer and head to the snow. Would you like to join us? Come and have a bit of fun and forget about all this of a few dias?" asked Elentari.

"That does seem a good idea, a few dias away with the family to rejuvenate. I will have Jahan and Torvi come too. They will need some time out from all this," replied Theonry.

"Excellent idea. I haven't had the pleasure of meeting Jahan other than a quick introduction at the janual. That dia is not one I wish to do again," said Elentari rolling her head.

"Bit daunting, was it?" asked Theonry with a smirk.

"A bit is an understatement. We must be off. I shall see you in a few dias Theonry," she said, looking at the Master waving frantically at her to hurry up.

"Bye, Elentari. See you in three dias," said Theonry.

Crowning dia finally arrived, and it couldn't come quick enough with Fendton's constant excitement and questioning about seeing snow and what would happen. Even though the rest of the group were looking forward to the trip, they certainly did not have the level of excitement Fendton had. The sun hadn't even risen when he came bursting into their casa, acting as a child on Christmas morning, eager to get going.

"Fendton, we are leaving after breakfast. Now get out of here," yelled Elentari from her bed.

"Why can't we go now and have breakfast there?" whinged Fendton from the bedroom doorway.

"Because we are leaving after breakfast AS ORDERED," yelled Rorien slamming the door shut with his power. "NOW LEAVE!"

"Ok, ok, ok, I get the drift. Can I wait here in the lounge?" asked Fendton.

"GET. OUT!" yelled both Rorien and Elentari. Elentari threw a pillow at the door.

"We are NOT having kids if this is what we have to deal with," said Elentari.

"Agree, especially if they are as curious as he is. How can I complete this without interruption?" asked Rorien as he nibbled her neck, his hands finding her breasts.

"Like this," she answered, raising a stone in the floor up to block the door as her hands moved down his body, finding his hardened malehood.

"Good morning, Princess, Prince. Are you all ready to depart?" asked the Movement Master. He sat at the table with Fendton and a pot of tea waiting for her as she entered their lounge, fresh from her shower.

"Yes, Master, as soon as I eat, we can go. Shall Awnrie and I attempt to transport ourselves and our bags?" asked Elentari. She and Awnrie had begun personal training with the Master to extend their abilities beyond transporting short distances and transporting more than one. They had both moved two to the East but had not attempted moving beyond this land.

"Yes, transport yourselves. I will take your bags over and maybe on the return trip. You can bring bags. We shall see how you fair first," said the Movement Master.

When all had finished breakfast, the group gathered in the lounge.

"If you are ready, please begin," said the Movement Master to Elentari and Awnrie.

To transport took concentration and energy. The further away, the more energy spent and how much was transported meant more attention. Elentari learnt if you are unable to succeed, your body blurs and flicks in and out of reality before it stops and leaves you with a massive headache. She discovered this the first time she attempted to travel to the East. Before, she had only practised movement around the cuedel and to the fields. Before personal training began, Awnrie travelled about 200 stadi by herself and 100 stadi with someone. It took some time to transport herself and Lorcan between Thoroneath and Rhunduin. Now both of them could travel 400 stadi taking two others without totally exhausting themselves. They aimed to transport themselves and five others between lands enabling the two of them to transport their group everywhere. This aim would give Elentari freedom to transport whenever and wherever.

"I shall see you there," Elentari said and kissed Rorien. She stood back, concentrating on the North royal hall. She felt her body go tingly, blackness flashed in her eyes, and when her eyes cleared, she was in the North royal hall as planned. Awnrie appeared near her, followed by the Movement Master with the rest of the group.

"How do you feel? Could you manage bags as well?" the Master asked, coming over to check them both.

"I feel fine, not drained and feel able to take on a little more," answered Elentari.

"I'm fine and could take someone with me," answered Awnrie, doing a little jump and jiggle.

"When you return, Princess, you shall take your bags with you, Awnrie. You can take Lorcan. Where is the King meeting you?" said the Master, scanning the hall.

"He said in the royal hall. I expect he and Prince Theonry will be here soon," answered Elentari.

"The other Masters are gathered in the Kings private meeting room. I shall take my leave and join them. Until the crowning ceremony," said the Movement Master as he bowed and left.

Theonry and her Father settled them into their rooms before returning to the royal hall in readiness for the crowning ceremony. The hall was bustling with beings chattering and finding the best spot to watch. The Kings and Princes were congregating at the front, where seats were placed for them. The rest of the hall was standing room only. Upon the pomp, the raised stone platform, was a new throne etched with earth symbols and emeralds representing Leopold's power. The crafts being carved a large L into the back of the throne. Elentari and Rorien made their way to the front with Jasper as their guard while the rest found a place to stand amongst the crowded hall.

The room became quiet as a green carpet runner was unfurled along the floor from the door to the throne steps, signalling the crowning was to begin. The Masters walked down the aisle and stopped at the throne stairs. They turned to face the crowd with the Element Masters standing to the left of the throne and the Spirit Masters on the right. Prince Leopold began his walk to the steps of the pomp and stood facing the throne. King Adtarian followed the Prince and stood behind him.

The air and sight Masters took their spots on the pomp between the Prince and throne. In the Sight Master's hand was the varita, a full-length delicately ornate staff laid with green stones and a silver royal crown set on top. The Masters read the ancient text.

The Prince replied, "I shall govern according to the ancient text."

The Sight Master placed the varita in the Prince's left hand, and the two Masters returned to their position as Earth and Shift Masters stepped forward. The Shift Master held the vorbola, a smooth green orb with four silver bands circling it, crisscrossing over each other and etched with earth symbols. The Masters read the ancient text.

The Prince replied, "I shall do my utmost power, maintain this land."

The Shift Master placed the vorbola in the Prince's right hand as the water and heal Masters stepped forward. The Heal Master held a green handleless cup etched with earth symbols and the letter L, the vasokop. The Master read the ancient text.

The Prince replied, "I shall use compassion in all my judgements."

The Heal Master put the cup to his lips to drink from before placing it in the throne cup holder. Lastly, the Fire and Movement Masters stepped forward with the Movement Master holding the velo, a green stone cylinder with a large L etched on it and a candle in the centre. The Masters read the ancient text.

"I shall uphold the ancient text and honour the King of all the Lands." He replied, leaning the varita against his side as he lit the candle. The Movement Master then placed it on the green pedestal beside the throne.

The Prince stepped up and stood facing the crowd in front of his throne. King Adtarian climbed the stairs of the pomp and stood in front of the Prince. The Prince sat, and King Adtarian held the new crown high above the Prince's head.

"I claim you King Leopold, King of the Northlands and a minor king of my lands. I shall sit with you and govern with you," said King Adtarian as he placed the crown on the new Kings head, stepped back and bowed. "Hail King Leopold."

The hall stood and bowed, repeating, "Hail King Leopold. King of the Northlands."

The new King waited for the noise to quieten down and stood. King Leopold nodded and waved to all in the hall before stepping down to greet them. The newly crowned King made his way to the courtyard and into the royal carriage. He sat in the open-top carriage to begin his journey as the new King and meet his subjects as he weaved his way through the cuedel.

CHAPTER 5

Rorien watched, laughing as Fendton slid down the slope, standing on his wooden sled, attempting to be the furthest sled ride standing up. Another competition to add to the dia of competitiveness. Games for furthest backwards, furthest kneeing, most enormous snowball, anything they could think of, they had made into a competition. Rules were enforced to stop powers from shifting their abilities. Eventually, it was agreed upon to instil a no powers rule. Elentari agreed to sneakily assist Rorien, giving him a little edge occasionally, a little push with air power or help with water power. Not enough to arouse suspicion but to win any way he could.

"I'm going to catch you, Fendton!" yelled Lorcan, surfing on his sled.

"Better go faster than that. I'm next!" yelled Jasper as he readied himself.

"You or me next, Theonry?" asked Rorien.

"You go. Want to see you all watching me as I beat you all," chuckled Theonry.

As Rorien stood on his sled, he heard a rumbling sound coming from behind him. A white tsunami of powder was coming quickly towards them. Snowstorm clouds exploded into the air and impacted over the top of them. One moment, the slopes were still and silent, and the next moment, they were quickly moving. Before the cry could escape his lips, the snow powder was all around him, battering him and unforgiving. The weight of the snow caused his momentum to be no longer under his control, and he tumbled over and over. Snow crushed him from all sides, breaking his bones.

He tried to use his airpower, but it was useless. He could not see and did not know which direction was which. He was tumbling, cold and battered and then darkness in a tightly confined space. He could not move, could not use his power. The snow was no longer soft against his body. The hard ice snow was constricted against his body, compacting tight against him. He was buried deep in the snow. His body heat quickly dropped, he was so cold, and he could not move to get warm. The snow was crushing him, keeping him from moving. His feet and hands felt like ice blocks. He yelled, but no sound could escape, and no sound could he hear. A few seconds either way would be the decision of his life or his death.

'Help me, I can't move, I can't see. I have broken almost every bone in my body, and there is no light. It is cold, so cold, and I can't get out, can't move. Help me, Elentari, help me quickly.' Rorien clung to their link

'I am coming as quick as I can. Hold on. I love you.' Elentari clung to the link holding him.

The snow was crushing him, the cold creeping quickly into his shattered bones, and it was hard to breathe.

'I am coming as quick as I can. I am just organising rescue crews. I love you,' said Elentari on their link.

'Hurry and be careful. I am so cold. I can't feel my legs. I love you,' said Rorien on their link.

He was struggling to stay awake, struggling to remain conscious. He could hear her calling to him, could feel her holding their link, holding him. He had to hold on for her, for them, but he was too cold. He knew he was slipping, falling into a deep sleep, and he tried to fight it.

'I'm here. I'm' was all he heard before the darkness came. He felt warm, but it was not enough, darkness engulfed him, and he went blank. He felt a warmth against his body but did not know where he was, could hear commotion around him as he was coming to and then the darkness again.

Her hands were warm against his body, and he tried to move to hold her. His body would not move. He called her name, but no sound came. In his head, he could hear himself calling to her, but his voice did not respond. Then the darkness came.

"Where am I?" he spoke, but no words came. He could not open his eyes. He could not move and didn't know where he was. He was confused and frightened, and he couldn't feel her beside him. He could feel her holding their link tight, could feel her need for him, but he could not respond. Then the darkness came.

Beneath his body, he felt softness, felt the blankets warming his chest, but he did not know where he was. He tried to speak, but the darkness came.

He heard them speaking, but she was not with them. He did not know who they were or where she was. He was scared and wanted her near him, where he felt safe. The males were talking about him, but he couldn't hear them properly. "I can't hear you!" he yelled, but no sound was heard. He thought he heard them say he was dying. No, he can't be dying. He can't die. She needs him. He struggled to move, trying to speak, but the darkness came.

He sensed that time and space did not exist in this space. Where he was, he did not know. There was nothing here, only feelings. Feelings of so much love and feelings of absolute serenity and so much peace surrounded him. He was floating on feelings of joy and patience, floating on softness and warmth. He felt alive, felt terrific, felt settled, felt incredible.

Was he missing something? Something niggled in his mind. What was that? Did he lose something? He could not remember if there was something before now. Nothing was there, but something kept scratching his mind? What is it that is keeping him from moving forward?

In the distance, he could see a white light radiating from something gently floating towards him. It was surreal, calming, and relaxing. He was mesmerised by it, watching it glide close to him as another light appeared behind it, and it floated towards him. He could see sparkles shimmering behind the first light, flickering over her face. He knew her. At another time, he knew her as Mother.

She floated gently around him, checking him before taking him in her arms, hugging as only a mother could. He tried to speak, but nothing. He was agitated, wanting to tell her he was sorry but unable. Why was he sad? He couldn't remember, but he knew he was sorry. It confused him. She shook her head and gently touched his face. It was as if she knew and was telling him it was alright. He relaxed and fell into her arms feeling such love and comfort. So much warmth and peace he could feel as her arms surrounded him.

The other light was his father. His shimmering face showed such happiness he had never seen before, a kind of proudness for him. His hand gently touched his shoulder, and serenity flowed through him. He felt such love.

As his mother hugged him, she turned him around to face how he came, showing him the way back. He did not want to go back. He wanted to stay. He tried to turn back, to face the way she came, but she kept forcing him to see the other way. He shook his head, saying no, he didn't want to go that way. His mother had her back facing the way he came, and she turned her face to glance over her shoulder. He followed her glance.

Who was that? She felt familiar, from another time and place. From where did he know her? He moved towards her, back the way he came and past his mother. He watched her, seeing she was in pain, in agony, screaming as the tears flowed down her face. He wanted to stop the hurt, stop the pain and make her smile again. Who was she? He was drawn towards her, wanting to hold her and love her. He glanced back at his parents as confusion set in. His mother nodded for him to go, waving him on, as did his father. They were telling him to go to her. He turned towards her, torn between staying and going. He felt a sharp jolt through his chest, and then another and another. What was happening? The darkness came.

He could feel the restriction and the heaviness of his body again. He could hear the voices calling a name, could hear her calling a name. Her voice, so angelic to his ears. He knew he loved her but could not see her. Another sharp jolt caused him to take a sharp intake of breath, and his eyes opened. He could see her over him, pressing down on his chest as the tears streamed down her face. She stopped at the sound of his breath.

"You came back," she said, grabbing him and hugging him tightly.

He could see three males and two females behind her. Who were they? Should he know them? They seemed familiar, but his mind was blank. He searched, but nothing was there. She was kissing him and hugging him. He put his arm around her. He knew she was glad to see him. Who was she? He couldn't remember.

"Rorien, it is good to see you," said one male.

She sat up, allowing the male to come close. The male was holding his hand out to him. He moved his hand to the male, allowing him to shake it. He couldn't remember his name. Was his name Rorien?

"Rorien, you scared us. Glad your back," said another male.

I must be Rorien. The other male said it too. Is my name Rorien? Yes, it is! I remember my name! Rorien. Who are they?

"Don't do that to her again or to us," said the third male.

"Rorien," said one female kissing his head.

He should know them, they were familiar, but nothing could he remember. He touched his chest, should there be something there? He felt like something was missing, but what?

"Our link snapped when you died," she said. "As did the oath."

He looked confused. Should he know what link is? Is it something he shared with her?

"I don't know if we can mend our link. The masters may find the answer," she said as she looked to the far side of the room.

He followed her gaze. Four males were all dressed the same but in different colours stood quietly. Should he know them? Are they the Masters?

"We will get through this together, Rorien. Together we will find our link again. You are alive. That is all that matters. You are alive," she said, hugging him again.

Her scent filled his nostrils, lotus flowers amongst the moss growing beside a waterfall. A memory flashed in his mind. What was that memory? It was too quick. He breathed deeply, trying to bring back the memory. The scent calmed him. He loved that smell, and he relaxed, breathing in her perfume. The memory flashed again, a bit longer this time. He could see the woods, and she was there. He was holding her. He did know her, but who was she?

"We need to get you home. Can you sit? Let's try and get you up and get you something to drink," she said.

The first male grabbed his shoulders while she moved his legs and sat him up on the side of the bed. He swayed, and the male caught him, steading him. She put her arms around him and leaned him into her.

"It's ok. Lean on me till you are strong. Sarina, can you get him a juice," she said.

Is her name Sarina? No, her name is not Sarina. That is the other female's name. He couldn't remember her name. He wanted to, but it wouldn't come to him. Why can I not remember her? I want to remember her. What is her name? He was frustrated and confused.

She took the cup and held it to his lips. He put his hand to the cup and sipped the juice. It tasted good, and his stomach groaned.

"You must be hungry as you haven't eaten for a while. Drink your juice, and we will try some food. Take it slow. Your body has been through a lot and still has a lot to go," she said.

He watched her. She was so loving to him. He knew he should know her, but he couldn't remember. He wanted to know her, for she made him feel safe. The cup was empty, and he could feel his strength returning. She held out some fruit for him. He took it, eating it slowly and watching her, waiting for more memories of her to return.

"We will get you home soon, Rorien," she said.

Was this not his home? Where was home? His eyes wandered the room. Where was he? She was busy fussing and organising everything. He liked how she was taking control.

"Are you ready to try standing?" she asked.

He nodded, not sure.

"Lorcan, can you help Jasper. Take him under his arms and raise him slowly," she said.

Which one is Lorcan? Another memory flashed in his mind. The male she called Lorcan was with him, and they had a cup in their hands. Where was it? He knew him before but could not remember now. The males took an arm each and picked him up. His head swam, and he swayed. She was in front of him and put her hands out to steady him.

"Sit him down. He is not ready," she said as she sat beside him. "It's ok. We will try again soon. How about you stay here and build your strength while I step out and complete some duties. It won't take long. Will you be ok without me?"

He nodded. He tried to scream, 'Please, don't go. I need you.' Where is she going? He began to worry.

"I won't take long. I have princess duties to do. Once I am finished, I can spend more time with you. Lorcan and Fendton will help you, and Sarina is here too. They will look after you. Ok?" she said.

He nodded. She kissed him, and he watched her walk out. Why does she have princess duties to do? Is she a princess? Who is Fendton? Should he know him? He kept watching the door waiting for her to return. He was agitated without her. She made him feel safe. When would she come back? He took more food from Sarina.

He watched as Sarina and the Master waved their hands near him. What were they doing? Why are they concentrating on him? What was happening? He felt strange.

"Shall we try standing again?" the male called Lorcan asked. Sarina and the Master moved away, and the strange sensation stopped.

He nodded. This time he didn't sway, and his head was fine.

"Well done. We are going to let go and see if you can stand by yourself," said Lorcan.

His legs wobbled, and he began to fall. They caught him.

"Ok. Let's sit you down again. We will try again soon. Let's get you standing by yourself before Elentari comes back. She will be thrilled," Lorcan said.

He nodded. He took the drink from Sarina and sipped it while he watched the door. When will she be back? How long does princess duties take? He was feeling anxious and just wanted her here so he could feel safe.

He watched the Master waving his hands near him. The sensation returned. What is happening? Tell me what you are doing? He struggled to understand. It felt good, but he was confused.

"Feeling like you could try again?" asked the male called Jasper. The Master moved away. The sensation stopped.

He nodded. They helped him stand and let him go. He was standing by himself. He felt happy.

"Try sitting down by yourself and see if you can stand up without us," said Jasper.

He sat. Could he stand without help? Was that something he could do before? She will be pleased if he could. He slowly raised himself and shakily stood.

"Excellent. Rest a bit, and then we will try to walk. Sit if you need," said Jasper.

Did he need to sit? He felt fine and didn't know what to do. He sat to think. Where was she? Would she return soon? He hoped so. He could hear footsteps, hoping it was her. He eagerly watched the door open, and she entered. He was happy, and he stood.

"Oh fantastic, you can stand by yourself," she said, her face beaming towards Sarina.

He saw she was delighted. He had made her happy, and that made him happy. Another memory flicked through his mind.

"Can you walk? See if you can move your foot forward. Lorcan and Fendton will catch you," she said.

He looked at his feet, not knowing how to move them. He felt a push on his leg to help him. He moved it forward, and he felt another push on the other. He moved it. He was moving closer to her where he wanted to be.

"Excellent work. We will get you moving in no time. Heal Master will help you move, and Sight Master will help you get your memories back. You have forgotten, haven't you?" she said.

He nodded. How did she know? She must know me well.

"I know because I can hear your thoughts. How about we get you home and continue getting you better. Are you ready to go home?" she asked.

He nodded. He wanted to see where he lived. Maybe it will help him remember. He hoped it did as he tried to remember her.

"Ok, Movement Master, let's do it. Does every being have everything? Where are our bags?" she asked as she scanned the room.

"I have them," the other female spoke.

Who was she, and how do they get home? Where is home? He was confused.

"It's ok. You just stand here with me, and the movement Master will do the rest. You will feel tingly, and everything goes black and your home. Very easy." She said with her arm around his waist.

Will she not be coming with him?

"I will be with you the whole way. It is ok. I won't leave you for the rest of the dia," she said, smiling at him.

He smiled and kept his eyes on her. The group surrounded him, and he felt tingly, everything went black, and as his eyes adjusted, he saw he was in another room. Was this home? A scent of honeysuckle filled his nostrils. The smell was familiar, and she said they were going home. It must be home.

"We are at home. Are you ok?" she asked.

He nodded.

"Let's get you settled on the couch, and then the Sight Master will see if he can help you unlock your memories," she said.

He nodded and, with help, shuffled to the couch.

"Are you comfortable?" she asked.

He nodded.

"The Master is going to go into your mind. Would you like me to show you what is going to happen? If you don't like it, we won't do it, ok?" she said.

He nodded.

"Usually, we just read what you think, but the Master needs to find answers and to do that, he needs to enter. Relax, and I shall enter your mind," she said.

He could see her in his mind, standing there beside him. In front of them were rows and rows of small windows starting at the floor and reaching just above his head. She spoke, but he heard no voice in his ears.

'I can talk to you through your mind. The Master will walk with you checking the windows, attempting to find the key. Come, let's see what he will do. All your memories are windows that have the shutters closed, which means the memory is blocked. I have jars for my memories which are stored on shelves as high as I can reach. Others have their memories stored in boxes or books or within balls,' Elentari said as she moved along the rows of windows. 'This window, you can see the light around the edges and is coloured. This means there is a memory, one you have unblocked. If you were to open the shutter, it would show you that memory.' As she opened the shutter, the shutter disappeared and he could see a picture. 'This is when you first met me. See you are standing at my door, and I open it to find you there.'

He watched the scene unfolding in front of him. He liked the feeling of seeing her for the first time. He could see the joy he had for her, meeting her for the first time. As he stared at the scene, he could feel something stir inside him, a feeling bubbling within.

She left his mind, and he opened his eyes.
"It wasn't too bad, was it?" she said, watching him.
He shook his head.
"The Master will read your mind and attempt to find the key to unlock all your memories. Are you ready?" she asked.
He hesitated, unsure if he was alright. He wanted to please her and make her happy. He nodded. The Master was in his mind, running through all the rows and rows of windows his mind contained, running this way and that, looking for something, and Rorien couldn't keep up. They passed many blank windows without colour, but the Master kept moving, moving deeper and further but didn't open any shutters. He just kept racing through

his mind, quickly moving and not stopping. 'Stop,' he thought, and the Master disappeared.

"I went as far as I could before he stopped. I found nothing yet and shall try again on the morrow," said the Master. "We shall leave you."

"Can you ask the King to come by, please? I don't want to leave him again," she said.

"Yes, Princess." The masters bowed and left.

"We shall go too. We will come back later and check on you. Supper here?" asked Lorcan.

"Yes. Supper here. Sarina, can you please organise the cook to make us something. I shall see you all later and organise where we go from here," she said.

Every being left the room, and he was alone with her. He liked being with her, liked how she made him feel, liked how she fussed over him. She made him feel safe and loved. He smiled as he watched her. How calm and happy he felt around her. He was so tired and could hardly stay awake. He wanted to stay awake and watch her but his heavy eyelids closed.

CHAPTER 6

It was the last dia of the third mesik, Lume, when Elentari woke to kisses on her shoulder and hands moving over her body. Rorien had scrunched her bed shirt up around her neck. She lay there for a moment savouring the feel of the kisses, how she had missed waking up this way.

The past few mesiks had been stressful, taking care of Rorien and helping him recover. She helped him to move, to find his memories and to speak. Her life was consumed with him and allowing him to become him again. He was able to move around and perform tasks without help. Each dia, more new snippets of memories came back, snippets of festivals and places and general things. Yet, his memories were few, and his emotions were missing. He showed little emotion in all he did. The laughter and happiness no longer danced across his face or on his words. He was distant and cautious, speaking in short sentences and asking general questions.

Each night, the Sight Master would visit with the Air Master to talk to Rorien and hopefully unlock his memories. The Sight Master would explore Rorien's mind looking for the key to unlocking his memories, but had not been successful. Rorien wouldn't allow him to venture far or go into certain places. No matter how hard the Masters tried, Rorien kept his guard up.

This morning was different. Elentari rolled towards Rorien. "You're back," she said softly, tears welling in her eyes and a smile on her lips. It felt wonderful to feel Rorien touching her again.

"Yes, I am," Rorien answered as he kissed her and his hands explored her body.

"I missed you," she said, removing her top before kissing him again. Her hands moved over his body, exploring him and once more, getting to know him. She had almost forgotten how good he felt, how good he made her feel when he took her, bringing them both to climax.

"I love you," she said.

"And I you," he replied. He looked up at the ceiling. "My memories came flooding back during the night. It felt like I was watching a movie of my life, lots of screens flickering all at once and showing very fast. My head spun with such an overload of information. It was like it exploded, blasting them all through my mind. When it settled, waves full of emotions flooded through. I was crying, happy, scared, angry, alone, and many other emotions all at once. It was exhausting. Emotions were flowing all through my mind finding a spot to seep. It was quite confronting. How long have I been out of it?" he asked as he turned his head to face her.

"Too long, it was the 10th when the avalanche happened and 11th when you died and came back, and now it's the last dia of Lume," she replied. Her head rested on his shoulder as her hand rubbed his chest. She raised herself onto her elbow. "But let's not discuss it todia. It's your first dia back as you, so let's enjoy it. We can recap another dia?"

"Nearly four mesiks," he said quietly, turning to stare at the ceiling. "Ok, we will recap another dia. Our link is gone?" he asked as he looked at Elentari.

"Yes. It snapped when you died. The Masters have been searching for a way to rebuild it, not on the high priority list for them. So, our friends decided to search as well. They are quite used to the ancient library after all." She smiled her chin on his chest, looking towards his face.

"It feels strange not to feel or hear you. Snapped?" Rorien asked.

"Yes, it does, and, yes, it snapped like a twig. Just broke apart before fading to nothing," Elentari said quietly before sitting up excited. "What shall we do todia, now you are back?"

He grabbed her, pulling her to his chest and kissed her. "How about we stay here and do this all dia?" he said as he retook her, giving them such pleasure.

"It sounds like a perfect dia," she answered as her breathing calmed. "Except, in a moment, the door is going to open, and our friends will be here. Time to get up."

He groaned as she pushed him out of bed towards the shower, hearing the door open and footsteps through the lounge. She knew it was their friends organising breakfast. She emerged from the bathroom to find Rorien dressed and sitting on the bed, waiting for her to greet their friends together.

"Morning E. Morning Rorien," said Fendton as he poured tea.

"Morning Fen," replied Elentari.

"So, are you claiming the sled ride before the avalanche as your win?" asked Rorien.

"Well, I was." Fendton stopped mid-sentence and turned to Rorien. "Hang on. Your back!?" said a surprised Fendton. "You are you again?"

"Yes, it's me," replied Rorien.

"Sarina, Jasper, he's back!" yelled Fendton as Sarina and Jasper entered the room. "Rorien is back!"

"Rorien, it is you?" asked Jasper.

"Yeah, I'm back," grinned Rorien.

"Glad to have you back," said Jasper, shaking his hand and bringing him into his chest.

"Glad to be back," replied Rorien, slapping Jasper on his back. "So, what's on the agenda todia?"

"Breakfast first. A visit to Papa next. Then we shall walk around the cuedel," said Elentari. "An easy, carefree dia until we begin duties on the morrow."

"Great. So, nothing fun then," replied Rorien. "I'm back, and you've got me greeting every being. No catching up with friends, just boring Prince stuff."

"Yes. So, spend this time catching before I drag you out," said Elentari with her hands on her hips and a smile on her lips.

The dia was spent wandering the cuedel and greeting beings, their faces lighting up to see Prince Rorien himself. Word spread quickly through the cuedel, and beings inundated them, wanting to see the

Prince. Cheers and accolades followed them everywhere they went. Their cuedel was terrific to be so supportive and accepted them as their future. Elentari was most pleased to be part of this beautiful community. It was very different to her city on Earth. Here it was more of a large family always coming together and supporting those around them compared to Earth, where everyone went about doing their own thing.

Life went back to normal the following morning, each off doing their duties and being her guard. She made Rorien take it easy and assigned a guard to him to make sure he rested. She would need to find a new guard to replace him. Then have her guards take the blood oath to be his guard as well. It was not usual for the royal's linked to have a guard, and as she was not typical, it fitted. Sharing their guard would enable them to assign them as required and give them more protection and information. For todia, her three guards were enough.

"Papa, I need a new guard to replace Rorien and want them all to take the blood oath to him, enabling us to share our guard and assigning them as required. I have an air yielder I wish to ask," said Elentari as she entered the royal hall with Jasper as her guard.

Both Lorcan and Fendton were with Rorien, making sure he rested and took it easy. Not that they need to watch Rorien as the elder females were doting on him and keeping him under control.

"I am sure Seneca will gladly take the blood oath to you, and having them all take the blood oath to Rorien is a great idea. As it is not a custom, it suits you. On the morrow, we shall complete the blood oaths. Inform Seneca and your guards, and I shall sup with you tonight," said the King.

"Thanks, Papa. I shall see you for supper tonight. Come on, Jasper. We need to find Seneca first and then the others before we get into duties," said Elentari as she began to head out of the hall. Jasper fell into step beside her.

"This means we will all have two oaths to keep?" asked Jasper.

"Yes, is this a concern for you?" asked Elentari, looking sideways at him, an eyebrow raised.

"No. We are with you both anyway, and it does seem logical. Just means I have three to summon me whenever they want," said Jasper with a grin.

"Not sure Sarina will appreciate that comment and, in the time I've known you, she has not summoned you," smiled Elentari.

"Wasn't game enough to fight you for me," grinned Jasper.

"Fight me for you!? She can have you. Three is nothing. Try having four to command and not just be summoned by," said Elentari with a little giggle.

"Wanting to make this a competition, are you?" asked Jasper.

"If I did, I would win again. You cannot beat me. Every time you bet against me, you lose, so give up now," smirked Elentari.

"For now, we shall table this discussion. Seneca is over there," said Jasper, pointing to Seneca.

The training area was in full swing. Not only was the army were practising their yielding, but beings were also practising their yielding, calling on the Masters and Apprentices for help. Elentari could hear the clanging of swords above the sound of voices as the army was training. She glanced to where Jasper pointed. She saw Seneca among the beings helping with yielding.

"Seneca, I have a request to ask you," said Elentari as she approached him.

"Yes, Princess, what is it I can help you with?" asked Seneca, bowing.

"I require a new guard who yields air. Do you have any suggestions?" she asked playfully.

"Other than myself, none who would be game to tango with you," Seneca grinned. "I would be honoured to be your guard Princess."

"Wonderful. Tonight, please join us for supper and bring your link. It will enable me to meet her and to get to know her. She should know us all a bit before you officially join the Princess' entourage," Elentari said.

"Thank you, Princess. Nea and I will be honoured to sup with you. Until supper, Princess," said Seneca bowing before returning to his duties.

"And the group grows to nine of us," said Jasper as they headed off.

"We are getting large. Lucky this is all. Oh, we still have one to come," said Elentari.

"Who?" asked Jasper.

"Fendton's link, whoever she is. Wonder if he will find her soon?" wondered Elentari.

"Who can tell. It took Rorien nine anoks to find you and Lorcan was four anoks. Has he tugged for her?" Jasper asked.

"Good question. I do not know the answer," Elentari said as they approached Rorien and Lorcan. She filled them in on oaths before finding Fendton.

"You know, the answer will be revealed when it is needed," grinned Jasper as they continued on.

"Yes, it will. And just for that remark, you are on extra duties," smirked Elentari, playfully jabbing him in the ribs.

The following morning, Elentari and Rorien found the eight Masters waiting for them in the royal hall, ready to conduct the oath for the Prince's guard and the Princess' new air guard. The King sat on the throne and watched her enter. His eyes moved across the group as they entered.

"Good morning Prince. Are you prepared for the oaths?" asked the King.

"Yes, my King," said Rorien, bowing as Elentari stood beside him.

"Princess guards, do you accept the honour of being the Prince guards as well as the Princess' guard?" asked the King.

"Yes, I accept," answered Lorcan, Jasper and Fendton in unison.

"Seneca, do you accept the honour of being both the Princess and Prince guard?" asked the King.

"Yes, I accept," answered Seneca.

"Masters prepare for the oath. Begin with Seneca and the Princess," said the King.

The Master of air stepped forward. Elentari and Seneca held out their right hands to the Master. The Master cut them both, and Seneca took Elentari's hand in his, their blood pooling together. The Master recited the ancient oath.

"You are my guard by the ancient oath," said Elentari.

"I am your guard by the ancient oath," answered Seneca.

They healed their wound and let go. Elentari reached up to her chest, touching her new oath. Seneca raised his hand to his chest, and Elentari felt his touch on the oath.

"Rorien, step forward," said the Air Master.

Rorien stepped beside Seneca, and they held out their right hands to the Master. Each of the Element Masters performed the blood oath as Elentari watched from her seat beside her father, her face beaming with joy watching her link receive his guards.

"The oaths have been completed. Spend the dia getting to know your guards," said the King.

"Yes, my King," answered Rorien bowing.

"Let's help Seneca and Nea move into their new casa before we relax and enjoy the dia," said Elentari as she stood. "Rorien's old casa is the perfect spot for you," she said to Seneca.

"Excellent idea, Princess. Nea was excited to meet you all last night, and she is looking forward to being part of the group," said Seneca. Nea had opened up quickly to the group and fitted in marvellously with the females. Her bright personality made it easy to get along with her.

"It was a delight to meet her," said Elentari, taking Rorien's arm before heading out of the hall. "Let's find her and help you move in."

Seneca and Nea settled into their casa. The group were chilling, glad for a little downtime after the past few hectic mesiks.

"E, can we not have any more excitement and disasters, please," said Fenton as they sat in the Princess parestala.

"What do you mean, Fen?" Elentari asked.

"Well, each mesik you have been here, something eventful has happened, be it good or bad. Your first mesik, we found out you yield every power, and we had to be wary of Rorien and his decision not to be with you. The second mesik you put us in grave danger meeting Hoofington and the fauns. The third was good with your linking dia, and you went away. The fourth was the King's death and avalanche. Rorien forgetting everything and having to help him, that was three mesiks. This mesik, we took oaths to Rorien, and now you turn 21 on the dia after the morrow."

"Jasper did say to Rorien the first dia I was here; life would never be boring. Guess I lived that up," she grinned at Jasper.

"Never thought it would be this full-on with you and expected you would be giving Rorien grief, not us," replied Jasper.

"Wasn't all me. Rorien put us through hell after the avalanche," said Elentari.

"Good point. But back to Fen's point, when can we get a break from all this madness?" Jasper asked.

"Was it this mad back on your world?" asked Fendton quietly.

"Not for me. Others would have lots happen to them and others who would have nothing. Life is very unpredictable. I never expected to be stolen and sent to another world, only to have my life changed by a stranger. It won't always continue this way, Fen," said Elentari, placing her hand on his arm.

"Can we stay in the Royal lands and not venture anywhere? It is safer here. Everything bad happens beyond here," said Fendton.

"No, Fen, I have to visit the other lands. Plus, I like adventure and excitement, not destruction, excitement. You were enjoying all the fun in the snow before the avalanche," Elentari said, placing her hand in her lap.

"Yes, but…" began Fendton as Elentari cut him off.

"No buts. It was fun, and we all enjoyed it. Think of the other exciting places we can visit and the fun we can have? Plus, you are my guard; you have no choice," she smirked, laughter dancing across her eyes.

"She has you there, Fen. It was fun, and you have no choice," laughed Jasper.

"The next adventure is my 21st and yours too, Fen. It was not great we missed yours, and what a fantastic idea to have a joint birth date celebration? We're both 21, and we are celebrating together, celebrating my 21st with my bestie," said Elentari, grabbing Fendton and hugging him tightly.

"Ok. I can handle our joint birth date celebration. Nothing bad should happen," said Fendton, untangling himself from her grip.

"What about a trip to my world? We can go for Donna's 21st, would you like that Fen?" asked Elentari.

"I know how you have fared in the past with celebrations. Their linking dia," said Jasper pointing to Elentari. "You seemed to have a lot of fun," Jasper said, nudging Fendton.

"Yeah, Fen. You never did tell us what happened to you on their linking dia? We saw how you ended up but not how you got there, so spill," said Lorcan standing above Fendton.

"Nothing happened. I drank, I danced, and I went to sleep," Fendton said, folding his arms across his chest, slinking down in his chair and hanging his head in an attempt to hide himself to avoid their questioning. It didn't work.

The males kept ribbing him and pushing for details. Even Seneca was joking around with them. Elentari sat back, watching her guards enjoy themselves thinking to herself. It had been a big anok. Her first anok in her homeland as the Princess, and to finish it off, her parents and Donna would be here soon. She left her guards to continue their banter as she headed to her casa with Rorien to relax before meeting her parents on the morrow.

"When will they be here?" asked Elentari to no one. She was pacing the floor in the ancient library, waiting for her parents and Donna to arrive.

Only a few Apprentices were in the library todia and had moved to the other side of the room when she started pacing in frustration. The first anok Apprentices hid in the passages as they continued to catalogue the books. It was their responsibility to organise the texts into subjects and document every book. The Scholar Apprentices had packed up and left to continue their recordings of new information in the library.

"They will be here," said Rorien as he half sat and half leaned on her table.

The table was a gift from the Masters and Scholars for opening up the ancient library. The library had brought them much joy and excitement that it was their way of saying thanks to her. Elentari's gift was a beautiful wooden table with carved dragons twisting up the legs with their heads supporting the tabletop. Power symbols were etched into the sides and set with each power stone. Across the top of the desk was an inscription. Her table sat in the far corner near the fire passage, where Rorien discovered her code.

"Why aren't they here now? This is agony waiting for them and not knowing when they are due to arrive. At least on Earth, the Arrivals board told you when they would arrive. This, turning up when you feel like it is not going to work for me," said Elentari in frustration.

"They will be here. They did say they would come in the morning, and there are still a few horis till high sun. Why not walk the full length of the air passage?" asked Rorien. Under his breath, he said, "that will fill in time and stop you whinging for a bit."

"And if they arrive while I am down there, I won't be here to greet them. No, I am waiting here. Plus, I heard that," Elentari said, stopping in front of him with her hands on her hips.

"Good. Stop whinging," said Rorien.

"I just want to be here when they arrive. It's my first time to meet them here," Elentari said.

"Then wait patiently. How about you read a book?" asked Rorien, picking up a random book off a nearby table.

"I can't concentrate on a book! I'm too agitated. I don't like to wait and hate not knowing," answered Elentari, shaking her head.

"You weren't this uptight when it was our linking dia. Sit down and stop pacing. You're wearing a trench in the stone floor," Rorien said, shifting the chair out for her to sit.

She slumped into the chair but not for long, again, pacing the floor.

"Finally, it is here," said Rorien as the portal appeared and Francis and Beth stepped through.

"Mum, Dad, you're finally here," Elentari said, racing to her parents and hugging them. "Where's Donna?" Elentari stared at the space where her parents arrived, waiting to see Donna appear.

"Hello, Dear. She didn't come with us," answered her mother as she hugged her tightly.

"Why? Where is she? She is coming, right?" asked Elentari, all agitated.

"I spoke to her yesterday, and she said she would meet us here," said Beth.

"She'd better not miss my birth date, or she is in big trouble," said Elentari, stepping back. "Come. Let's settle you into our place and find the King. Papa is looking forward to catching up with you both," she said as she headed up the stairs, talking nonstop. She led the way to their place and settled them in before finding the King. The King began filling them in on all Elentari had accomplished since they were last here and all the happenings in the cuedel. Elentari left her parents with the King to check on preparations.

Elentari checked on the parestalas for the 21st birth date before finding her parents and spending the rest of the dia with all three of her parents. It was well after supper when Donna finally appeared.

"Thank goodness you don't lock your door," said Donna as she stepped through the door of Elentari's casa, dropping her bag onto the floor.

"Donza!" yelled Elentari.

Both girls erupted screaming, racing towards each other, talking rapidly over the top of each other, questioning, answering, explaining, hands flailing about, hugging and touching each other, not breathing, holding two different conversations at once.

"Not again," groaned Lorcan. "I'm not putting up with this. I'm off to bed." Lorcan slapped Rorien on the back and headed out the door. The rest quickly followed behind except Sarina and Jasper.

"Elentari, we need to get Donna settled in," said Sarina placing a hand on both Elentari and Donna's shoulder. "You can continue this on the morrow. It is late." Sarina grabbed Donna's arm and pulled her out the door.

"Ok. We shall settle Donza in and catch up on the morrow," said Elentari as she bounded out the door with Donna in tow.

Elentari and Donna continued their rapid talking as they settled Donna in at Sarina's casa. Even after Donna was settled, the girls continued. As hard as Sarina tried, she could not stop them or get Elentari to leave. Sarina gave up and left them, heading to bed and leaving Jasper to continue. It was late in the night when Jasper finally managed to kick Elentari out and peace filled the casa.

The sun was beginning to rise as Elentari bounced out of bed and raced into the lounge room. "It is the 4th of Erde and my birth date!" she yelled over and over as she raced through the casa.

"Happy birthday Dear," said her mum appearing from the guest room, rubbing her eyes.

"I am 21 todia! 21 todia. Which makes me an adult!" she said, dancing around the room.

"Happy birthday, girly," said her dad as he hugged her.

"What is all the commotion?" asked Rorien, appearing half asleep in the bedroom doorway.

"It's my birth date! Todia, I am 21! Woohoo!" she said, jumping up and down.

"Is she always this excited?" groaned Rorien.

"No, not always. When she turned 18 and could drive without us, she got this excited. On Earth, 21 is a big deal and being her first birthday here, she will be excited," said Beth watching her daughter going crazy through the casa.

"Anza, it's your birthday!" yelled Donna bursting through the door, grabbing Elentari and jumping around in circles.

"Yes, I know. I'm 21!" she said as both girls were running excitedly on the spot.

"When will they stop?" groaned Rorien as he headed into the kitchen.

"Tomorrow. Tomorrow, they will stop. Don't expect them to stop before then," replied Francis as he sat at the table, waiting for his coffee.

"What's wrong?" asked Fendton racing through the door. Elentari had called him on the oath.

"It's my birth date and our combined 21st!" yelled Elentari, and she and Donna grabbed Fendton, spinning him around with them.

"Woohoo! My 21st party!" replied Fendton joining in with their merriments.

"On no" groaned Rorien collapsing against the kitchen bench. "Not you too, Fen." He watched the three of them go crazy before racing out of the casa screaming. "So, where are they going?" He had a look of concern on his face.

"Usually, they run around the block screaming. Here, I am not sure where they will go," answered Beth. "Maybe around the North area or maybe around the whole cuedel. Only they know."

"So, we have a few moments of peace, great. Tea anyone?" asked Rorien, holding up the teapot.

Elentari, Fendton and Donna raced their way around the cuedel, yelling and screaming, jumping and dancing. Letting every being they met know it was the Princess's birth date and her and Fendton's combined party. Their merriment was contagious and beings began to join in. They finally made their way back to have breakfast, open gifts and dress for the dia before again racing through the cuedel. Presents kept arriving in the Princess parestala for Elentari and some for Fendton. The three of them excitedly opened them together, presenting and discussing the gift between them with anticipation and enthusiasm. Beth quietly wrote the thank-you cards for each gift.

By the time their party kicked off, the three of them had hardly stopped. Their excitement and gusto hardly waned all dia. The East parestala kicked off the celebrations and was decorated in varying sized balls in a chained garland forming arches around the parestala. A large wooden 21 stood in the middle of the parestala. Tables were filled with antipasto platters, fruit platters, cakes and biscuits, and a cake in the shape of 21 took pride at the end of the parestala. Those from the east filled the parestala and congratulated the Princess and Fendton as they entered, throwing petals over them and joined them in their merriment.

In the South parestala, streamers hung down from the top in various lengths filling the whole parestala. Streamers reached down to touch beings heads and shoulders, and Elentari and Fendton ran through with their arms raised. An enormous wooden 'E' and 'F' stood in the middle of tables covered in food platters. Cupcakes were joined together to spell out 'ELENTARI' and 'FENDTON' and took place at the end of the parestala. Again, they were covered in petals as those from the south congratulated them. All had much fun as they ran hands stretched up through the streamers.

The West parestala was filled with flower garlands hanging from the top, and on daises were candles of fluctuating sizes, creating beautiful lighting throughout. The tables were filled with food and biscuits, and a four-tier cake decorated with filigree icing spelling their names and the number 21 sat on the table at the end of the parestala. Beings threw more petals and congratulations, more frivolities and excitement.

The fauns and minotaurs were gathered at the North parestala to celebrate with them. The parestala was decorated with ball garlands, lanterns and candles. A jelly cake sat pride of place in the centre of the parestala, an awe-inspiring, unique and edible work of art. The jelly cake was a purple 21 on a sparkling base with colourful fireworks motifs injected into clear jelly to create the illusion of a 3-dimensional cake. Stars adorned the top as if they were suspended in mid-air. A group of fauns sat in the corner playing music on flutes while others danced. At each parestala, they danced and sang and drank, enjoying every moment.

Every being sang the tradition birth date song as they stood together with their arms linked.

It is your birth date, the dia you were born.
It is your birth date, a dia filled with joy.
It is your birth date, another anok has passed,
and we wish you many more. Hoorah!

They spent the night moving from parestala to parestala with their friends, the princes and fauns. Beings were lost as the night wore on, picking a parestala to stay at or taking their leave to rest. It seemed only Prince Sven and Princess Anya had kept up with Elentari. Even her guards had decided to stay at the North parestala as she continued. Elentari, Fendton and Donna were the only ones sitting in the princess parestala as the night began to change.

"E, the sun is going to be coming up soon. Our celebrations are over," said Fendton.

"Ok. It's bedtime," said Elentari, standing up.

"Or we could just keep going," said Donna.

"If we keep going, then we have to help clean up. Plus, I want some sleep before having to greet the Kings to say goodbye. Don't want to look bleary-eyed for them," said Elentari, grabbing Donna's hand and pulling her up.

"Sven and Anya will. They were not in a good state when they headed off. Red eyes and sore heads for them," grinned Donna.

"But not for us. Glad we have always had the 'stop drinking after midnight' rule," Elentari said as they began finding their way to Fendton's.

"Best rule we've agreed on and made. It has got us out of all those idiotic ideas at two in the morning," said Donna.

"So, a few horis of shut-eye before we get found, and I have to be host," said Elentari.

"Bed it is." They all said in unison.

"I'll take the spare bed," said Elentari, heading into Fendton's spare room.

"Me too," said Donna, following her. "Night Fen."

"Or morning," said Elentari as she closed the door.

CHAPTER 7

Anticipation had been building for a few days in the lead up to the Jiwebola Final. From what Elentari's dad could gather, it was the equivalent of an FA Cup Final, Superbowl, or Grand Final of the AFL or NRL. He was always keen to understand new sports. He was thrilled to be allowed to attend as a special guest of Elentari and the King. East would be playing West in the Final. This was also Elentari's first look at their traditional game. Her mum chose to stay at the casa and spend time with the other females.

The shape of the playing field was the first thing she noticed. There were four independent rectangular playing fields, positioned in the form of an 'M', out in the grounds in front of them. The main grandstand was set at the bottom of the 'M', with the King's seat located right in the middle, allowing the best view of all four fields. Other beings were scattered around the outside of the fields, scampering for any view they could obtain. The group found their spots in the Kings area and settled in, waiting for the games to begin.

Out in the fields, they could see some younger beings pretending to emulate their heroes who were about to take the field for the main event.

"Right," said Francis to the males. "What do I need to know about this game?"

They all seemed eager to answer the question and started talking over the top of each other, each wanting to show that they were the expert in their local sport!

"One at a time, please, Lads," said Francis, slightly laughing. The same thing happens at Footy games, he thought to himself.

Lorcan took the lead in the explanations. "Each field represents one of the powers. We start with Earth power on that field," he said, pointing to the field to their far left. "Then Water power on this field on the angle to our left. Firepower on this field on the angle to our right, and finally Airpower over to our far right."

"Each team has to move the ball past their opponents and into the goal at the end," Lorcan continued.

"Yes, but each team has their own ball," Rorien jumped in.

"Yeah, I'm getting to that," said Lorcan. "Each team has their own ball, and as they move the ball through various obstacles, they score points based on the difficulty of the obstacle. The catro ends when a goal is scored."

"Catro?" asked Francis.

"Think of it as a Quarter Dad," replied Elentari.

Suddenly, there was a roaring cheer as the players entered the grounds. Each of the teams had 16 team members in total, four for each power. The players waved to the crowd as they made their way to their designated field. Eight players in green robes made their way to the first field, four with the letter E on their backs and four with W. When in position, they waited nervously, ready for the big match to begin.

The tradition was for the King to open the games with a yielding ball. The King rose from his chair and held his arm high to signal the crowd to quieten. The crowd hushed, and the King yielded a fireball, throwing it high, signalling for the games to begin. A rush of adrenaline had the crowd on their feet, cheering for their team. West's ball was blue, and East had the red ball. The earth players began to move their ball, only using yielding as they stood on their platforms. No team members were allowed to step onto the field or off their platforms.

The two balls began to move from either side, both balls heading across the field in a seemingly random pattern as both teams tried to secure points on their way to goals. A coloured hole in the ground marked the goals, East's goal was red, and West's was blue. East was moving their ball away from the grandstand and West toward the stand. Attacking players were trying to get the ball through tunnels for extra points while defenders were blocking and endeavouring to stop their opponents' ball for points.

As they scored points, the crowd roared for their team, abusing the Umpire for what they thought was foul play and screaming tips to their players. A hubbub of continuous noise filled the air. It was full of energy, contagious energy that you can feel and hear zinging through all, an energy that vibrates beneath your skin. You could not help but be part of the excitement.

'*A typical Footy crowd*,' thought Francis.

East had managed to secure control of West's ball as well as their own. Both balls were moving towards East goal, and they looked destined to score a goal. However, just as East were about to score, West blocked and took control of one of the balls. They didn't appear to go on the attack, though, and the ball lay dormant at the edge of the field, waiting for West to take control.

"What is happening? Why is the other ball not in play?" asked Francis to Lorcan.

"The ball is in the zone of the West defender and the East attacker. Only they can control the balls in their zone. Other players are not allowed into their zone," answered Lorcan.

"Unless the players from the other zones control the ball when it moves between zones," said Rorien.

"Yes, but that's not the case here," replied a frustrated Lorcan, concentrating on the action.

"So, the West defender needs to move Easts ball into the next zone so West can retake control of the ball?" asked Francis.

"Yes, but right now, the West Defender is trying to make sure that the East Attacker doesn't score a goal. You are right, though; if the defender can somehow get the ball into the next zone, then his teammates can go on the attack again," said Lorcan.

The battle between West Defender and East Attacker to maintain control of the red ball continued to play out, while the other players were anxiously waiting, ready to take control of the other ball if it came into their zone.

The West Defender was doing an excellent job in preventing the East Attacker from scoring a goal and somehow managed to move the ball a long way from the goal. Sensing the chance to progress the other ball into an attacking position, he moved the second ball back into play, passing it on to his teammate in the next zone.

That slight distraction was enough for the East Attacker to try a long-distance shot at goal. Score! The East supporters erupted, stamping and cheering for the goal. East added 10 points to their score for the goal, taking their tally for catro1 to 19. West had only managed 6 points for catro1.

"Now we move to catro2 on Field 2. This is water yielding," said Lorcan.

"So, a goal ends the catro?" asked Elentari.

"Yes, catros can take a long time or a short time," answered Lorcan.

"You're a Water Yielder, aren't you, Jasper? Any good moves we should watch out for?" asked Francis. Elentari smiled at her dad with pride as he immersed himself in her new world.

"I like it when the defender sends a fast water twister to stop the ball. That can look great if it throws the ball into the air," said Jasper.

"What!?" questioned Elentari.

"Watch. Every game, there is at least one twister that shoots the ball high. You will know it when you see it. It's called a tordopio shot," replied Jasper.

"Got it, watching for a tordopio. Ok. How is the court staying rectangle?" asked Elentari, looking at the tall wall of water.

The field was a giant fishbowl, without any sides holding the water back with tunnels floating within. The goal was a coloured hoop in the centre of the end walls.

"The Master keeps the water in place," said Lorcan.

The umpires threw the balls into play, and quickly each team began to yield water to move their ball. The field was swirling and bubbling with currents flowing at different speeds, with twists and turns. Eddies were churning like hurricanes, creating a vortex for the ball to pass through rapidly. The balls were being tossed and turned with all the movement of the water. Balls tumbling down before flying to the top. Hiding the ball within the bubbles or whirlpools was a tactic to cause the opponent to lose focus and enable control.

All around the stadium, beings were leaping to their feet, shouting and screaming, raising fists in rage and flaying their hands in the air. East was moving their ball towards the goal when West blocked, causing the ball to rise high into the air beyond the field before falling back. The water movement, a tight spiralling twist of water, came from nowhere and with such force to punch the ball out of play and into the West end.

"And that is a tordopio," said Jasper, his hand forcefully pointed to the field.

"Oh, wow! That is unbelievable," said Elentari, her eyes wide. "Can you do that move, Jasper?"

"Not as strong, but I can. Guess you want me to teach you?" asked Jasper.

"Yes, please," replied Elentari.

The tordopio move gave West the distraction they needed to punch their ball through a whirlpool and directly into their goal, scoring a vital 10 points to even up the game at the end of catro2.

The Water Masters then updated the scoreboard for all to see
East 23
West 21

"That wasn't very long," said Francis, a bit disappointed.

"Catros are not timed. Once the ball is in the goal, the catro ends. Some catros can take a long time and others, SECONDS. The shortest catro was 8 seconds by North, and the longest was nearly two horis when South played North. That game almost lasted all dia," replied Lorcan.

"They explained that last catro, Dad! Geez, keep up!" Elentari said, clearly enjoying herself.

"Anyone want anything to eat or drink?" asked Jasper.

A chorus of yes please from everyone, as Jasper wondered why he had to ask.

"Does someone bring them, or do we need to go get them?" asked Francis.

"Elentari could probably waive her hand, and someone would bring them, but more of an experience for us to get them ourselves," smirked Jasper in Elentari's direction.

"Great, I'll give you a hand," said Francis, as he and Jasper made their way out of their seats to find food and drink.

"Your Dad seems to be enjoying himself," Rorien said to Elentari after Francis was out of earshot.

"Yeah, he just loves sport. Any sport, especially if he sees the best of the best," replied Elentari.

"Maybe one day in the future, when things quieten down, I could travel to your world, and Francis could take me to one of your Football games?" added the King, which surprised everyone.

"That's a long way off, Papa. I cannot imagine things quietening down any time soon," answered Elentari.

The King sat back and nodded, albeit with a tiny grin on his face.

"I'd like to see that too," continued Lorcan. "Francis was telling me about football and that you have completely different games, and they are all still called football. How odd is that? I think he said Soccer, Gridiron, Rugby and the other one called Australian Rules. Australian Rules is the one I'd be keen to see. Francis was so enthused when he was talking about it."

Lorcan and Elentari continued to discuss Jiwebola & Football's merits, with Lorcan still adamant that there would be no better sport than Jiwebola.

"Hey, your back," said Rorien, as Jasper and Francis appeared with food and drink for them.

"What's this?" asked Elentari as Jasper handed her a Jiwebola Special.

"It's a Jiwebola Special. No meat in it, so you can have it, but beyond that, you'd need to ask Jasper," answered Francis, eager to show his newly acquired knowledge.

"Try it and see. You'll like it," Rorien added.

A Jiwebola special was a red ball-shaped rice bowl that fitted nicely in your hand. It was filled with a gooey blue substance, a bit like melted marshmallow, and thin rectangular rice biscuits to dunk into the goo. Elentari dipped a biscuit into the blue substance and took a bite. It tasted a bit like orange-lemon-cherry-raspberry-apple-blueberry-blackberry-lime with a touch of vanilla. The flavour was most unusual and tough to describe, very hard to pinpoint a specific taste. The smooth, creamy pudding texture melted in her mouth. Even the rice biscuits melted on her tongue, keeping the soft, flowing texture. It was not as sweet-tasting as she expected but more of a refreshing and cleansing taste.

"This is amazing!" said Elentari dipping her biscuits in goo, enjoying the new experience and taste. Following the others' lead, she broke the bowl and dipped it in the remaining goo when she finished the biscuits, leaving nothing to clean up.

"So, this is only available during Jiwebola? What a shame," said Elentari.

"Yeah, you should be able to have it whenever you want. Too good," said Fendton dipping his fingers into his goo and sucking them.

"Back on Earth, we have meat pies and hot dogs at games. Which yielding is next?" asked Elentari.

"My favourite, FIRE!" answered the King, his eyes massive and smile wide. "Play is about to start too!"

The umpires rolled the balls onto the field, and the players used fire yielding to move the ball in the direction of their goal. Fireballs exploded around the field, lines of fire snaked across the field and fire whips cracked from the players' arms. Fire lines pulled the ball along tunnels, and fireballs would be thrown at them, knocking them offline. Cracks were formed from the fire heat drying out the surface. The players then used these cracks to run the ball in their direction.

"This is exciting. I like this catro," said Elentari.

"Yes, both teams are playing extremely well." replied both the King and Lorcan.

A cacophony of cheering, hollering, and stamping of feet buzzed through the charged air. Beings were electrified, soaring to new heights of emotions, their fists in the air and eyes flung wide. They were screaming with passion watching the balls continually shifting direction, never stopping, rolling this way and that, back and forwards, around and around but never in a straight line.

Eager for their team to lead at the end of the third catro, both teams' supporters took their noise level even louder than before. West had managed to remove Easts ball to the far end, with West's ball teetering on the goal's edge. The East Defender was flinging all his firepower to stop it toppling over as the West Attacker was pushing equally as hard. The ball was wobbling but not moving. Concentration imprinted on their faces, sweat seeping from their pores, teammates stiff, poised, ready for action, waiting. The ball was teetering. Neither could budge the ball, both pouring everything into their yielding, their power equally balanced. Suddenly from nowhere came a fire whip, cracking against the ball, giving it that final edge and tipping it into the goal. The crowd went mad, every being up on their feet, part of the crowd yelling abuse and others cheering for the goal. Banging and crashing filled the arena as part of the mob became angry.

"What is happening?" asked Elentari, noticing the umpires had not given the goal and were locked together in discussion.

"Possible ball interference," answered Lorcan.

"How?" asked Francis.

"The fire whip. Only the attacker can have control of the ball, and it seems another player used fire whip to assist," said Lorcan.

The Umpires called the Attacker and Defender to them, and the crowd hushed, ears straining to hear the Umpires. Whispers rose and fell around the arena as all watched the defender's hands, pointing and moving about as he explained his view. Umpires nodded and turned to the attacker. He pointed towards Elentari as he spoke. All eyes in the stadium turned to her.

"Mmm. I do not like this," said the King toward Elentari. "Did you do something there?"

"No. Honest, I didn't," answered Elentari as the Umpires made their way toward her.

"Guess we're about to find out," said Rorien.

"My King. Princess," said the Umpires bowing.

"Umpires." They answered.

"Princess, the attacker has said you showed him a move. We wish to confirm it is correct," said one of the Umpires.

"Please continue," the King answered the Umpires whilst glaring toward Elentari.

"He says you showed him how to use both hands to yield?" asked the Umpire.

"I do use both hands to yield, mainly using fire and water, but I can use both for one power," replied Elentari. She could feel every eye on her.

"Did you show him?" asked the Umpire.

"I have practised with many over my time here, and many have watched. I have not personally shown him how. But I guess he could have seen, and by default, I have shown him," said Elentari

"Can you yield a fire force and a whip?" asked the Umpire.

"Yes," answered Elentari.

"Please show us?" asked the Umpire.

"Please ask the attacker to show you. It is his skills which are in question," said Elentari.

"Yes, Princess," said the Umpire.

The Umpires bowed and headed back to the players. All players from both teams were huddled together beside the field. The Defender and Attacker in question were standing alone, quietly waiting.

"Gee E, you seem to like getting us in trouble. Even at the games," said Fendton.

"Oh, shut up and watch," snapped Elentari.

The attacker moved back to his podium and yielded a fire force. The Umpire nodded, signalling for the attacker to also yield a fire whip. He did so, proving he could yield both at once and, therefore, no interference. The Umpire signalled the end of catro3 and a goal to West.

The Fire Master then updated the scoreboard for all to see.
East 32
West 36

"Wow, this is close. Any sides game from here. East is normally pretty strong in Air yielding, so we should be in for a good finish," said Lorcan.

"Air won't have as much happening, will it?" asked Francis.

"No. It is boring to watch after all the others, no extra elements to view, just the ball moving," replied Lorcan, grinning at Rorien.

"Hey. Air is cool," snapped Rorien. "It's where the hard work happens, not that flashy stuff that you guys put up! Unless, of course, Elentari has more surprises we don't know about!"

"Shut up and watch, the lot of you. You are destroying the experience for me," said Elentari abruptly. She would never admit it, but Elentari had felt a little embarrassed to be queried on the powers. She was hoping to sit back and enjoy the contest with her Papa and Dad.

There seemed to be an eery hush in the crowd as everyone awaited catro4 to begin. Everyone could feel the tension and nerves as the players prepared themselves for the biggest catro of the year.

The airfield was exposed for all to see, with the ball rolling and changing direction frequently. There were no places or elements to hide the ball. Those spectators with Air powers could marvel at the subtlety of air currents' movements in the atmosphere and then anticipate the impact these currents would have on the ball.

'*A Purist's view*!' thought Francis. Trying to find the Earth sporting analogy, they were like those who enjoyed Test Match Cricket over T20.

The ability to move air meant the ability to slightly see currents in the atmosphere, see the air curling and the wisps of wind, and see how the currents gently meander down to the ground before rapidly twisting into the sky.

In the air catro, the Masters awarded points based on ball spin and rapid direction changes. West had taken full advantage early in Catro4 and jumped out to an 8-point lead. West only needed a couple of more points for the victory. If they could increase their lead to more than 10, then even an East goal would not be enough to steal victory away from West.

The West supporters were more vocal than they had been all game, whilst a nervous tension seemed to grip the East supporters.

East had managed to steal West's ball and was moving both in the direction of Easts goal, claiming back a couple of points in the process. West's lead back down to 6!

In an unprecedented move, Wests Yielder fired multiple currents in the direction of the ball. Most were deceptions, with the 'real' Air current securing back West's ball. Scoring another point with the move and the lead jumped back up to 7.

East's ball was not far from their goal, and the East Attacker and West Defender were fighting hard for control. A goal for East would end the game, securing the win. There was a lot to take in all at once, with West continuing to score points with their ball whilst East were attacking goal with their ball.

All players were concentrating fiercely, watching intently, trying to figure the best strategy to overcome their opponent.

And then it happened. In the blink of an eye, East changed the direction of their attack, moving the ball sideways and then straightening toward the goal. The ball seemed to take an eternity as it headed in the direction of the goal.

The raucous crowd noise from only seconds ago was silenced as everyone watching paused with nervous anticipation.

"It's in!" was the sound that broke the silence as the East crowd erupted with jubilation. Strangers were shaking hands and patting one another on the back. Wests supporters were slumped in their chairs, pondering missed opportunities and what might have been.

"And that is Jiwebola," said Lorcan, standing up to applaud an excellent final. The others joined his applause, recognising outstanding performance by both teams in the Final.

Both teams made their way to Grandstand to await the presentations. The King would present the Trophy to the winning team, and Elentari had the task of presenting the medal to the best player performance.

Elentari announced to the crowd. "The best player today, showcasing the ability to Yield with both hands, goes to Bradlett". This gave the West crowd something to cheer about, whilst the jubilant East crowd seemed happy to cheer anything and everything.

After the King handed over the Trophy to the winning team, the celebrations started to kick off. This was the cue for the King, Elentari and the rest of the group to make a quiet exit.

"Who's staying for the celebrations, and who's coming with us?" asked Elentari.

"Celebrations!" replied Fendton, without looking back as he jumped the fence onto the area.

"Yep, me too," said Lorcan.

"Yeah, I might stay for a while, too," said Jasper.

Lorcan and Jasper followed after Fendton while the rest of the group made their exit.

"Dad, how did you enjoy the game?" asked Elentari as she transported them home to find Mum.

"Loved it. It will be a memory that lasts forever. It will need to. Something tells me they will not bring out souvenir DVDs," said Francis, chuckling at his little dad joke.

CHAPTER 8

Jasper was with Rorien, and Fendton was with Elentari in the ancient library. Fendton searched through a book as he meandered through the outroom while Elentari was looking in the fire passage.

"Have you had any response from your link?" asked Elentari from the passage.

"No. I'm starting to understand Rorien's frustration at not getting a response. It's been four anoks, E, four anoks since we were 21, and I started pulling. Why won't she answer?" asked Fendton from the outroom.

"It will happen. If you pull enough, you will annoy her just as much as you annoy us, and she will answer," Elentari smirked.

"Thanks. Great help you are," Fendton said, slumping against the table. He kept flicking through the book he was holding.

"I found it!" yelled Fendton, suddenly, down the fire passage. "How we can rebuild the link. It is here!" He walked back to her table and placed the open book on her desk.

"What?" asked Elentari as she appeared from the passage. "Don't mess with me, Fen." She waved her fist at him.

"I'm not. The link rebuilding. It's here," replied Fendton, pointing to the book open on the table.

Elentari rushed over to read. She lifted her head to look at him. Her eyes sparkled with joy and her grin wide.

"Fantastic! Let's find Rorien and then the Master's, and let's get our link back. I have missed talking to him and feeling him," said Elentari. She placed her hand on Fendton's arm for a moment before saying, "This is awesome! Let's go." Elentari dragged Fendton from the library, heading towards the training field chatting excitedly about the rebuilding. Neither noticed the archway they stepped through until they were in a strange room and stopped. She had felt tingly, like the sensation of movement, and blacked out but thought nothing of it. Now she realised somehow, they had been transported here, but she was confused as to how. She looked to Fendton, and he was just as confused as she.

"What!?" they both said in unison.

Elentari grabbed hold of Fendton's arm and pulled on the oaths. She felt nothing. She did not know where they were and tried to yield movement but failed. Panic began to rise in her as she realised she had no easy way to get home.

"Welcome to my casa," said a female voice behind them.

They both slowly turned to the voice to find a female and male grinning at them. The male had a sinister look about him, causing her to tremble. A table of stone sat in the centre of the bare, large room with plenty of space between it and each wall.

"So, this is Rorien?" asked the female as she began to circle them, looking them up and down.

Fendton stood in front of Elentari, protecting her, his arm holding her back, her arm holding his.

"I expected you would have a better male than this," said the female, grinning as if she had won.

"This is not Rorien. This is my guard," said Elentari.

"You should have chosen better, Annie," the female sniggered with such a menacing tone that sent shivers down Elentari's spine.

"My name is Elentari," she said as she straightened up to stand tall and strong.

"Yes, and on your world, it was Annie! Shall I tell you how you became Annie?" the female snarled. "Have a seat."

The male pushed them against the wall, shoving them to the floor. Elentari tried to yield air to force the male away, and nothing happened. She sat beside Fendton on the ground, their backs against the wall and their bodies close together. Elentari's arm was tight around Fendton's as she began to feel helpless without her ability to yield. She turned to Fendton, her face full of shock and confusion as she discovered she was powerless. Fear began to creep across her face as she realised they were trapped. Her mind began to search for ways for them to escape.

Fendton's eyes were wide, concern for her safety written across his face, he too realising they were in trouble. He had tried to use earth yielding and failed. He searched the room, trying to find a way to get out. There was only one door, but he could not see what was beyond it.

"Don't be gentle with them. We can't have them comfortable," the female said to the male with a broad grin on her face.

"What do you know of my world?" growled Elentari.

"I know how you got there, and I know you should have stayed," replied the female.

Elentari desperately wanted to know what happened and focused her attention on the female, forgetting for the moment about escaping. She wanted to hear what the female knew.

"Go on," said Elentari.

"Are you uncomfortable? Good, I shall begin," the female said without pausing and took a seat on the chair.

"As you know, Queen Elena bore twins, Leelan and Gornack, and Leelan became king. Elena hated Gornack, but he was the rightful twin, the firstborn, and should have been king. Gornack was linked before the brothers' war and owned a casa in each of the lands. His linked preferred the casa in the Northlands and spent most of her time there. His family did not know about her. They kept their lives separate as she was not one for the limelight and preferred a simple life. Before the war began, Gornack's link fell pregnant and bore a son. Gornack went to war after his son was born as he wanted his true line to be on the throne. The evil fauns stormed the Royal land casa to free Gornack's workers, destroyed the casa and killed Gornack. No one knew he had more than one casa, and that kept any being from finding his linked and son, who were safe in the North. The son bore a son, who bore a son and so on until me. Gornack is my great, great, great, great, great grandfather, and I am to sit on the throne," said the female.

"No, you won't be. It is I who is next to sit on the throne," replied Elentari defiantly. The male slapped her hard across the face.

"Do not speak to the future Queen that way, and do not speak unless she questions you," the male said and slapped Elentari harder again.

Elentari tried, again, to use her powers against him but failed. Her yielding was useless. Fear crept in as she began to search for a way out.

"Yes, I will be the future Queen, for you will be dead," said the female.

Elentari went to speak, and Fenton quickly put his hand on her leg to stop her. His eyes told her to be quiet.

"Your guard protects you this time. Next time, you will both be punished," the female said laughing. "Now, where was I? Yes, I am the future Queen. I have lived between Gornack's casas waiting for the right time to claim my throne. Life was going well until you were born. You threatened my plan and had to be removed.

As you know, no being can kill you and neither can I except in war. But any being can remove you to another world. Amongst the casas, Gornack had ancient texts, and I found the way to another world." The female straightened herself in her chair and continued.

Elentari held Fendton closer. Fendton grasped her hand in his. They both knew their life was about to change but unsure of what was to come. Fendton could feel Elentari's heart racing and knew her mind would be going crazy trying to figure a way home. His mind was pinging, trying to find a way out, but he had nothing.

"I crept into your casa and stole you, which was easy after I drugged your parents. I then opened a doorway to your new world, changed my look, and tried to find some beings to keep you alive. It was getting close to time to return when a couple came along the trail. 'Please take any-name-but' I said and whispered 'Elentari', and they thought your name was Annie." The female and the male laughed, a deep uncaring laugh from within. The female enjoyed the thought of Elentari being named wrong.

"With you being called Annie, no being from this world would be able to find you. You were out of my way, and the path for my family to return to the throne was set. I returned to this world and have lived between my casas waiting for that wrongly crowned king to die," the female said as hatred dripped from her words. "Your mother pleased me by dying quickly, and I hoped the old fool would follow." The female's face was angry, and the males terse. The male slapped Elentari again.

"That punishment is for your father's insolence," the female said and paused. "And then your stupid link had to go and find you. He should have given up anoks ago, but no, he had to go and find you," the female snarled as the male, again, hit Elentari.

Elentari's face was sore, and blood was seeping from her nose. She used her sleeve to wipe the blood away. She was not sure how much more she could take and needed a way to escape.

"Because of your linked, I now have to be rid of you again. As you may have noticed, you cannot use your power here," the female said, her hands pointing around the room. "As the ancient Masters brought us to this world and brought us the ancient texts, they also brought yielding. Through the texts, I found how to nullify it. In this room, I have nullified yielding. Your link will not work either, for it is nullified. You have no way of being found. My casas are heavily guarded, and no being can enter without my knowledge and approval."

Elentari wanted to wipe the smug look off the female's face. The Bitch's face. Fendton rubbed her arm to calm Elentari as her anger began to surface.

"My link was snapped when Rorien died in the avalanche," Elentari stated, knowing she would be hit again.

The male moved to hit her, and the Bitch put out her arm to stop him. "You say your link died?" the Bitch questioned.

"Yes. He was caught in the avalanche that also killed Prince Theonry and died the following dia. That was when our link snapped," said Elentari.

"Yet, you still wear your linking ring," said the Bitch.

"Yes, it reminds me of our linking. You do know, most keep wearing their ring," said Elentari.

"And because he was revived," said the Bitch. "I know he still lives. You cannot fool me. He has been alive for four anoks and not dead."

The Bitch grabbed Elentari's arm. Elentari tried to pull her arm away, but the Bitch had it tight. The Bitch inspected her linking ring, studying the gems before dropping Elentari's arm. The male stood watching the Bitch with his hand on his sword and ready to fight given the signal.

"He will not be trying to find you or coming for you. We shall leave your ring to remind you of how you won't be saved from this place," said the Bitch sitting down with a sinister smile.

"Now, you know why I stole you. Your time here will be brief," said the Bitch, tapping the arms of her chair. "You will be begging to die before my well-trained Torturer is finished with you. You won't last a vika against his devices." She stood and left as four males walked in.

The males grabbed Fendton and dragged him across the room. Fendton struggled against them, but the males were strong and held him tightly. It was no use Fendton fighting against the four of them. He couldn't move.

"No, leave him alone!' screamed Elentari, scrambling after them. She grabbed a male to pull him off Fendton. The male elbowed her hard in the chest, and she fell backwards into the original male, her Torturer to be. Elentari struggled to breathe.

"I am going to enjoy my time with you," the Torturer sneered in her ear. He held her arms behind her back, and the more she struggled, the tighter the Torturer held her.

Unable to move, she gave up and looked to Fendton. The males had chained Fendton's arms and legs to the wall with his arms stretched wide. The whole wall was filled with chains at different heights and lengths. Her Torturer pushed Elentari towards the males, and they held her facing Fendton. The Torturer stood between Elentari and Fendton, looking from one to the other, a half-smile on his face. His look was not one of pleasantness, and she was beginning to dread what was to come.

"I am going to enjoy this, and your guard is going to watch everything I do to you. I hope he enjoys it as much as I will," the Torturer sneered.

Fear was in her eyes as she looked at Fendton. He was struggling to move, to get free of the chains and help her. Across his face was fear, fear for what was to happen to her. He had to save her, had to help her, but he couldn't get free.

"Let her go!" Fendton yelled.

The Torturer stood facing her. He laughed as he ripped Elentari's dress from her body, exposing her breasts. She was trying to move against her captors, to cover herself, feeling humiliated at being so exposed. Her struggling was futile against the males. No matter how she struggled, she couldn't move her arms.

"NO. NO. Don't. Please don't!" Elentari screamed, begging for them to stop as tears flowed down her face.

The males removed the remnants of her dress still hanging from her.

"Please. No. Please." Elentari kept begging, and the tears kept flowing.

"Stop it!" yelled Fendton, still struggling against the chains. His wrists were beginning to bleed as they chaffed against the chains.

"I have only just begun, and I am not going to stop until you take your own life. Until then, YOU. ARE. MINE!" the Torturer laughed. He walked around Elentari, staring at her and making her feel defenceless. He stood in front of her as he ripped her panties off her leaving her fully naked and vulnerable.

Elentari struggled harder against her captors to cover her nakedness. She moved her knee up to cover herself trying to curl up into a ball, but a male grabbed her leg to stop her. She was exposed and unable to move. Fear seeped into her, anxiety as to what was to come.

"Let her go!" yelled Fendton struggling to free himself. Blood seeping from his wounds where the chains chaffed his skin.

"Shut him up," said the Torturer.

A male left the room, returning with something in his hand. A wide wooden stopper with leather straps through one end was in the male's hand, and he shoved the stopper in Fendton's mouth and tied the straps behind his head. Elentari could see Fendton was choking, his mouth stretched wide to fit the gag, and he was convulsing, shaking his head, trying hard to remove it.

"Much better. Now strap her on the table," said the Torturer.

Elentari wanted to yell and scream for them to stop but was not game to say anything. The gag frightened her. Instead, she silently fought back, kicking and struggling to get free as tears flowed down her cheeks. She was scared and feared what they were to do to her. No matter how hard she fought, they quickly laid her on the table on her back and strapped her wrists and ankles to the table. The straps were threaded through holes and buckled tight underneath. She had little capacity to move and hoped what she thought was to come wouldn't.

"Until the morrow Annie," said the Torturer as his finger gently ran down her arm. "And then the fun will begin." He left, closing the door, leaving them in darkness.

Elentari twisted her head towards Fenton, unable to see him in the dark.

"I'm sorry, Fendton," said Elentari. She heard him shuffling and banging against the wall, trying to communicate with her. "How about I ask you Yes/No questions, and you answer one tap for no and two for yes?" She heard two taps.

"Are you ok?" She heard him move, but no tap. "Ok stupid question, guessing you're looking at me saying 'really?'." She sighed as he tapped twice.

"I'm not sure we are going to be able to get out of here alive, and I am terrified of what is to come on the morrow." She heard two taps.

"We need to find a way to get out of here without yielding."

Tap. Tap.

"Did you see the guards at the door?"

Tap. Tap.

"They are too big for either of us to fight, and we are defenceless against their swords."

Tap. Tap.

"Any ideas?"

Tap.

"Me neither. We have all night to think before we face the morrow when it comes."

Tap. Tap.

CHAPTER 9

"Something is wrong with Elentari," said Jasper, a concerned look on his face.

"What do you mean something is wrong?" Rorien asked, puzzled.

"Our oath has gone slack like there is no one on the other end. I can still feel she is here but can't reach her."

"Something is wrong," yelled Lorcan as he came racing up to Rorien and Jasper.

"Your oath slack too?" questioned Rorien with grave fear.

"Yes, like it is blowing in the wind without being attached to something," answered Lorcan.

"Where was she last?" asked Rorien.

"With Fendton and Sarina, I think," answered Lorcan.

"The oath to Fendton is strange. It is there but not answering. Whatever happened to Elentari has happened to Fen too," said Rorien. He began to pace.

"Sarina said they headed to the ancient library over an hori ago," said Jasper grabbing Rorien and sprinting off. Lorcan quickly following behind.

"Has anyone seen the Princess?" asked Rorien as he hurried down the stairs and into the ancient library.

"Yes. She was here not long ago with Fendton. They raced out as Fendton had found what they needed. I thought they headed off to find you at the training area. Did she not find you?" asked one of the Apprentices.

"No. Not long ago, the blood oaths slackened, and her guard can't reach her," replied Rorien. "It seems she is missing."

The Apprentice checked the open book on the Princess' table. "This is the book they were looking in when. Oh. They found 'How to build a link'," said the Apprentice. He looked up at Rorien. "That's why they raced out of the library and why she was so happy and excited to find you. She found how to relink with you. I will call the Masters and Apprentices and have them search for her."

"Have only the Masters meet us at our casa. Say nothing and tell no being until we know what happened. Don't want a mass hysteria if it is nothing. We will check the royal hall and gardens and head to our casa," said Rorien.

"I will find the Masters and have them meet you," said the Apprentice.

"Remember, say nothing of this to ANY being," said Rorien sternly.

"Yes, say nothing," said the Apprentice as he followed them out.

Rorien began to fear the worst as they left to search the royal gardens before seeking the King, making sure not to worry him unnecessarily until confirmation she was missing. He headed home to meet the Masters and the Masters arrived not long after, all confused as to what was happening.

"Thanks for meeting us here, Masters. We may have an issue concerning the Princess. It seems she is missing, and her guards cannot reach her. The oath is slack and not attached. Any solutions to why?" asked Rorien.

The Masters began to speak to one another, confusion on their faces, searching for a reason. Rorien sat quietly, watching and waiting for them to answer. Lorcan and Jasper stood behind Rorien, waiting for the Masters.

"It seems, Prince, we have no answer to what is happening. I shall check the book which explained 'pulling up' and check if there are any other sensations, specifically slackness. Can you explain further?" asked the Air Master.

"It feels like it is like a piece of string blowing in the wind. Attached to me but not attached to anything else. It's like it's searching for her," said Lorcan.

"Yes. It's like she is still here, but it's unable to connect to her. If she were on another world, it would pull up, wouldn't it?" asked Jasper.

"Yes, and if she were no longer with us, it would snap. It suggests she is alive and, in these lands, somewhere. We shall head to the library and find an answer," said the Air Master bowing before leaving. The other Masters bowed and followed the Air Master.

"So, she is here, alive somewhere in these lands, but it doesn't explain where she is or why she is missing. Should we tell the King?" asked Lorcan.

"Let's see what the Masters find before we burden him with this. He has lost her once. Let's make sure she is truly missing before we give him the news she is lost again," said Rorien. He started to pace the lounge, frustrated and concerned.

"I will call Sarina and have her meet us at the library, and we can help search. Is Fendton with her?" asked Jasper.

"He was, and I assume whoever took her took him too. Otherwise, he would have informed us. Neither of them was on the path between the library and training area. How about we start at the training area and walk directly back to the library. Check for any signs of what happened, a clue to help us locate them," replied Lorcan.

"Good idea Lorcan. Hopefully, we will find something to help us," said Rorien.

Rorien, Lorcan and Jasper headed back to the training area and slowly walked the path directly to the library, checking for any signs. It wasn't far from the library when Lorcan spotted something. There were strange markings on either side of the path as if some being had removed something. The markings weren't deep or large, just four small holes on each side of the path, looking like four small chair leg marks. Jasper noticed Elentari's heel marks finished at the markings.

"It seems this is where they got to before they vanished," said Jasper as Sarina met up with them. "Whatever was here, took them without a fight. There are no scuff marks or any other marks."

"Lorcan, grab the air and sight Masters to show them. Maybe they may know. Also, grab the Movement Master. Movement leaves no marks, so maybe someone took them using movement," said Rorien, shrugging. "Who knows?"

"Can't hurt. Anything right now could help," said Jasper.

Lorcan shrugged and quickly headed off.

"We will find her, Rorien," said Sarina as she gently placed a hand on his arm. "Or she will find a way back to us. She won't leave you. You do know that, don't you?"

"Yeah, I know," replied Rorien. His shoulders slumped over. After everything they had been through these past anoks, he wondered if they would ever get any time together.

The Air Master began searching the area looking for anything out of the ordinary, anything unusual, while the Sight Master attempted to visualise what happened. The Movement Master looked for traces of movement. Air Master came up with no new clues, not even another's footsteps, and other then the holes in the earth, there was nothing to say they were transported somewhere.

"I can only get snippets of them from different perspectives and of no one else. It does seem as though they vanished as they reached this spot," said the Sight Master. It was easy for those who yielded sight to have the ability to see images of past events in others' minds. The Master, Apprentices and very few others were able to receive pictures from locations. The ability to see from sites was one reason Masters picked them as Apprentices.

"I can sense a slight trace in the air, but it is so faint I cannot track it." said the Movement Master.

Directly after transporting, there is a trace from one location to the next enabling movement yielders to track the yielder to their destination and follow. The trail begins to fade shortly after. Too much time had passed since the Princess went missing, and them finding the location. The trace was almost gone.

"It seems to be far. I would guess the Princess is in another land, West, East or South most likely, definitely not North," said the Movement Master.

"That narrows it down, only three lands to search, and they would have to be the biggest ones," sighed Rorien. "Guess we had better inform the King we have lost the Princess again."

"I worked out last time what happened. I can inform him if you prefer?" said the Air Master.

"No, I shall inform him. Masters, you can give him the details. Guess the army is going on a search," said Rorien.

No being moved. No being wanted to tell the King. No being wanted it to be true. And so they stood rooted to the spot.

"We should go," said Sarina, gently taking Rorien's arm to move him on.

"Yes," he said as he hesitated to take a step.

As they reached the hall entrance, Rorien paused to compose himself before entering and heading to the King.

"My King," said Rorien, one knee on the ground bowing. The rest of the group followed his lead. "We have news, bad news. The Princess is missing, and we believe she has been kidnapped. The Movement Master believes she is possibly in the South, East or West lands. The Masters have more detail on what we know," Rorien said with his knee still on the ground, waiting for the King to allow him to rise.

"What do you mean the Princess is missing?" roared the King leaning forward towards them, his face red with anger. "You are her guards. How can you let this happen!?"

"I was with Rorien when our oath went slack, and we were unable to contact her. We traced to where she went missing, and the Masters have confirmed the spot where she was last," replied Jasper. He had one knee on the ground and his head bowed, afraid to stand.

"My Lord," said the Sight Master as he stood. "We have found the spot where she was taken. I have seen images of her and Fendton walking from the library to the training area, and as they reached this spot on the path, they disappeared. I am unable to see what was on the path or how they disappeared."

"My Lord," said the Movement Master standing beside the Sight Master. "The trail is too weak to trace. It is far, and I believe it is in the East, West or South. I know she is not in the royal land or the Northland."

"She is still alive?" asked the King.

"Yes, my Lord. She is alive as the oaths have not snapped. They are searching for her to attach," answered Jasper, still kneeling.

"Find the Generals now. We will send out a search for her," said the King to Rorien, Jasper and Lorcan.

"Yes, my Lord," they answered heading quickly out to find the Generals, leaving the Masters and Sarina behind.

"Sarina, find the cooks and have food and drink brought in. It could be a while," said the King. He sat back in his chair and began to stroke his chin. His brow furrowed as he thought.

"Yes, my King," Sarina answered as she headed to the kitchen, glad to be dismissed.

"Masters, what else can you tell me?" asked the King.

"Not much else, my King. The Apprentices and other Masters are all searching the text to see if we can find why the oaths have slackened and maybe help locate her," replied the Air Master.

"Alright. Keep searching. Let the Apprentices know this is a top priority. Everything else is to be put aside until I say so," said the King.

"Yes, my Lord," said the Air Master. He headed out to inform the Apprentices.

The Generals had gathered in the hall, standing beside the Masters with Rorien, Lorcan and Jasper.

"Generals and Masters. The Princess is missing. We need a plan to find her," said the King.

"Do we know where to look?" asked a General.

"East, West and South lands is all the Masters know. No leads on exactly where in these lands," said the King.

"This is a big task," said the General, concern on his face.

"And it needs to be completed without any being knowing, other than those here now," said the King. "Do not breathe a word of her disappearance until I announce it. Not even to your linked!" The King glared at those around him.

The Generals began discussing and hatched a plan to search for the Princess without drawing attention to her kidnapping and alarming every being. It was hoped she would return before they activated the strategy, even some news of Princess's whereabouts. The proposal was to split the army into thirds. One third was to travel to the West in two dias time, to train throughout the West as a cover while searching in secret for her. Two dias after the west army leaves, another third would travel to the East to train. Again, searching in secret and two dias later, all the rest of the army to the south for training. One General and twelve soldiers would stay in Thoroneath with the King as his guard. It was late when the King dismissed every being, with instructions to meet each dia at lunch to discuss any findings and adjustments to the plan.

Lorcan stayed each night with Rorien to keep him company and offer support as needed. It was on the dia of the army leaving, Rorien heard a knock at the door. He opened the door to find Duggit standing there.

"Come in, what brings you here?" Rorien asked puzzled, shuffling Duggit in.

"I came with a word from Hoofington. We heard about the Princess, and Hoofington wants to meet with you to discuss what we can do to help. He is at the edge of the woods in the North," said Duggit.

"How did you hear? The King gave strict instructions not to breathe a word," asked Rorien

"We have many ears, and not all ears belong to beings. The King cannot quieten the animals and birds," replied Duggit.

"Point. He does not rule the animals. Ok. Wait here with Lorcan while I get Jasper. Lorcan call Awnrie to help," said Rorien as he dashed out the door. He returned with Jasper and Sarina a moment before Awnrie came in the door.

"Duggit, we will go quickly but not too quick to draw attention to ourselves. Let's keep this quiet for the time being," said Rorien. "The cuedel doesn't know of her disappearance, and we need to keep it that way. Or they may know and are not saying, after all, you all know."

"Ok," answered Duggit.

"Chat and laugh amongst ourselves to stop suspicion," said Rorien.

"That shouldn't be too hard," said Jasper. "Been a while since we saw you, Duggit."

"Yes, but not much has happened," said Duggit heading out and leading the way to the north woods and Hoofington. Each found it challenging to stay upbeat and to keep the conversation going. Luckily, not many beings were in the North area.

"Hoofington, it is good to see you," said Rorien, extending his hand.

"And you. What is it we can do to help find Elentari? Do you know where she is?" asked Hoofington in his usual matter of fact style as he shook Rorien's hand.

"Either in the West, East or South lands. The army moves out todia and over the next few dias to train in these lands while secretly searching for her. Do you have contacts in any of the other lands?" asked Rorien.

"I do. I shall send word to see if anything unusual has been seen. Meet me here in two dias, same time, to exchange information. Until then, stay safe, Rorien," Hoofington said and left with Duggit.

"Well, Elentari did say they may be useful one dia. She wasn't wrong. Fauns and minotaurs will have the woods covered and see what we don't. We have a bigger army looking for her, Rorien. We will find her," said Jasper with his hand on Rorien's shoulder.

"He certainly is direct," said Lorcan.

"Yes, we will find her," Rorien said as he began to walk back. "Head back to what you were doing, keep this quiet. If asked, say I need to get away, and you all came as protection."

"Not sure what protection I can give you," said Awnrie.

"Movement if needed and Sarina, healing. Say anything you need to keep this quiet," replied Rorien. "Head off, and I'll see you tonight."

CHAPTER 10

Are you awake?" whispered Elentari shivering on the stone table, her back aching from not being able to move and legs tense from being so cold.

Tap. Tap.

"You didn't sleep either?" asked Elentari.

Tap.

"Did you think of anything to get us out of here?" asked Elentari.

Tap.

"Me either. What is going to happen to us?" asked Elentari.

Tap.

"I am scared Fen, what if we can't get out of here?" asked Elentari.

Tap. Tap. Tap.

"Is that 'I don't know?' tap?" asked Elentari.

Tap. Tap.

"Guess we will find out soon. Footsteps are coming," said Elentari.

Tap. Tap.

The door slammed open, causing them to squint against the blinding light streaming in. Elentari could make out three shapes enter and move through the room. One figure lit the lamp hanging from the ceiling as the other two made their way towards her.

"What a fabulous morning to be torturing you," the Torturer said with happiness in his voice. "You are the reason my Queen cannot sit on the throne, and I shall enjoy every hori I spend torturing you for taking her away from her rightful spot." Hatred dripped from his words.

The other two males undid the straps and handcuffed Elentari. The males yanked her off the table and dragged her across the room, directly across from Fendton. A chain hung from the ceiling, and the males hooked her handcuffs onto the chain. Her hands stretched high above her head, and her feet just touched the floor. She looked at Fendton and could see tears rolling down his face and fear on his face.

"What shall I use this morning?" asked the Torturer.

On the table, Elentari saw four different whips. She gasped and began to sob, understanding Fendton's fear of knowing what was to come.

"Please don't. Please? Please?" Elentari begged, watching Fendton struggling against his chains.

"Oh. I am Princess," the Torturer laughed. "For a whole hori, I will be. The question is, do I just use one type or all of them todia? How about each morning I will try a new one, so you know what they all feel like and then start mixing?"

"Please no," Elentari said through sobs. She kept pleading with him.

"The whip, the cat o'nine tails, qilinbian or the chain whip? Let's start with the whip," the Torturer said as he grabbed the end of a whip made of leather and cracked it a few times.

A muffled scream came from Fendton as he struggled harder to free himself. He kept working to free himself and trying to scream for them to stop. The restraints digging into his wrists. The Torturer walked behind her as the other males left.

"No. Please. Don't, Please. No," Elentari cried out.

CRACK! Elentari screamed as the whip hit her across her back.

"NO!" yelled Elentari.

CRACK! Another scream escaped Elentari's lips as the whip hit her.

"STOP. Please. Stop," Elentari begged.

CRACK! Again, and again Elenatri felt the whip across her back. The Torturer was continually changing directions across her back. She was screaming as the whip hit her. Between screams, she begged for him to stop. He kept going, whipping her straight across her back, whipping her diagonally down her back, whipping any way he could. The pain was so excruciating to Elentari. She lost control of her functions and wet herself.

"Please. Stop," Elentari whispered between sobs. Her throat was hoarse from screaming and struggling to breathe. Her breaths were short and quick as she dangled from her wrists, unable to stand.

"I will stop when the hori is over. Until then, hang there and enjoy." the Torturer laughed.

She could feel the blood running from her cuts down her legs to pool at her feet. She dared not look down and closed her eyes, trying to block out the world.

CRACK! This time the whip hit her legs. Again and again, relentlessly attacking her legs. The more she screamed, the more the Torturer laughed. He enjoyed hearing her scream. The whip paused, and she hoped he had stopped. Her wrists were bleeding where the cuffs dug into her skin. The cuffs chaffing as she involuntary moved when the whip cracked against her skin. There could be no skin left for him to whip. Her back and legs were pounding, and her head fuzzy and cloudy.

CRACK! Elentari felt the whip across her stomach before she passed out. She woke to find a female healing her as she still hung from her wrists.

"Water, please," Elentari croaked. Her throat ached from screaming, and her head and body exhausted from the pain. The female shook her head and continued her healing, confusing Elentari. There was no yielding in the room, yet the healer could heal her. She was too exhausted to think. The healer left when she finished healing Elentari, and a faun entered, placing food and water just inside the door against the wall. Her stomach growled. Elentari looked puzzled at Fendton, wondering how they could eat if both were chained up? Two males entered, yanked Fendton from his chains, and he fell to the ground crouched over. Reaching behind his head, Fendton untied the gag and gasped for air as he removed it. The males uncuffed her, extinguished the lamp and left, closing the door behind them. Elentari and Fendton were in darkness with only a small slither of light under the doorway.

"Can you move Fen?" Elentari asked, her voice husky.

Tap. Fendton was still gasping for air.

"I will bring you food. If I can find it," said Elentari as she began to slowly move along the wall towards the food, letting her eyes get used to the dark. She brought the food to Fendton, and they sat huddled together. Both were silent as they sat on the floor with their backs against the wall. Their sides were touching to comfort each other. Here they sat and ate the bread and an apple, sharing bite for bite. There were no cups, and they drank straight from the jug of water.

"You ok?" Fendton quietly asked her when the meagre breakfast was gone.

"Depends," Elentari said as she felt his arm wrap around her. She snuggled into his warm body. "Thanks, I'd ask for your top, but if they found me with it, we'd both be naked. At least I have you here to warm me.

"Yeah, I thought that too. At least I can warm you a bit. Imagine if you were alone," Fendton said quietly.

"Hate to be here by myself, but then I don't want anyone here to endure what is to come," said Elentari quietly. She shivered at the thought of more torture.

"I don't want to think of what is to come," Fendton said. He rubbed her arms and back to warm her.

They sat quietly waiting, their anticipation building, not knowing what was to come. Neither wanted to think about what was next. Was it over for todia, or was there more to come? Footsteps approached, and the door slammed open, revealing three males, including the Torturer. The other two males carried a large, heavy tub and placed it on the ground inside the door. The males then grabbed Fendton as the Torturer grabbed Elentari's neck, yanking her to her feet and holding her arms behind her. The males chained Fendton to the wall and left. This time, his hands were chained above his head.

"Time for some more fun. You can swim, can't you?" the Torturer laughed.

He dragged her to the filled tub of water. She realised her next torture was dunking. He pushed her to her knees in front of the tub and shoved her head under the water. She was struggling to breathe as her hands searched for the tub edge, screaming into the water and thrashing her head about, trying to find air. He released her, and she lifted her head gasping for breath.

"How long can you stay underwater, Princess?" the Torturer taunted as he shoved her back under the water.

This time he held her down longer. Again, and again he dunked her. Eventually, she stopped fighting and started to count, trying to find a pattern to help her. The dunking was erratic, which made it hard for Elentari to breath. She attempted to slow her heart rate.

"Seems you have gotten used to this. Let's change it," the Torturer said with an evil tone. He began to dunk her quickly, dragging her up by her hair and promptly slamming her back down. She had little time to catch a breath as he shoved her down, dragged her up, only to shove her down again. He kept going snickering to himself. She couldn't take a proper breath and started to breathe in small breaths and exhale into the water. She felt dizzy and light-headed. The water was trickling down her body, and she knelt in a pool of water. Her hair and body soaked with water, and she began to shiver. The shivering made it harder for her to breath properly. He pushed her deep into the tub, and her face hit bottom before he let go. She was unbalanced, and her feet struggled to grip the floor. She moved one arm into the tub, finding the bottom and pushed herself out. She collapsed to the floor in a ball, coughing and spluttering, her breath quick and shallow.

Two males approached Elentari. They grabbed her and strapped her onto the table, dripping wet before leaving them in darkness. She was shivering and coughing, unable to catch her breath.

"I won't survive this," Elentari sobbed quietly, between coughs.

"Yes, you will, E. I am here with you," said Fendton quietly, glad they didn't gag him again.

He was trying to sound upbeat as the water began to drip from the table. Drip. Drip. Drip. This new torture was torture for them, both the sound of dripping water. When the dripping finally stopped, the door swung open, and a faun entered, placing food against the wall. Two males entered to remove their shackles before leaving them in darkness. Elentari heard Fendton shuffling along the wall as she sat up, watching his dark shape move to their food. She moved to the furthest corner away from the door. Here she sat on the floor with her back against the wall. Fendton made his way to her and placed the food on the floor. They huddled together with their knees up, and he wrapped his arm around her. Her arm hugged his knee.

"Gee, that was not good. You could hardly catch a breath, and the dripping from the table was annoying," said Fenton.

"I don't want to think about it. Glad you here to keep me company. What will be my next torture? Hopefully nothing else todia," said Elentari, between bites of bread and half an orange each.

"Don't think. Just find a memory that makes you happy and concentrate on it. It might help you get through it, hopefully," said Fendton. Fendton had a hand over his mouth when he spoke to keep his voice from being heard. Neither knew if any being was listening and didn't want to risk it. They kept their conversations quiet just in case.

"Thanks. It could work for a bit. I will try anything," said Elentari. "Do you think that is it, or will I be tortured more todia?"

"The Bitch did say you would be tortured and would beg to die before he finished. Guess there will be more to come," replied Fendton.

"Great. What more could he possibly do?" asked Elentari.

Fendton shrugged.

When they finished their food, they sat huddled together in silence. They waited silently for the door to open, waiting for the next torture in their horrific dungeon of no escape and not knowing when or what was to come next—their anxiety building and becoming mental torture to them both. Time dragged as they waited. It seemed forever, but it wasn't that long before the door opened. The males chained Fendton to the wall, this time with his legs spread wide, before cuffing Elentari and chaining her to the ceiling hook, the same one they used when the Torturer whipped her. She couldn't cope with more whipping. The Torturer entered with hammers. He sorted them on the table in order of largest to smallest. One of the males placed a large basket on the floor at the end of the table.

"Time for more fun. I have a multitude of items I would like you to try, hammer, drilling hammer, sledgehammer and blacksmith hammer," the Torturer said. He picked each up as he called their name.

"There are also all these rocks to try, too," said one of the males. He picked up a rock and threw it into the air, trying to catch it in front of his face. However, the stone was too heavy and went straight through his hands, smashing into his face and breaking his teeth.

The Torturer roared with laughter at his helper's misfortune. The Torturer turned to Elentari.

"This is nothing compared to the pain you will suffer. What would you like first? Maybe I should just use one todia and let you get a feel for it. But which one?" the Torturer chuckled as he stopped in front of the hammers. He dropped the rock and picked up each hammer to inspect, banging it against the table to test it. To her, they all looked the same, just different in size. The drilling and sledgehammer had two faces, while the blacksmith hammer and hammer had one face with a claw on the other side. Each sounded different, with the hammer sounding the lightest while the sledgehammer sounded heavy. None sounded good to hit against the body.

"Let's try this one," the Torturer said, picking up the hammer and circling her. He banged it up and down in the air as if hitting an imaginary nail before moving behind her. She tensed, waiting for the hit.

WHACK! The hammer hit her shoulder, and Elentari screamed as the pain instantly shot through her body.

"NO!" Elentari shouted. Tears fell to the ground.

"STOP IT" Fendton yelled. He struggled against the chains, unable to break free.

WHACK! Elentari felt the brunt of the force in her other shoulder and heard a bone crack. Searing pain followed. She screamed, as did Fendton, both screaming for the Torturer to stop.

WHACK! Elentari tried to think of anything to make her happy, anything to focus her mind. The Torturer worked his way down her back and hitting her in every spot possible, except her spine. Elentari screamed at every hit, and the Torture enjoyed her pain. The pain was unbearable, shooting up and down her body as he moved onto her legs.

"No more," she begged. "No more. Please. No more."

"Only you can stop it," the Torturer said as he smashed the hammer hard into her thigh.

It became so intense, Elentari passed out and woke to find the female healer healing her broken bones. She lay face down strapped to the table with her head sagging over the edge and her feet towards Fendton. She groaned at the sensational feeling of her bones moving to heal, the tiny fragments shifting to meld back together. Her legs had no feeling in them, and she guessed he might have hit her spine.

"Water?" she questioned, but no answer came. Quietly she lay face down, giving her body rest. She was enjoying the sensation of her bones healing and hoping it would take time. More time to heal meant less time for the torture to happen. Her legs tingled as the blood flowed into them as the healer mended more bones, the full feeling in her legs returning once all the bones healed.

"Fen?" asked Elentari.

Tap. Tap.

"You ok?" asked Elentari.

Tap. Tap.

"Guess you have the gag again," said Elentari.

Tap. Tap.

"Does he continue after I pass out?" asked Elentari.

Tap.

"Maybe I should fake passing out," she sighed.

Tap.

"Have they hurt you?" asked Elentari.

Tap.

Footsteps approached, and Elentari groaned "Please no more todia," she said.

"Princess, you are awake and ready for our next play session? Wonderful. I am sure you will enjoy this game," the Torturer snorted. "You can stay where you are. No need to move."

Elentari could feel heat near her feet but could not work out from where it came. She could hear Fendton struggling against his chains and guessed it was terrible. Her heart rate increased as panic set it, panic at not knowing what was to come and what it was.

SSSSsss. Elentari let out an agonising scream, throwing back her head, as the hot coal touched her back. Burnt skin filled her nostrils, causing her to gag at the smell.

"No. Please. No more. I can't take it. Please stop," Elentari begged between screams.

"When you ask for the knife to end your life, that is when I stop," the Torturer said as another coal fell onto her back.

She howled. She watched as her tears fell to the floor, trying to change her focus. The pain was excruciating, and the coals were burning deeper into her skin. She couldn't focus on anything other than the searing pain through her body.

"Your skin smells so good when burnt," the Torturer chuckled.

Elentari threw up, and another coal fell onto her back. The smell of vomit mixed with burnt skin filled the room, causing Fendton to choke. Her heart went out to him. With the gag still in his mouth, he was unable to vomit. A lump of coal dropped onto her leg, and she thrashed, trying to shake it off, howling at the pain. Another coal found her other leg. It felt like the coals were burning their way to her bones. He kept placing coal after coal onto her with a gap of 30 seconds between each drop until she passed out. As she came to, the healer finished and left.

"Fen?" asked Elentari.

Tap. Tap.

"I don't want to do this anymore," Elentari said.

Tap. Tap. Tap. Tap. Tap. Tap. Elentari heard in quick succession.

"I know I have to hold on. It is just so hard," Elentari said.

Tap. Tap.

"I hope that is it for the dia," said Elentari.

Elentari heard footsteps approach. Again, a faun left food while the male removed their bonds. Neither moved until they could no longer listen to footsteps. Fendton ripped off the gag, grabbed the food, more bread and an apple, and joined Elentari in the far corner. He huddled into her to comfort her, putting a protective arm around her as she hugged his knee.

"Thanks, Fen," she said softly. "You are so warm."

"Let's hope this is it for the dia as this is dinner. If you can call what we are given meals," Fendton gently replied.

"I hope so. We need to find a way out of here or a quick way for me to cope. I don't want to go through another dia like todia again," Elentari said.

Fendton pulled her closer, knowing he had no way to help her. They sat there in silence, waiting, knowing it wouldn't be long before they would be chained again.

Tonight, she was strapped and gagged. The gag was expanding her mouth beyond its usual size, causing great agony through her jaw and into her ears. Her teeth bit into the wood, causing discomfort in her teeth. Her tongue seemed to be lost in her mouth, and she fought to find a spot to rest. She wanted to swallow and couldn't. Saliva sat awkwardly in her mouth. It was going to be a long night of restlessness and distress before another agonising dia.

CHAPTER 11

"Elentari, something has been playing on my mind," said Fendton quietly, covering his mouth as they sat huddled together, eating more bread and a piece of fruit again.

"What?" Elentari asked, muffling her words.

"The Bitch said she broke yielding and the link. What about your bite? I know you found the ancient text to speak into your bite when you complete your linking. Did you speak the text?" asked Fendton.

"We did. Why?" asked Elentari.

"Would it work the same as the link?" asked Fendton.

"Don't know. Do you think it could work like the link?" asked Elentari.

"Don't know. Try it. What can happen?" Fendton shrugged. "If you can contact Rorien, then it may be our way out of here if it works."

"Possibly could work. Suppose it won't hurt to try," answered Elentari, staring across the darkroom, lost in thought.

"Anything is worth a try to get us out," said Fendton.

"Ok. Later, when we are alone. I will try then," replied Elentari.

They sat in silence, finishing their food before the males chained Fendton to the wall and her to the table. It had been two full dias of torture since they arrived with no escape and no way of knowing what was happening in the outside world. Nights were long without the ability to talk to each other. Each night, the Torturer would gag one of them and tonight was Fendton's turn. As the night grew late and the light under the door went out, they would quietly ask yes/no questions to each other just to keep the boredom at bay. They were doing anything to try and change their focus from the dia. It hadn't worked as they ended up asking something about the dia. Tonight would be different. Elentari was waiting for the light to be extinguished and quietness to approach before she spoke again.

"Ok, I will try to communicate on the bite. I guess I do it the same way as the link?" said Elentari.

Tap. Tap.

"Here goes," Elentari said as she closed her eyes. She began searching for the bite feeling in her body. She felt a weak sensation of love and togetherness and began to concentrate on it, attempting to make it stronger. She fell asleep, touching the spot feeling happy and content and woke to the door slamming open and coming back into reality.

"What a fabulous dia it is to be torturing you...then again, every dia is fabulous to torture you," snickered the Torturer.

The males unstrapped her from the bench, only to chain her to the ceiling hook.

"Which whip shall I use todia? You've experienced the single whip and the cat o' nine tails, so will it be the qilinbian or the chain whip? Let's use the qilinbian todia," the Torturer grinned as excitement filled his eyes.

The Torturer picked up a handle wrapped in leather with a lash made of steel rods inking together. Each link was decreasing in size, with a leather cracker at the end. He cracked it a few times as if to show Elentari how it worked. Tears began to roll down her cheeks in anticipation of the pain she was to endure, and she closed her eyes, waiting for the whip to hit.

CRACK. Elentari felt the leather crack across her back and screamed. She had given up begging for him to stop, knowing it got her nowhere and screamed in agony.

CRACK. This time Elentari felt the steel rods slash across her back and could feel the blood starting to run down her back as the whip again hit. She bit her lip, trying to think of anything but being here and began to play out their linking dia in her mind. The whip kept coming, and she kept screaming. It kept slashing across her back, her legs, and her arms until it felt like it had hit every part of her. Just when she thought he had stopped, the Torturer turned her around to begin on her front. She found her bite spot and concentrated on it.

'*Rorien, I miss you,*' she said as her mind focused on her bite and the whip cracked against her stomach.

'*Elentari?*' She heard, and her eyes sprung open, and her face dropped. It worked.

'*Not yet. I will talk when I can. I love you,*' Elentari said on their bite.

'*P*lease tell me what is going on? I'm worried,' replied Rorien on their bite.

'*I can't just now. I will explain everything tonight,*' Elentari said on their bite.

'*Ok. I will wait,*' said Rorien on their bite.

Elentari closed her eyes to hide her happiness. Tears of joy began to trickle down her cheeks. The whip couldn't inflict pain anymore as her body went numb and hope-filled her. She managed to endure the whipping session and was eager for the healing to be over to enable her to speak to Rorien.

The food faun arrived, and they were unchained. Elentari was anxiously waiting for the footsteps to disappear to tell Fendton. She quickly moved to sit by the wall, and as Fendton sat, she whispered into his top.

"It worked, happened when I was being tortured, and he answered," said Elentari.

"It did? What happened? asked a wide-eyed Fendton.

"I spoke, he answered. It was quick. I will talk to him now, ok?" replied Elentari.

Fendton nodded.

'*Rorien, I have a little time to talk, you there?*' asked Elentari on their bite.

'*Yes. Where are you?*' asked Rorien on their bite.

'*We don't know. Fen is with me. We were transported here by a descendant of Gornack. She used the ancient text to nullify yielding and the link. Fen thought of this idea, using our bite,*' said Elentari.

'Glad he did, I have missed you. We have actioned a plan to search the East, South and West lands. The Movement Master believes you are in one of them,' replied Rorien.

'Have the Master look for bring yielding and nullifying it. I need to find a way to bring it back. Is the bite giving you any direction to me?' asked Elentari.

'Nothing,' answered Rorien.

'Have to go, speak tonight when I am alone,' said Elentari as she heard footsteps approaching.

"Princess, time for play," said the Torturer as he entered the room.

Two males followed him in and chained Fendton to the wall. This time, the males chained Fendton with his right arm chained straight out and his left chained over his head towards his right. He looked awkward, bending towards his right as if completing stretching exercises. Elentari stifled a laugh at the sight of him.

"This play session, you can lay back and relax…without me," the Torturer grinned at her. "Bring in the water." Two males entered carrying a wooden contraption on a small table and placed it at the stone table's top.

"Let's get you comfortable," said the Torturer. He grabbed Elentari's arm and dragged her to the table. She lay down, giving up struggling, knowing it was no use and waited for what was to come. Above her head was a funnel, and sitting above the funnel was a large bucket with different-sized holes in the bottom.

"Are you comfortable? Because you will not be soon," said the Torturer as he poured water into the top bucket to fill it.

Water began to drip through the holes, into the funnel and onto her forehead. Drip. Drip. Drip. Each hole leaked at different speeds, causing the drops onto her head to be erratic and unpredictable. The inconsistent pattern of dripping causing her brain to go foggy and the drips to echo loudly through her head. It wasn't long before Elentari began wriggling her head, trying to change the drip spot, trying to change the BOOMING sound through her head. BOOM. BOOM. BOOM. The woodblocks positioned tight against her head intended to keep minimal movement gave her no relief. She was sobbing and screaming for the water to stop. The water ran into her eyes, mixing with her tears and into her hair and ears. The boom aggravated her, and the water into her ears was maddening. She began to struggle to free her hands and banging on the table in frustration at not breaking free.

Elentari could hear Fendton humming softly, struggling to hum a tune to the drops as if trying to distract her. He was trying to create something pleasant from something irritating. It was sort of working. His voice was soothing, and she tried to hum with him. By the time the water ran out, her mind was screaming, and her head kept pounding. The water soaked her hair and surrounded her head and shoulders. Water began to drip onto the floor, causing a new irritation. It was not as pounding as the drops on her head but still infuriating.

"Thanks, Fen. Your humming helped a little," said Elentari.

"Anytime E. When will..." Fendton paused, not wanting to say it out loud in case ears were listening.

"Let's just say hawk, one word, one meaning, hawk," said Elentari.

"Hawk?" asked Fendton.

"Later when it is quiet," answered Elentari.

Elentari knew the food would arrive soon, followed by torture with hammers or stones. Next up was suffering by hot coals or burnt before supper and rest. The previous two dia routines had been the same, and she guessed it would continue. Now she had hope and had to endure the final part of the dia before she could enjoy hearing Rorien's voice.

'Rorien, speak to me,' said Elentari on their bite.

'Elentari, what has been happening. Why can't you talk?' asked Rorien on their bite.

'You don't want to know the details. I don't want to know the details. Just know you have given us hope, great hope. What is happening?' asked Elentari.

'The army's split into three and is being dispatched to the East, South and West to search for you,' replied Rorien.

'NO! Stop them! If the Bitch finds out the army is not in Thoroneath, she may attack. It is the throne she wants,' said Elentari, panic in her voice.

'One group has been dispatched todia. I will call off the rest,' said Rorien.

'Good. Keep Papa safe. She is counting on his death. Are the Masters searching?' asked Elentari.

'Yes. Not only the Masters and Apprentices but other beings have offered their time to search. You can hardly move in both the library and the ancient library. Also, Hoofington has sent word to his contacts, and they are searching for you too. Your disappearance was to be kept quiet,' said Rorien.

'Like no being would not notice me missing. Of course, it wouldn't be kept secret. We are underground somewhere and will be in one of Gornack's casas. He has one in every land. Is there any way of finding who owns the land?' asked Elentari.

'I will check with the King on the morrow. There may be something in the royal books about Gornack's lands or lands belonging to royals,' replied Rorien.

'Ok. Keep searching for bringing yielding and finding who owns the land. We'll talk again this time on the morrow. I love you,' said Elentari.

'And I you. Until the morrow,' replied Rorien.

Despite their efforts, time slipped by. It had been nearly a mesik since Elentari and Fendton had found themselves captured, and nothing changed in routine. Each morning Elentari was whipped before breakfast, tortured with water before lunch, hammered and battered after lunch and burnt before supper. She realised the Torturer used devices to represent each elemental power to torture her, air, water, earth and fire, and never combined them. Elentari and Fendton used their taps to communicate when gagged and huddled together when not chained, always keeping their voices low and muffled. Fendton would hum in an attempt to bring a sense of peace to Elentari. The best part of each dia was speaking to Rorien and listening to the outside world's happenings.

Elentari loved watching the eagerness of Fendton the following morning to hear the latest news. It gave them both hope of escape. Todia was the first of Augavesi, the second month, and in eleven dias, it will be Fendton's 25th birth date. Both hoped they would be home to celebrate. They knew the possibility was very slim, but they needed to look towards something.

"Welcome to a new mesik, Princess. Shall we start the dia with the chain whip?" the Torturer asked. He picked up a handle with several metal rods joined by rings to form a flexible chain and a metal dart at the end used for slashing. "We will use this on your back, the cat o' nine on your legs and the whip on your front. Now, this sounds like a fun activity, doesn't it?" The Torturer sneered in her ear and stepped back.

CRACK! Elentari felt the metal dart slash down her back, slashing her from head to tail. A scream escaped her lips as she knew it was going to be extra painful todia. Every whip would slice through the slash, causing excruciating pain. She had to stay strong and focused on what Rorien spoke about the night before. She remembered this was the worst, and it would get better. More screaming came from Elentari, and more pain through her body followed.

"What type of bath would you like todia? Shall we use the Chinese water torture, dunking or maybe the deep tub? Let's have the deep tub todia and make it extra cold," the Torturer chortled.

The males brought in the 2-meter-tall wooden tub and began to fill it with ice and water. It was hard enough having to struggle to stay above the water without it being filled with ice as well. With the width so small, it was hard to tread water. Every time she grabbed the sides, a mallet would come down hard on her fingers and sometimes broke them. She would slip back under the water. She tried to sink to the bottom and push up above the water, and the Torturer would shove her back down before she emerged, causing her to suck in water. Other times she just managed to hold her breath before he dunked her and would pant for air when she surfaced. Having to struggle against the icy cold water as well as stay above water triggered Elentari to hyperventilate.

Tap. Pause. Tap. Pause. Tap. Fendton was signalling her to stop and calm.

Elentari tried concentrating on her breath, unable to bring it under control before the males lifted her into the tub. Tap. Tap. she replied, letting Fendton know she was thankful. Just as she thought, it was much harder to breathe and more challenging to stay above the water with the ice pressed against her chest. The icy cold water quickly caused her muscles to tense and tighten. She began to use one hand to hold the tub, letting go as she saw the mallet come down and reached up with her other hand and was able to stay above water a bit longer. That was until the Torturer shoved her hard and down deep into the tub. Every time she found a way to cope, the Torturer would change the game.

"I think you need a bit of a rest after lunch, Princess. How about you lay down instead of standing? You look so tired," said the Torturer, sniggering.

Elentari knew she would not be resting but wasn't sure what he would do to torture her. The males strapped her to the table and left, returning with a large flat rock and placed it on her.

Ooff. The air was squeezed out of Elentari as the weight of the rock squished her. The rock lay on her stomach above her hips and on her ribs just below her breasts. Her abdominal muscles were tense, attempting to stop the rock from crushing her insides. Her breath was shallow and only able to fill the top part of her lung. How long she could keep her muscles tense, she was unsure. She tried to wriggle the rock further down to sit on her hips, but it was too heavy. She managed to twist slightly onto her side, and the rock moved to give her a little ease. It was still heavy against her, and she was unable to breathe deep, but it was easier to cope with, especially with Fendton humming to distract her.

"Since you froze in the water todia, how about we warm you up?" the Torturer said as delight played across his eyes.

Elentari was unsure and petrified about what was to come. The males brought in a large spit roast. *Surely this was not going to be rotisserie-style torture?* She panicked.

"Let's get you comfortable in your new bed," said the Torturer.

The males placed a thick pole against her back, tying her to it before putting it on the spit and began to turn it. She had guessed correctly; her new torture was being roasted alive. She struggled against the bonds, trying to free her hands. The males had tied the ropes tight, and she had little movement.

"The best part of your new game is your guard is going to play too. He will keep you moving so you don't burn," the torture laughed from deep within as he shoved the stopper gag in her mouth.

Elentari felt like a pig being roasted. The males removed Fendton from his chains and chained him to the spit roaster.

"I'm sorry, E. I'm sorry," said Fendton over and over again. His voice was full of sorrow and anguish at having to be the one to torture her. Tears were falling from his face as he sobbed. She couldn't respond.

Elentari felt dizzy and nauseous at being spun around and around. Her skin and hair were searing from the heat of the coals. Her eyes stung at the force of the heat, and her throat went dry from breathing in the hot air. Her skin felt like it was severely sunburnt, and her hair almost burnt off. She was removed from the spit and healed before he threw a dress at her. She caught it but confusion set in as she held it, unsure if she was to put it on or not.

"Put on your dress. The future Queen is coming and does not want to see filth and scum," said the Torturer.

She obeyed. Her skin ached as the fabric touched it, still tender from burning. She stood back against the wall, looking for something cool to ease the heat. Fendton stood beside her, the back of their hands touching and their pinkie fingers entwined together, giving each other comfort in knowing they were not alone.

"Welcome to a new mesik. Are you ready to die yet?" said the Bitch as she waltzed into the room and took a seat.

WHACK. The Torturer slapped her across the face.

"Speak," said the Torturer.

"No," Elentari answered.

"Oh dear," said the Bitch with a pout. "And I was so hoping this would be the dia you would give in. It has been almost a mesik since your games began. Surely your tire of them by now?"

"No," answered Elentari.

"Then we shall increase the pain, and by next mesik, you will. I don't like waiting," said the Bitch. She stood and left with the Torturer following, blowing out the lamp and closing the door.

Fendton quietly grabbed the food and met her in the far corner.

"At least you have clothes…for now," said Fendton.

"That is until bedtime," said Elentari.

They sat waiting and anticipating when they would be chained for bed. It grew late, and the light under the door disappeared.

"Did they forget us, E?" asked Fendton.

"I don't know, Fen. Let's get some sleep and worry about it if and when they return," answered Elentari. She lay down on the floor, and Fendton lay behind her wrapping his arm around her waist. They fell asleep quickly but woke at every noise with the expectation of being chained again.

"Morning Princess. I am most sorry you were not tucked into bed last night. Let's get you out of that horrible outfit. You must be uncomfortable," said the Torturer.

Elentari took off the dress and threw it at the Torturer.

"Isn't that much better? Now your guard is overdressed. He needs to take off his clothes," said the Torturer with a grin.

Fendton and Elentari looked at each other, apprehension on their faces. It seemed there was new torture to be had. Fendton removed his clothes as Elentari turned her gaze to the Torturer knowing Fendton would be feeling humiliated and shamed just as she had been. The males grabbed her and chained her to the wall, her arms stretched high above her head.

"Todia, we are changing the games. You can sit and watch," the Torturer snorted as the males grabbed Fendton and chained him to the ceiling.

"NO. NO. PLEASE. NO. Not him. Please. NOT HIM!" Elentari screamed, struggling against the chains to get free. She realised todia Fendton would be tortured instead of her. Fenton's torturing was her new torture, watching Fendton tortured because of her.

"You know what you have to do to stop it. Just say the right words, and I will stop," the Torturer grinned, staring at her waiting for her to speak.

"Give me…" Elentari started to say before Fendton cut her off.

"No. Elentari, no. I am not worth it!" yelled Fendton.

WHACK. The Torturer slapped Fendton across the face.

"What were you going to say?" asked the Torturer pacing back and forth in front of her.

Tap. Pause Tap. Pause. Tap.

Elentari shook her head, dropping her eyes away from Fendton.

"If you have nothing to say, I shall start with the chain whip," the Torturer said. He knew this was the whip she hated most.

Tears were streaming down her cheeks as she sobbed, knowing what Fendton would be experiencing and not wanting him to participate. She knew the only way to stop it was to take her own life, but she also knew he would kill Fendton before her body hit the ground. She had no way to save him.

She closed her eyes, trying to block out the image of Fendton, not wanting to see what would happen to him. It was bad enough to know the feeling. She heard him scream in anguish and felt the pain down her back. Her eyes squeezed tight at the sound of his scream. With every whip, he cried, and she screamed. She began to sink into despair, knowing she was the reason for his pain and unable to stop it. It had been silent for a while before she managed to open her eyes to see the healer healing Fendton. A faun was cleaning up all the blood splattered everywhere as the healer returned Fendton's blood to his veins.

"You ok, Fen?" Elentari asked when they were alone.

Tap. Tap.

"Guess we both know what each other has been going through. Next time, don't give in. I can handle it. You have, and so can I," said Fendton, his voice sounding gravelly.

"Ok. Guess this is my next torture, to watch you going through what I have been through," said Elentari

"Guess so," answered Fendton.

Footsteps approached, a faun to bring them food and males to remove their shackles. Elentari felt uncomfortable being so close to a naked male who was not her link as they sat together eating the bread and apple. She tried not to shift and was careful where she put her hands. Usually, she would wrap her arm around his knee, but this seemed too intimate. Even Fendton was unsure if he should put his arm around her and held her hand instead.

"Shall we continue with the games?" said the Torturer as he entered, followed by two males carrying the Chinese water torture device.

The males placed it at the table's head and chained Elentari to the wall with her legs spread wide. More humiliation and embarrassment, as she felt very exposed and open in her female area. She hummed while they were alone, as Fendton did for her, knowing he would be feeling a boom echoing through his head. She watched him wriggling, trying to stop the sound through his brain, knowing what he was going through and knowing she was defenceless to help.

"Do you have anything to say?" asked the Torturer as he entered the room after lunch.

"No," said Elentari.

"Then the games continue," said the Torturer.

The males chained her to the wall with her arms stretched wide and chained Fendton to the ceiling hook. The Torturer pounded Fendton with the sledgehammer, and she closed her eyes to avoid seeing the pain and anguish on his face. She screwed up her face at the sound of his screams. She knew his legs would collapse, causing more pain in his wrists, and after a long silence, she opened her eyes to see the healer leaving and Fendton watching her.

"How you doing, E?" asked Fendton.

"Don't ask. You coping with your new games, Fen?" asked Elentari.

"About as good as you, I would say," said Fendton,

"Guess his little scheme hasn't worked todia," giggled Elentari. "One to us. Go us!"

"There is still one more torture to happen for the dia. Let's not get too cocky," replied Fendton.

"Come on. At least let us have a little something," said Elentari looking at him sideways.

Footsteps approached, and they knew fire torture was coming.

"Lovely dia, it has been. I have enjoyed my games todia. Are you both enjoying the fun?" said the Torturer as the males brought in the spit.

Both Elentari and Fendton groaned at the thought of spit roast, torture causing both of them to cringe.

"Let's get you ready for the Princess to cook you," the Torturer chuckled as the males bound and gagged Fendton to the pole. The Torturer made his way to chain her to the spit. "Enjoy," the Torturer said and left the room.

"I have no tips to help you cope with this. You will get dizzy, but I can't stop turning, or your skin will burn. We will get through this. Stay strong," said Elentari. She had tears running down her cheeks as she kept turning. Her arms became tired, but she had to keep going swapping her arms to give each a rest. She hummed to herself between sobs to ease the burden for them both.

CHAPTER 12

Routine changed with Elentari and Fendton never knowing who the Torturer would torture. The Torturer kept changing who would bear the brunt of his torturing device. There were dias when one of them experienced all tortures and other dias where they took turns. Dias where one had the morning sessions, and the other had after mid sun sessions. Their anxiety grew, not knowing what to expect, and their hopes waned at being saved. Rorien gave them no news. The Masters' search to bring yielding was not progressing, and to find who owned land without suspicion was proving troublesome. Fendton's 25th birth date came and went with no cake, no gifts and nothing to recognise his special dia except Elentari wishing him well.

Augavesi passed, and Lume came. Again, the Bitch visited them on the first. Lume came and went and Erde, her birth month, approached. Another visit from the Bitch on the first and a special visit on her birth date. Her birth date was a dia of no torture. Elentari and Fendton were no closer to being free.

Fendton had the morning torture with all four whips as Elentari cringed strapped to the wall. The Torturer chose Elentari to dunk and chained Fendton to the ceiling hook to watch. Later, Fendton experienced the hammering while Elentari had her back to him. The Torturer strapped her bent over the table with her hands tied, and her butt was facing the doorway. Her feet were free to move. They were waiting uncomfortably for the dias last torture to begin and heard only one set of footsteps approaching. Elentari strained to turn her head towards the door.

"Greetings, Princess. It is lovely to see you," said Prince Cormac as he swung open the door in a grand entrance.

Shock flooded Elentari's face as Cormac entered through the door. Fendton looked perplexed.

"Yes, Princess. Prince Cormac has come to visit you. Don't get any ideas that I am here to save you," Cormac laughed. "No. I am here to watch your torture. I too hope you die soon, for once you are gone, and the future Queen sits on her rightful throne, she will name me King of all the Lands," said Cormac, his voice full of excitement.

"Get out!" Elentari yelled as she twisted, trying to break free.

"Oh, Princess. I thought you would be glad to see me. I am hurt," said Cormac. He pulled a sad face and placed his hand on his heart before laughing at her. "You look ravishing," Cormac whispered across the table.

Elentari moved her feet, feeling very anxious at what he was planning, not liking the look of lust he was giving her. Her feet touched the small table the Torturer used for coals to sit on. Cormac began to move around the table seductively, running his fingers along the top while licking his lips. Elentari struggled more, trying to break free of the restraint. She kicked him as he came within reach. Cormac rubbed his chin and grabbed her thigh.

"You in this position is perfect for me to have my way with you," Cormac whispered in her ear as he spread her legs and leaned over her.

Elentari could feel his malehood hard against her backside. Panic welled up inside her. She did not want to be with another male, did not want to be taken this way.

"No. Please. Please don't," Elentari whimpered. Tears fell from her eyes, and she struggled even harder against the restraints and trying to kick him off.

"Leave her alone!" yelled Fendton as he fraught with removing the chain from the ceiling hook.

"Oh. I do love a female who struggles. I am going to enjoy you, and neither of you can stop me. I always take what I want and who I want. Right now, you are what I want," Cormac said, pressing his groin into her, again and again, so she could feel his hardened malehood as his hands rubbed over her body and backside.

"NO!" she screamed as she heard him removing his pants. The restraints were digging into her wrists, cutting them. She did not care. She kept pulling and twisting, trying to break free from him.

"Get off her," yelled Fendton. He was jumping to try and reach the hook to remove the chain.

Cormac laughed and continued to remove his clothes.

"RORIEN! HELP ME!" Elentari screamed, struggling even harder, not caring the straps were ripping into her skin as they broke. She twisted around, slamming her fist into Cormac's face, the leather strap whipping his head. She grabbed the small table swinging it high against Cormac's head. Cormac blocked her, but she didn't stop. Her eyes were fire as anger raged through her, throwing the table at him over and over. Until she eventually hit him hard enough, and he slumped to the floor. She dropped the table and began to punch him with her fists.

"ELENTARI! STOP!" yelled Fendton. He had stopped struggling and was watching her. He knew he had to stop her before she killed him.

Cormac lay unconscious on the floor, covered in blood. Elentari looked up.

"You can't kill him, remember," Fendton said as two males came racing in, grabbing her and chaining her to the wall. One ran out, returning with the healer.

Elentari grinned at her little win, oblivious to the blood running down her arm from her cuts. The healer fixed Cormac enough to enable him to be removed to another room before healing her wrists.

'*ELENTARI ANSWER ME!*' Rorien yelled on their bite.

'*Sorry, Rorien. When I screamed, I guess I grabbed our bite, hoping for you to save me, and you did. Cormac came to visit me. He is on the Bitch's side. The Bitch has promised him a seat as King,*' replied Elentari on their bite.

'*You must be in the South,*' said Rorien.

'*Or anywhere else. The Bitch transported me here, remember. What's to say she didn't transport him here too,*' said Elentari.

'*True. What happened?*' asked Rorien.

'Please don't ask me to explain what we are going through. It is bad enough we are living it without having to explain it,' replied Elentari.

'Sorry. I love you and want you safe back here with me,' said Rorien.

'And I you. Out of curiosity, has anyone checked the book Fendton and I were searching, the one with rebuilding the link?' asked Elentari.

'No. We left it on your table. I am going now,' answered Rorien.

"What happened?" asked Fendton.

"When I screamed 'Rorien' hawk," answered Elentari.

"Oh, you weren't hawk?" asked Fenton.

"No. Instinct, I guess. That book you found…"

Tap. Tap. Pause. Tap. Tap.

Elentari and Fendton hung across from each other, waiting for their punishment for hurting Cormac to begin. Night came, and no being had entered. No food came, and the light under the door went out. They woke with a start to the door slamming open with such force it almost came off its hinges.

"YOU DESERVE TO DIE! How dare you hurt the future King of all the Lands. Punishment to both of you, together, and extra sessions added. YOU will be begging to die before the mesik end in 10 dias," said the Bitch. Her face was red with rage, her eyes large, and her body stiff and tense.

'Elentari, we found it!' said Rorien on their bite. *'I hope you are awake.'*

'Sshh. Wait,' replied Elentari on their bite.

"Sorry, my Queen. I shall behave," said Elentari, in an attempt to throw the Bitch and get her out the door quickly.

"Then you will take a knife and end your life," the Bitch said as she stormed out the door.

'Good. What do I need to do?' Elentari spoke on their bite.

"Hawk, Fen," Elentari said aloud.

'Repeat the ancient text. I shall read it to you. Are you able to move? You will need to make the basic element moves, you know, the ones when you were first tested?' asked Rorien.

'I can move very little. Let me see what I can do,' answered Elentari. She moved her wrists and hands in the basic movements of each element. *'Yes, I can just make every basic move.'*

'Ok. In each new sentence, you will do a different element and spirit yield. It starts with air and sight, water and healing, earth and shift, and fire and movement. Ready?' asked Rorien.

'Yes,' replied Elentari.

Rorien read the text with Elentari reciting it while completing the actions and mind movements.

"Quick, footsteps are coming!" said Fendton in a hushed hurried voice.

Elentari kept going. She was finishing the last yield as the Torturer stepped into the room and spotted her arms moving.

"They are sore," Elentari said, quickly finishing the move. "We've been stuck here a long time."

"If you weren't so stupid, you would not have been stuck here," the Torturer said as a faun brought in their food. "Breakfast first, and then we will begin. I will bring the healer in to check on you."

The two males standing guard at the door, armed with swords, stepped inside as the Torturer removed their chains. The Torturer left, and the guards stepped out, closing the door.

"Did it work?" asked Fendton.

Elentari shrugged as she grabbed their food and met him in the far corner.

"Eat first. If it did, we need our strength to get out of here, not that bread and orange is much," said Elentari.

Elentari and Fendton ate silently as the healer checked her over. Elentari tried yielding her sight power and could hear the healers thoughts. A smile spread on her face; it had worked. The healer's heart was light, and her mind pure. Elentari knew the Bitch held against her will.

"Can you talk?" Elentari asked the healer.

The healer shook her head and left.

"It worked, Fen," whispered Elentari. "Are you ready?"

"Do you need to ask? Get us out of here! Now!" replied Fendton jumping to his feet.

"Ok. We take the healer with us, and when we are in the open, I will transport us a distance away before changing into my animal spirit and get out of here. Let's go," said Elentari as she stood up.

Fendton stood and grabbed Elentari's hand, racing for the door. She used her air power to blast through the door, throwing the guards against the wall and knocking them unconscious. Fendton grabbed a sword off the guard as she began running the tunnel towards the exit. She was checking each room on the right as Fendton checked the rooms on the left. Fendton found the healer, grabbed her and dragged her with them. As they neared the exit, the Torturer stepped into the tunnel entrance. Elentari blasted him with such force that sent him flying through the air and into a tree. The exit was clear for them.

"STOP" yelled the Bitch

They heard the Bitch yell as they took two steps into the outside world. Elentari turned to face the Bitch.

"I will meet you on the battlefield in war, Bitch. You against me, the south battlefield on the royal land on the last dia of the mesik. Until then," Elentari waved goodbye and transported them away to the foot of the mountain. She pulled the oaths and felt them pull her North. It felt great to feel her guards again. She changed into her dragon animal spirit, grabbed Fendton in one claw and the healer in the other before leaping high into the sky and heading North as fast as she could. Elentari had been flying for three horis when she spotted the ocean in the far distance, and hori later, she landed on a secluded beach to rest.

'Rorien, we're are stopping to rest. We have hit the ocean. How far is it across from the South to the Royal lands?' asked Elentari on their bite.

'About 3,500 stadi,' answered Rorien.

'I don't have enough energy. Have Lorcan call Awnrie and bring the Movement Master,' said Elentari. She kept looking back over her shoulder, making sure no being was following them.

'Lorcan has called her. They will be here soon. Are you hurt?' asked Rorien.

'No. Both Fen and I are not hurt. Have the Master concentrate on us, and hopefully, he can pinpoint us. We are standing on a deserted beach, looking North,' replied Elentari. Her eyes scanned the bush, looking for movement.

'He is coming,' said Rorien.

"Master, you are a wonderful sight to see," said Elentari as the Master appeared before them. It felt like horis since she landed and the Master appeared, but it had only been moments.

The Master looked from her to Fendton, his cheeks turning red, and shifted his gaze to the trees behind them.

"Princess. It is good you are alive," the Master replied, trying not to look at her.

"Take us to Rorien and then home, please. I need clothes and a good bath before meeting with the King," said Elentari.

"Yes, Princess. As you wish," the Master replied. He transported them to Rorien.

Elentari leapt into Rorien's arms, grabbing hold of him tightly and sobbing into his chest. Relief flooded her body. Rorien's arms wrapped tightly around her as his cheek rested on her head. He sighed. All the stress melted from him, and he felt calm. Elentari had forgotten her nakedness until she felt a shirt draped over her shoulders. She turned to see Jasper as she put her arms in the sleeves.

"Thanks, Jasper. I forgot about our nakedness," said Elentari, still clinging to Rorien. She turned to the healer. "Can you talk?"

The healer shook her head.

"Ok. We need to get back and get you safe until the war," Elentari said, holding up her hand to stop the questions about to come. "I'll have a dungeon set up with comforts, and you will have the key. Jasper will set you up with Sarina. Jasper, please have Sarina set up the largest dungeon with comforts and activities for our new friend."

"On it," Jasper answered.

Elentari whispered into the healer's ear, "Let no one in except Jasper and those with him. Do not let me in if I am not with him. Do you understand? No being but Jasper," Elentari said with a look of 'you understand' across her face.

The healer nodded.

"Jasper, when we get home, take our friend to her lodgings and settle her in before finding me either in my casa or the royal hall. Lorcan, find the Generals and have them meet in the royal hall in an hori and Master, round up all the Masters, Apprentices and Scholars and have them meet in the royal hall in an hori. Awnrie, get us some food, no bread or apples. Now Master, take us home," said Elentari.

The Master transported them into her living room. Jasper left with the healer while Lorcan went to find the Generals. Awnrie set off to get food and the Master to fulfil his order. Elentari headed to her bathroom, yielding water to fill the tub. She was desperate for a good soak in a warm bath to remove the dungeon's stench and enjoy the feel of being covered in clothing.

"Fen, you want a shower? I can fill it for you?" Elentari asked as she stepped into the bath, sinking deep into the warm water.

Tap. Tap.

"Sticking with the tap-tap, are we Fen?" asked Elentari. "Rorien, can you get some clothes for Fen, please?" asked Elentari.

"Yes. So what? It's just…" said Fendton.

"It's ok, Fen. Just remember we are home now," cut in Elentari.

"Ok," said Fendton.

Elentari heard the shower run as she began to wash her hair or what was left of it, relishing in the smell of the oils as she cleaned her head. She scrubbed her body, removing all traces of the past four mesiks. Rorien returned with clothes for Fendton, and she topped up the shower.

"You ok?" Rorien asked, his voice soft as he sat on the edge of the bath.

"I am now. I have you," answered Elentari. She reached up and kissed him. "I have missed you."

"Remember, I am here," yelled Fendton from the shower.

Tap. Tap. Elentari tapped the edge of the bath, not wanting to ruin her moment with Rorien.

"I shall enjoy being with you tonight," Rorien said, kissing her.

"Still here," said Fendton.

"Mmm. Tonight can't come quick enough," replied Elentari, stepping out of the bath and watching Rorien taking in her body as she wrapped her towel around herself. She enjoyed the softness against her skin. It felt so wonderful to have soft, fluffy fabrics against her skin. The shower stopped, and Elentari threw Fendton a towel and stepped into her robe. She ran her hands through all her hanging clothes, appreciating and touching them all. She had missed her dresses and took her time to dress.

"Fen, when I changed into my spirit animal, all that we had been through seemed to have happened to someone else. It was like it never happened to me," Elentari said as she stepped out into the living room dressed as a future Queen should and found the King waiting for her.

"Papa!" Elentari raced to the King to hug him.

"Daughter, you're home. You are home," said the King wrapping his arms tightly around her. Tears welled in his eyes.

"Yes, I am. We will eat and then meet in the royal hall with the Masters to fill every being in on what is happening," answered Elentari.

"Ok. I shall see you soon," said the King as he kissed her and left.

"Is that how you managed to cope and keep going? By changing?" asked Fendton.

"Yes. It was like I had been watching it happen from a distance, someone else's dream. It felt great, almost like being free," Elentari said.

Fendton looked at her, not sure what to do.

Elentari nodded.

Fendton changed into his cheetah form and sat on the couch beside her. She reached over and patted him.

"Hello. You big fluffy kitty," Elentari said, rubbing her face against his fur. "Kitty is so soft." Cheetah Fendton purred, rubbing his face against her. "It feels much better, doesn't it?"

Tap. Tap. Fendton's paw tapped her leg.

Elentari kept patting cheetah Fendton and talking to him until Awnrie appeared with food, and he changed back.

"Food," Elentari said, making a bee-line for the table and the bowls of stew.

"Food," Fendton said, chasing after her.

Elentari sat with her knees up on the chair and with her back to Rorien and the door. Fenton sat beside her and put his arm around her, sitting together as they had been. She put her hand on his knee, and his arm draped around her.

Tap. Tap. Tap. Fendton tapped with his mouth full of food.

Tap. Tap. Elentari replied with a full mouth. Tap. Tap. Tap.

Tap. Tap.

They sat in silence, eating the stew from one bowl before moving to the second bowl.

Tap. Tap. Elentari tapped.

Tap. Tap. Fendton replied.

"Elentari?" asked Rorien quietly, unsure of what to make of Fendton and Elentari.

Elentari and Fendton both jumped at the sound of Rorien's voice, and she clung to Fendton as they both turned around.

"Oh, I'm sorry Rorien. We coped by huddling together when we were alone and eating," Elentari said as she removed herself from Fendton. "It may take us a bit of time to break these habits and adjust back to reality. Hard to believe we are home."

"I didn't mean to startle you, but it is time to meet the Generals and Masters," said Rorien. "We have to go."

CHAPTER 13

"Masters, Apprentices, Scholars and Generals. Thank you for meeting with me. I have called you all here for I am to go to battle on the 40th. I will be fighting against the Bitch who took me and require your help to fight her. The fight will be her against me and no other being, and it is to the death," said Elentari. Her eyes were looking directly at each of them as they stood in the royal hall. She had her hands resting on the table they were working form, which her guards had brought in for them. Her face showed no emotion. She meant business. A few moved slightly, unsure if they should speak up.

"Much work and training we have to do before we go to war, and we shall begin on the morrow. Between now and then, every available being is to see if they can find a way to create a shield wall, a wall to stop yielding. The room where the Bitch held us had all yielding removed. This wall you are to build will allow power within but not to exit or enter. Somehow you are to find a way to build a wall around me to protect me from any other beings yielding. Not only is it to protect me, but every being on the battlefield, for I do not trust her. Her power will not exist beyond the wall to harm any being, nor will any power enter to harm me. Is that clear?" said Elentari as she stood straight and tall. Her face was tense. Her eyes scanned every being as they nodded their understanding.

"Right. Generals inform the army they will be training this vika heavily. If I fail, they will need to take the Bitch down, but I do not plan to fail, for I have the best of the best here in this room, and I expect you will not fail me!" said Elentari.

All heads nodded.

"Excellent. On the morrow, I shall explain my plan and have your input. Any questions?" Elentari asked as she scanned the room.

"Princess. If I may, I wondered if it is not any trouble. If you would, can you explain…" the Air Master struggled to find the words?

"Just say what you want and stop faltering," said Elentari. She crossed her arms.

"Yes, Princess. What happened?" asked the Air Master.

She leaned both hands on the table and lowered her head to steady herself. Fendton moved beside her and put his hand on the table beside hers linking their pinkie fingers.

Fenton gently tapped on the table. Tap. Tap. Tap. Tap.

Elentari spoke softly. "I shall say this once and once only as I do not want to relive it. As we," she nodded to Fendton, "left the library heading to the training area, we found ourselves in a room, suddenly. The Bitch explained who she was and why she kidnapped me as a babe. She kept us in a large room which was void of yielding, where each morning before breakfast, I was tortured with different whips, healed, fed and then tortured with water. After lunch, I got to be hammered and beaten before healing and then burnt different ways before dinner. This is on top of being strapped to a table or chained to a wall. By the second mesik, we were both tortured. I was stripped naked, humiliated and tortured. The expectation was I would take my own life. All because a descendant of Gornack believes she is the rightful heir to my throne." She looked up. "Does this satisfy you?" Elentari asked with anger and disgust in her tone.

"err…I would…yes, Princess," the Air Master said as he hung his head realising, the Princess had been through hell, and he had reminded her of it.

"Any other questions?" Elentari asked as she scanned the room. "None? Good. Now get to work. We meet here after breakfast." She raised herself and waved her hand to dismiss every being as she approached the King.

"Papa, do you have any questions?" Elentari asked as she took her seat beside her father. Her fingers ran over the royal chair, taking in every detail. It felt so good to be back in her rightful spot.

"Elentari, Rorien says Cormac was there. What happened?" asked the King.

"You don't want to know. Just know Cormac is working with the Bitch," Elentari said as she felt Fendton hand on her shoulder.

Tap. Tap. Tap. Tap.

"I do want to know. He is next to be sitting on the South's throne, and I need to know if he is the right male to be on the throne. If he is not, then things need to be put in order," said the King.

She sighed before speaking. "Papa, Cormac spends more time with other females. When he was here, and I searched his and his linked minds, I could not find a time they have been together of late," said Elentari.

Fury raged across the Kings face, and Elentari saw Rorien stiffen as Fendton's hand squeeze her shoulder.

"Did he hurt you?" growled the King. His hands were gripping the hand rest of his throne, his knuckles turning white and his body moved forward, ready to attack.

"No. He didn't. Instead, I found a great surge of strength and broke my restraints and took him down. If it weren't for Fendton, I would have killed him then and there," said Elentari. Her face was red with rage.

The King looked to Fendton, questioning. Sorrow flitted across his face, yet his eyes showed anger.

"He didn't touch her. He tried, but as E said, she took him down. I wanted her to kill him but yelled for her to stop, and she did," Fendton answered quietly.

"He has committed a crime against a future crown and will be dealt with accordingly," said the King moving back in his chair.

"Papa, leave it until after the war. If he's there, as I expect him to be, then our troubles will be over. We are in a war, and he can be re-moved during a war without consequences, remember?" said Elentari.

"When the war is complete, we will broach this subject again. Just make sure you win. I do not want to lose you again," sighed the King. "It seems you leave just as you arrive."

"I have no desire to lose, Papa. Who will look after every being in our lands if I am gone?" Elentari smiled. "Plus, I have an advantage with the Masters, Scholars, Generals and with Rorien able to communicate with me."

"What power does she hold?" asked the King.

"I have no idea. Maybe the healer will know. On the morrow, the Master will search her mind to find any tips to help us. Right now, I want to go home and enjoy my freedom before having to deal with this vika and what is to come," Elentari answered. She stood and kissed the King before heading off.

"Until the morrow future Queen," the King said as he watched her leave, wondering how he could change the situation without her going into battle. He sought the Masters' council and was no closer to solving the issue before the morrow came.

Elentari and Rorien arrived at the royal hall to find it filled. The full hall was a good sign. Every Master, Apprentice, Scholar and General stood waiting for her, ready to assist her in what she required. All ready to standby their future Queen.

"Good dia to you all. Firstly, has there been any progress in finding a shield wall?" asked Elentari.

"No, Princess," answered the Sight Master. "We have found the text on nullifying yielding but nothing on building a shield. As you know, you generally use yielding to stop another's yield."

"Ok. Keep searching. Can we have a map of these lands?" asked Elentari.

"Yes, Princess. I shall get one for you," said Cornel. He bowed to the Princess and headed out.

"While he is gone, is there any being who is not happy with being a part of this war?" asked Elentari. She searched the faces and read their minds. She was searching for any being who was not entirely dedicated, giving them an out. Only those who wanted to help her would be able. All beings' minds focused on the coming war and the job at hand.

Elentari could not find one doubt. This dedication pleased her, knowing she had every being's support.

"Princess, here is the largest map we have, plus, I have brought parchment and ink for you," said Cornel entering the hall.

"Thanks, Cornel. Most helpful," replied Elentari.

Cornel placed the map in the centre of the table and parchment beside her.

"The battle is to take place on the south battlefield, here," Elentari said, leaning on the table and pointing to the map. "This area here is where I want the shield wall to be." She circled an area on the map with her finger. "I will be here, and Rorien with the Masters and my guards shall stand here." She moved her fingers to each of the spots. She stood up.

"Their role will be to stand here and not move, feeding me any information I need and relaying anything out. I need to see Rorien and know I have support. Any information you need to pass on, speak to the Masters. Anything I need, Rorien will be my communication to get it," said Elentari. She paused before looking to Cornel.

"Cornel, can you please make up a large map of the battlefield and have it ready on the morrow?" asked Elentari.

"Yes, Princess," answered Cornel.

"Excellent. Sight Master, can you please search the healer's mind and seek any information which will be helpful. Specifically, if you can find what power the Bitch yields. Jasper will take you to the healer," said Elentari.

"Yes, Princess," replied the Sight Master.

"The idea is to have sight, air and earth yielders working together to save those who have a light heart and unwillingly captured. These will be the Unwilling. Sight yielders are to search their minds and have the air and earth yielders gently encourage them to move towards us. Movement yielders, when the Unwilling get close, let them know you are here to save them and transport them to the camp, which will be over here," Elentari said. She pointed to a spot just off the battlefield. "The Heal yielders and Shift yields will stay at camp to help the Unwilling.

Apprentices who are next to be Masters of each power will be in charge of the field. Use this time to work together to hone getting the Unwilling to safety."

"Yes, Princess," answered the Apprentices.

"Now, those with dark hearts, we will move them here in this centre area directly behind the Bitch. Those without a task will spread out and scatter yourselves around here," said Elentari. Her finger moved over a section of the map. "Keep moving around, erratically moving fast and slow and stopping constantly. I want it to keep changing so as not to arouse suspicion that the Unwilling are missing. Those whose hearts are not fully light or fully black, move them to the sides." She paused, checking to see if every being was following and waiting for any questions.

"Once the shield wall drops, take out those with black hearts. I want none of them alive. The wall will drop either when I die or when I kill the Bitch. Capture those with partial hearts and see where their loyalties lie before you give them their punishment."

"Yes, Princess," answered every being.

"This plan centres around finding a shield wall," said Elentari. She stood straight.

"What is the plan if we do not find one?" asked an apprentice.

"I have the best within all of the lands right here. I expect you to find one," glared Elentari.

"Yes, Princess," answered the Apprentice with his head down.

"Princess, maybe we should have a backup plan. The Bitch may nullify the wall or create a crack in it to enable her power to flow through. She may have her wall. Let's make sure we have every possible outcome covered," said a General.

"Ok. We shall work on this as the main plan and have back up plans. Think of any possible scenarios which the Bitch could overcome, and we will find a solution to them all. Fendton, if the Torturer is there, which he will be, you may take him out when the shield wall drops. Use what you need to complete the job. If it takes you a few horis, so be it. Do not let it take more than eight horis," said Elentari.

"Thank-you. No more than eight horis and whatever I want," Fendton replied.

"Yes. Rorien, if Cormac is there, he is yours," Elentari growled. "Do whatever you need to remove his existence."

"Yes, Princess. Any requests to how you wish him to die?" asked Rorien.

"No. Just make it so no being can revive him," Elentari said. She paused, taking a deep breath before continuing.

"Is there any adjustments or other ideas we can use?" asked Elentari.

"Yes, princess," said one Apprentice.

Ideas began to fly around the room as they started to fine-tune the plan. The Sight Master left after lunch with Jasper to seek information from the healer, and the scholars went to draw a new map. Those without a task headed to the library to search for a way to build a shield wall. Elentari was alone with her guards and the King in the empty hall.

"Papa, what are your thoughts?" Elentari asked as she approached the King.

"You have thought this out thoroughly and actioned it with the strength of a ruler," the King answered.

"I did have plenty of time to think about my revenge," said Elentari staring at the entrance doors.

"You will make a great Queen, Elentari. You are proving yourself worthy to sit on this throne," said the King.

"Papa, I will not be Queen for many anoks. There is still much life in you, and I am too young to govern just yet," said Elentari.

"Yes. I still have many anoks left in me yet. Still, you will make a great Queen," answered the King.

"Papa, when this is over, may my guards and I have time away?" asked Elentari.

"Why?" asked the King.

"I need a little time out to settle. What we went through was hard, and I need to rebuild," said Elentari.

"Where do you want to go?" asked the King.

"West, maybe to the giants. Not out of this land," answered Elentari.

"How long?" asked the King.

"A vika, maybe two?" said Elentari.

"After this war is over, you may have one, ONE, vika with your guard and only in the West. You may spend time in Chelista and only there. Is that understood!?" replied the King. He had one finger up to enforce one vika.

"Yes, Papa. One vika in the West," said Elentari.

"Chelista," said the King.

"Fine, only in Chelista," said Elentari. "You are becoming a bit too protective, Papa."

"And why shouldn't I? I have to protect the future of my lands and throne. There is only you," said the King. "Now, is there anything else? I have other business to conduct."

"No, Papa. We shall take our leave," said Elentari as she stood. "I need some time to think and recover. See you at supper."

CHAPTER 14

"It was horrible, no, horrible is like a walk in the park compared to what happened," said Fendton. He shook his head, trying to find the right words. He was sitting on the floor with his knees up, hugging them to his chest. Rorien, Jasper, Lorcan, Sarina, and Awnrie quietly sat on the chairs, watching him, unsure of what to do. Elentari was elsewhere and had gone off wanting time by herself.

"It was frightening not knowing where we were or what was happening, and it just got worse from there. I wanted to punch the Torturer's face when he hit her," Fendton said, his face full of anger. "But I couldn't," his voice was low. "He was brutal and showed no sympathy. We had to listen to the Bitch's story and sit there, waiting to find out what was going to happen. The Bitch liked that I wasn't you, Rorien," Fendton said, glancing to Rorien before putting his chin back on his knees. "And that your link was gone. E told her you died but not that you were revived and lived. She kept that quiet. I guess as a way to save us, but the Bitch knew you lived." Fendton paused.

"They grabbed me and chained me to the wall. The Torturer held E so she couldn't move. He threw her at the males and taunted her before ripping her dress off her. I struggled but couldn't break free. There was no way I could help her. Nothing I could do help her. I couldn't help her. I couldn't help her. No matter how hard I struggled, the chains would not break. I couldn't move. She was trying to cover herself, but the males were too strong. She was screaming and struggling against them. I was yelling at them, but they gagged me with a stopper, so large my mouth was stretched wide. They tied her to the table and left us in the dark. I couldn't talk to her, couldn't help her, couldn't comfort her as she cried for most of the night. I could hear her shivering, her teeth chattering from being naked in the cold room, and I couldn't help her," said Fenton. His chin was on his knees, and he was staring at the floor. His friends said nothing.

"The torturing began in the morning while they left me still chained to the wall. The whips were relentless against her skin. She was screaming and begging for him to stop. I couldn't move to save her or even yell. I was just as helpless as her, but I should have been able to help her. I could do nothing. The more she screamed, the more the Torturer seemed to enjoy it. She just kept screaming so loud. It was so loud, so loud", Fendton shook his head.

"The blood splatted against the wall and was pooling at her feet. There was so much blood, so much blood everywhere. She just kept screaming and begging him to stop, but he kept going enjoying her misery. I kept trying to break free, to scream for them to stop, but couldn't. I couldn't stop him, couldn't stop him. When she passed out, he left her to hang from her wrists, just dangling there limp and lifeless. The healer would come, and a faun cleaned her blood. There was so much blood, so much blood. One of my hands was released to relieve myself before I was chained again. They showed no emotion and no care, and they wouldn't look at her or me. We were treated as nothing, uncaring and distant," Fendton said.

Fendton started to rock back and forth. His friends sat quietly, watching and listening to him, unsure of what to do.

"When she came to, and they released to eat. Bread and water with one apple was the standard meal. That was all they gave us. I could hardly move from standing stretched out all night. It was hard to breathe properly, and I just crawled. It was nice to eat, to hold her and warm her. She was so cold, so cold. It didn't last long, and the Torturer would begin again. This time was torturing with water. He kept dunking her in the water, holding her down, seeing how long she would last. She would struggle to breathe, and water would splash out everywhere. When she began to cope, he changed the way he dunked her. Dunking her fast and hardly allowing her any time to take a breath before shoving her under again. He stopped and left her so far beneath the water she was struggling to get out. I couldn't help her as her legs and arms were searching for something to grip to steady herself. I watched her struggle, struggling to stay alive and couldn't help her," said Fendton.

Sarina moved to sit beside Fendton, wrapping her arms around him as a tear ran from the corner of her eye. Awnrie sat on his other side and held him, holding back the tears. Both females were trying to comfort him. The males sat quietly and still, unsure of what to do or think.

"The hammers were brutal on her body. She screamed so loud as they hit her, begging for him to stop. He kept going, swinging again and again, hitting her and enjoying her misery. I could hear her bones break and watched as she slumped, dangling from her wrists and unable to stand. The screaming just wouldn't stop. Her constant screaming and begging did nothing to help, and it was never-ending. It was a relief when she passed out. The screaming stopped, and the hammering stopped." Fendton paused.

"Am I wrong to be glad she passed out? Am I a bad person?" Fendton asked, looking up at Sarina.

Sarina shook her head and hugged him tighter. Awnrie rubbed his arm.

"The smell of her burnt skin was overpowering, the coals burning into her back and legs as she screamed even more. She couldn't see it coming, couldn't see the coals as they fell from the Torturers tongs. She only felt it. I could see them, see the red-hot coals, see them above her and unable to stop them falling, watching them fall and hit her skin. The Torturer would often look at me before dropping the coals, smiling at me as he dropped them. The smell caused her to choke and vomit. The smell was atrocious, the mix of burnt skin and vomit. Lucky her head was off the table, and she vomited on the floor and not all over herself. I was gagged and couldn't throw up, having to swallow my vomit. It would seep out around the edges of the gag and run down my face, almost choking me. She just kept screaming and begging, and he wouldn't stop. I couldn't save her. I had no way to stop him. It wasn't right," said Fendton. His eyes focused on the floor, and he continued to rock back and forth.

"We ate bread and orange for tea. I kept my arm around her to warm her. I wanted to make it stop. I wanted to take her away, but there were guards at the door. We couldn't leave. We were powerless, and there was no way to save her." Fendton said.

Sarina stoked his back and held his arm, trying to soothe the pain. Awnrie stroked his head. The males watched on silently.

"She was so distraught and wanted it to stop. She wasn't coping, and neither was I. She got gagged for the night. Sometimes it was me gagged, and sometimes it was her. It kept coming, torture after torture. He was relentless and lived on her agony, delighting in her screams. I hated her screaming, dreaded her screaming. It was deafening. I wanted her to shut up, to be gagged just to shut her up. Her screaming was ear-piercing and just didn't stop. It was horrible," said Fendton. He paused.

"Every morning, he whipped her, alternating between four different whips. She just kept screaming. She wouldn't stop, and I couldn't help her. I was glad every time she passed out, giving me relief. I hated myself for feeling that way, but she wouldn't stop shouting. I started to hum to myself to block out her screaming, anything for relief. She thought I was doing it to help her, but I wanted to block her out. I am the worst friend to think that way, wanting to block out her agony?" Fendton looked up at Sarina.

Sarina shook her head and kissed his forehead, hugging him to her bosom. She rocked him. Awnrie placed a hand on his back.

"She didn't scream during water tortures, but I had to watch her struggling to breathe, watch her almost drowning. I couldn't break free to help her. I've never felt so helpless. He had different ways to drown her, dunking, the tall tub where she could hardly stay above water. The dripping device onto her head. She was always freezing afterwards, and her teeth would chatter as she shivered. It was annoying listening to her freeze and not able to give her a blanket to stop the chatter," said Fendton.

Sarina stroked his hair and began to hum softly.

"After lunch, not that bread and a piece of fruit is a meal. We did get stew or some runny gravy every few dias. I guess it was to keep her strength up. So, lunch then hammering. It was like the whips. The relentless screaming. Nothing I could do to stop him or save her. He had four different hammers and rocks. He kept swinging those hammers against her body, so persistent were the hammers, repeatedly pounding her, and she kept screaming. There was so much screaming, so much screaming. She just wouldn't stop. I hated the screaming, really hated it, knowing her agony and unable to stop it," said Fendton, sobbing. He clung to Sarina's leg.

"I couldn't believe it when Cormac came in. I thought we had been saved but was I wrong. That was the worst, knowing what he wanted to do, and I was helpless to stop him. The strength she found to stop him was phenomenal. She seemed to find a surge of strength that broke the restraints when he started…"

"FEN, enough," Elentari said. Her voice was stern and strict. She appeared from the bed room. "No more. No more," said Elentari quietly as she knelt in front of him.

Fendton raised his head and looked at her.

"We are no longer trapped, and we have a war to fight in eight dias," said Elentari. She placed her hands on his knees.

"It's hard to forget. The pictures keep coming. I keep thinking we are still there. Waiting for the next torture to come," said Fendton. He dropped his head and kept his arms crossed.

Awnrie went and sat on Lorcan's knee, looking for comfort. Lorcan wrapped his arms tightly around her, tears running down his cheek. Sarina sat between Rorien and Jasper. Jasper wrapped an arm around her, holding her tight, and Rorien took Sarina's hand in his. Tears ran down the male's cheeks.

"Ok. How about this. Every evening, go and see the Sight Master for an hori and tell him everything that played on your mind. During the dia, push it aside until you meet with the Master. Ok?" said Elentari.

"Why?" asked Fendton.

"It will help to talk about it, and the Master can see what happened. He can help change it and make it easier to cope. Talking about it with someone helps to heal and helps to realise it is over," replied Elentari.

"It is over?" asked Fendton. He uncrossed his arms.

"Yes, Fen. It is over," said Elentari. She gently rubbed his knees.

"Ok, I will. It does seem logical to speak to the Sight Master," said Fendton as he looked at her. He placed his hands on hers.

"Now, always finish on a positive. Finish the story. The Masters had found a way to bring back the yielding, and Rorien relayed it to Elentari. With yielding back, she," Elentari paused, sitting back and waiting for Fendton to finish.

"Blasted the door, and we raced for the exit and got free," said Fendton quickly.

"Bit more than that, Fen. Tell the end like you told the rest," said Elentari looking at him sideways.

"You heard!?" Fendton said, surprised and a little uncomfortable.

"Yes, Fen. I heard and read your thoughts," answered Elentari.

"How are you so composed?" asked Fendton. He looked at her puzzled.

"I wear two hats and have fallen into the role of Princess and future Queen to help me cope. I can't begin to relive it, not yet. I have every being to think about at the moment, and that keeps me going. Plus, I sought the Master. So, finish the story properly. This is the bit I want to hear," said Elentari smiling. She moved and sat beside him. She wrapped her arm around his leg. He wrapped his arm around her.

"Ok," said Fendton. He paused. "You blasted the door and knocked the guard's unconscious. We raced towards the exit, checking each room for the healer, and as we got to the entrance, the Torturer stepped in front. You blasted him backwards and into a tree, clearing the exit. As we stepped out of the exit, the Bitch spoke. You told her you would meet her in a war before transporting us away. Changing into a dragon, you flew us towards Rorien and home, stopping at the ocean to rest. You had the Movement Master find us and bring us home to safety. Home to safety. We are home, aren't we? This is real?" asked Fendton, squeezing her hands.

"Yes, Fen. We are home and safe. Maybe kitty cat can help you as Dragon helped me. If it feels too much, change for a bit and compose yourself. Utilise the Sight Master to help you," said Elentari.

"Why are you doing this? I wanted you to shut up, and you're helping me?" asked Fendton

"Two reasons. One – you are my bestie, and two - you are my guard. I need you to be yourself again. I need you strong and able to fight for me. There was nothing you could do. If you weren't there, Jasper, Seneca or Lorcan would have been there, and they wouldn't have been able to help either. It was you who saved us, Fen. You who came up with the idea. You who connected us with Rorien. You who found a way to free me. Fen, you freed me, freed us. Remember that you found a way to free me as my guard should. You protected me, putting your arm around me, holding me, giving me a little extra food, said Elentari.

"You knew?" asked Fendton, surprised.

"Yes, Fen. I knew," replied Elentari, shaking her head.

"I saved us and protected you?" asked Fendton.

"Yes, Fen. You saved us and protected me. Now let's move on. On the morrow, we are to start training and getting ready for war," said Elentari.

"Ok. Time to move on. Do you think I should see the Master now?" asked Fendton.

"If you need to, then, yes. See the Master if you need it. I have told him he needs to give us both time when we approach him. We are first and for most," replied Elentari. She shifted away from him and sat sideways.

"Ok. You don't mind?" asked Fendton, turning to face her.

"No. Would you like Lorcan to walk over with you?" asked Elentari. Fendton nodded.

"Come on, Fen. Let's go," said Lorcan as he took Fendton's hand and pulled him up.

Awnrie took Fendton's arm and walked with him and Lorcan to find the Master. Sarina helped Elentari up before hugging her tightly.

"I am here for you," said Sarina as she let go of Elentari and took her hands.

Elentari nodded. "I know."

"You don't have to do this alone," said Sarina.

"I know. Time for me to get some rest. Talk on the morrow," said Elentari kissing Sarina on the cheek.

Jasper took Sarina's arm and led her out. "Until the morrow. Sleep well, E," said Jasper as he closed the door.

CHAPTER 15

Eight dias till the war.

War council met after breakfast, and a new map filled the table. The scholars completed a map of the battlefield with assigned areas. Beings found no further information regarding the shield wall, and the Master found no useful information in the healer's mind. Upon capture, the healer had been imprisoned and only released to heal as required. Her entrapment meant she knew nothing of the life of the Bitch.

After counsel, every being headed to the training area to practice yielding air. Every air yielder within Thoroneath was present, including those not part of the army. Every being who lived in the cuedel wanted to help and be a part of the battle. Elentari agreed every being should train with them and help where they could. She would not force any being to fight and every being had the freedom to choose to participate. Every being was able to choose their path in this war.

Beings were grouped according to their ability and trained together. Elentari trained against the strong yielders and increased her opponents to practice quicker reflexes and reactions. Her guards, Masters and Apprentices all training as she did, training with her and against her.

In the library were the beings who did not want to fight. The books were searched and scoured, looking for a clue to building a wall. Any little thing a being found that could help was brought to the Scholars. The Scholars recorded every detail to present to the council.

The dia was long and satisfying, and supper was had together in the Princess parestala before retiring for the night.

Seven dias till the war.

The war council had no news on the shield wall. The Scholars presented a few details on yielding but nothing of value to help build the wall. A new way to yield water was discovered, and the council agreed to bring it into training.

Again, beings not in the army joined them and the Generals grouped accordingly based on ability. Water training was better when the weather was warm, especially if you ended up soaked from misjudging shielding. Shielding was the ability to use your power to block an opponent's yield shot. Many beings were drenched, yet none were left wet. The bonus of yielding water was you could always dry yourself quickly.

It was hard on Elentari when she ended up soaked as flashbacks of her water torture came thick and fast in her vision. The first time it happened, she screamed so loud the whole training area stopped. All eyes turned to her. Elentari was struggling to breathe, kneeling on the ground, as panic set in.

'*You are safe, Elentari. You are no longer being tortured. I am with you. See me,*' said Rorien on their bite. He knelt beside her, lifting her face to his.

'*You are with me. Stay where I can see you. I need you,*' said Elentari on their bite as she reached up to hold him.

'*I will always be here,*' said Rorien on their bite. '*Listen to my voice and focus.*' He hugged her tight and helped her to her feet.

Elentari nodded and took her stance, ready to battle.

The Masters wanted to change their attacks against her, but she wouldn't budge. She knew she had to keep going, push through the pain and panic. There were no time outs in battle. There was no middle ground in war, and she had to overcome her fears if she was to win. She battled on with Rorien, calmly speaking on their bite to comfort her and remind her where she was. His voice kept her grounded and focused.

Again, the Princess parestala held supper for every being. With so many attending, beings spilled out onto the paths surrounding the parestala. Much joy filled the air as Elentari and Rorien slipped away quietly.

Six dias till the war.

It was great news. The library team found a way to build a wall to shield yielding. They set to work to build a shielding wall to block all powers with the knowledge of nullifying yielding. The Scholars and Masters worked with Elentari and her guards to create an invisible, high, circular shield wall, testing and completing adjustments to strengthen and reinforce. They spent most of the dia building the wall, testing, rebuilding and testing. Many walls were constructed to get it strong enough to keep yielding from exiting or entering.

Many beings were excited by the new toy and came to test their yielding against the wall, enjoying trying to crack the barrier. Beings offered advice to help the Masters make adjustments to correct weaknesses. Surrounding the wall were many beings yielding all the elemental powers. Every element yielding was thrown at the wall, different ways to yield thrown and different strengths at yielding.

The Scholars and Masters kept adjusting the text to account for each element power. When the Masters strengthened the wall for one element power, another elemental power found it could enter. The Masters and Scholars worked tirelessly to perfect the text as beings worked hard to break the wall.

When the Masters finalised the wall and the final text perfect, the Scholars entered it into the ancient texts. The Scholars gave a new parchment with the text to Shift Master for safekeeping. It was a joyous moment, and many beings celebrated long into the night. Elentari, her guards and those part of the war council left not long after supper to rest and rejuvenate.

Five dias till the war.

The war council had no new news or anything to discuss, and the meeting closed quickly. The war council were sent away with the task of contingency planning, looking at what to expect from the Bitch. This cleared agenda left a full dia to train. With the shield wall established, Elentari trained within using air in the morning and water after high sun. Many came by to test their yielding against the shield wall as Elentari trained.

This yielding tactic caused Elentari's focus to be distracted and changed the way she trained. She was most thankful for the distraction, for if it happened during the war, she knew she would be dead. Elentari's focus had to be entirely on the Bitch while the army dealt with any enemies attempting to attack her.

Apprentice found you could use the wall to bounce or run yielding along. Beings changed their yielding tactics and found new ways to yield utilising the wall. The Scholars added each of the different ways to yield to the ancient text. Beings enjoyed the recent change and began to play around to see what they could do. Yielding using the wall was happening on both sides. A water yielder stood on one side while a fire yielder stood on the other. They yielded at the wall and caused their power balls to race along the wall, racing against each other. A new game began.

Prince Lannis arrived during the afternoon and trained with them.

"It is good to see you, Lannis. Will you be staying long?" asked Elentari over supper.

"As long as it takes. I am here to help you win this war. I intend to let every being in the East know I stand with you and that you are my future Queen. You are the rightful heir to the crown, you know," said Lannis.

"Thank you, Lannis. We shall include you. On the morrow, we have more training to do, earth training. You are to join us for council after breakfast in the royal hall," said Elentari.

"Thanks, I will," replied Lannis.

"I will take my leave. Training all dia is draining," said Elentari as she stood.

"Sleep well, E," said Lannis.

"Sleep well and rest up, Lannis. On the morrow, we train," said Elentari as she left.

Four dias till the war.

The war council had a few ideas and discussions on tactics before heading out to train with earth power. First, the Masters established the wall, and Elentari trained within. Beings battered the wall with their elemental power from all directions, hitting the wall from every direction. Fire and water, as well as air and earth, beat upon the wall. Great splatters of fire, water and earth kept hitting the wall as each being tried to distract Elentari. Beings loved the idea of trying to destroy the wall. Each being wanting to be the first to breakthrough.

It was a great way to train her focus and trust the Masters' ability to write texts. Elentari was not afraid to be hit with earth. With being battered during her torture, Elentari had trained enough and was able to heal herself quickly, giving her little time to pause. Elentari trained with Lannis, and he showed her a few moves, including one to protect herself if she fell, a way to recompose before returning to fight.

Beings helped by finding new ways to yield using the wall. Even those with little ability were offering advice. The Masters were grateful for every comment and suggestion, no matter how minor. The Masters used even the smallest adjustment to a yield to build a better result. More and more ways to yield was being found and added to the ancient text. The Scholars were busy transcribing all the new yields, and Elentari continued to train with her guards and army.

Three dias till the war.

Fire training was the best training dia. Elentari and Lorcan lapped up the dia learning new techniques with their fire and generally having fun. Sven and Jahan arrived before lunch, and Sven joined them. She enjoyed watching the fire race around the shield wall, and it was here a General noticed a flaw in the plan as yielding could go over the wall.

The whole time, every being had focused on a direct route and had forgotten yielding could bend. The Masters set to work to adjust the text and build a dome shield as Elentari continued to train. Even though during her torture, she was burnt daily with fire, she still loved fire yielding. It did not scare her. Fire was her favourite power, and nothing could change that.

Sven, Lorcan and Elentari finished the dia off with a fireball fight, similar to snowballs, only using fire, fun and non-harmful way to end the dia before collapsing in laughter.

"Sven, Jahan, what brings you here?" asked Elentari as they supped in the Princess parestala.

"We come to aid our future Queen, you," said Prince Sven pointing to her.

"Excellent. I shall include you as well. On the morrow, we will have more training, swordplay," said Elentari.

"Are you ready?" asked Prince Jahan.

"I have to be," replied Elentari, sighing. "Every being is counting on me. I have the best here to train me, so I am ready," said Elentari.

"What about Cormac?" asked Sven. "Yes, we've heard."

"He is Rorien's to do as he pleases," growled Elentari. "Until the morrow." She quickly stood and left the group, heading to her room.

"She is a bit touchy on that subject," said Rorien. "That is the only subject she will not elaborate, not one detail. Avoid it."

"Are you able to fill us in on what happened?" asked Lannis.

Rorien glanced around, checking to see where Fendton was before explaining what he knew about their imprisonment, including Cormac's appearance.

Two dias till the war.

Elentari spent the dia training with different size swords and against humanoids with differing skill sets. At one time, she had four other beings attacking her from all sides, giving her training in moving swiftly. Elentari practised a kill shot move with Seneca until she had it perfect and tried it against others to ensure it would work.

The Masters worked on the shield dome, perfecting the text. Late in the dia, the Masters constructed the shield dome, and Elentari stood inside. All around, yielders bombarded the dome attempting to break it.

'I see you.' A voice said in Elentari's head.

"Stop," yelled Elentari.

Every being ceased yielding and looked to Elentari.

"Is there a sight yielder amongst you, and are you yielding?" asked Elentari.

"Yes," a being answered stepping forward.

"Well done on testing a spirit power," said Elentari to the being. She turned to the Masters. "Masters, we need to adjust the text for spirit powers. Sight can get through. Can a movement yielder please transport to me?" asked Elentari.

A yielder appeared beside her.

"Thanks. Please return," said Elentari. "Masters and Scholars, you have work to do."

The Masters and Scholars quickly left to adjust the shield wall to stop spirit power from entering.

The dia ended with a kill sequence using all powers, designed by the future Masters, using the shield wall. Elentari had trained in every power and perfected the kill sequence. Now there was not much left to do except rest and rejuvenate and wait for the coming war dia.

One dia till the war.

The war council met to fine-tune the plan and present contingency plans. Each in command was relaying their role and actions, taking on advice and adjusting accordingly. An Apprentice raised the idea to search the opponent's camp. A general gave the position to a sight yielder and movement yielder to explore the base, save any light hearts, and find anything useful. Discussions continued on how they would fight once Elentari dropped the shield dome, and two different plans were formed, one for if she failed and one if she won.

"Prince Lannis, Prince Sven and Prince Jahan, you are not required to attend. You do not have to fight this war," said Elentari.

"We know. We are here for you. You are who we wish to sit with, to govern the lands and to work with," said Sven, speaking for them all.

"Prince Emmett, you are NOT going to the battlefield. You are staying here with the King and keeping an eye on him. If your brother is there…" Elentari said with her hands on her hips.

"He will be," answered Emmett, cutting Elentari off.

"I don't want you there with him. He will take you down," said Elentari.

"I know. I had no intentions of going to battle with him. I will stay here with the King. One of us has to look out for him." Emmett grinned

"Ok. That's settled. Princes, what rolls do you wish to have?" asked Elentari.

"We will support your guard and the Masters. Show all beings we stand with you," said Jahan.

"Done. Rorien will inform you of your tasks once the wall falls. Any further issues?" Elentari scanned the room. "None? Good one last training session before rest."

The Masters constructed the new wall, and spirit yielders spent time attempting to breakthrough. Adjustments were made to the text, and by mid after high sun, the wall was complete. The Masters designed the wall to be an extension of Elentari, living and breathing as her. It would drop when she died or was severely injured, and Elentari could drop it when she needed it. The Shift Master held the final text.

A final training session finished the dia off before Elentari retired to rest. She clung to Rorien as if it would be their last time together as she fell asleep.

CHAPTER 16

Elentari stood alone on the battlefield, waiting for her opponent to arrive, her army in place behind her. The air was still and quiet. Not even the birds chirped. Her opponent's army came into view over the horizon, a mix of humanoids, fauns and dwarfs. The enemy was led by the Bitch on a silver litter with patterned curtains hanging down the sides, the covered portable couch mounted on two poles and carried by four fauns. If the Bitch did it to intimate Elentari, it didn't work, for she cared not how her opponent would arrive. Elentari only cared about the outcome of the battle to come.

The army stopped at the edge of the field while the litter continued towards the centre. The fauns placed it on the ground. Elentari scanned the enemies faces noting it was a mix of emotions from scared and wanting to flee to those ready for battle. She knew there were beings forced to fight and did not want to be here. Her heart went out to them. Elentari straightened herself and returned her concentration to her opponent, knowing her army would begin to scan the opposing army. The Torturer took the Bitch's hand and helped her from the litter as Elentari watched, unfazed by the act. The fauns picked up the litter removing it from the field as the Torturer fussed over the Bitch before waved him off, and he left the area.

Elentari nodded to her opponent, who stood 50 cani away from her, a signal for the Masters to act. The Fire Master yielded a ring of fire as large as a football field around Elentari and the Bitch, setting the area as the Master of Shift built the dome shield. The royal army began to shift around the fire ring, taking their spots as arranged. As planned, in Elentari's peripheral vision, she could see Rorien standing with her guards, Princes and Masters. Elentari felt glad for their support, knowing they stood for her, and she was not alone.

"So, Annie, shall we begin?" the Bitch smirked.

"I am ready," Elentari said, her face void of all emotion. She would not let the Bitch get to her.

"Good. Todia is going to be a fabulous dia for me. Let us start with air yielding, shall we?" the Bitch's mouth twisted into a half-smile.

"As you wish," said Elentari, taking her stance.

The Bitch yielded first, just as Elentari wanted. Elentari took the defensive pose, as planned, to draw out the Bitch's ability and find her weakness. The Bitch threw everything at her, and she responded with shielding or yielding power.

'Why would the Bitch say let's start the air? Can she yield more?' Rorien asked on their bite.

'I have no idea and guess the Bitch does. We shall find out soon,' said Elentari on their bite.

Rorien gave Elentari tips and advised her where the Bitch's weak spots were as the Masters spotted them. Elentari had fallen a few times, and this time when she fell, Rorien spoke.

'Stay down and act as if you're badly hurt. We have a solution. Let the Bitch come to you,' said Rorien on their bite.

'And do what?' asked Elentari on their bite.

'When I say to, use your feet to yield and hold it,' replied Rorien on their bite.

'What?' asked Elentari on the bite.

'Yield the same as your hands but with your feet,' said Rorien on their bite.

Elentari stayed low on the ground, faking an injury, and watched as the Bitch drew closer. The field between them getting smaller. The Bitch was closing in quickly, and Elentari began to worry. She had to trust the Masters, and before she could ask, she heard Rorien.

'Now yield and hold, hold, hold, bring your knee in and kick out towards her,' said Rorien on their bite.

The force of Elentari's yield sent the Bitch flying across the battlefield, landing on her back and sliding to a stop. *'Nice. Like the new* move. *The Bitch is better than me in air yielding,'* said Elentari on their bite.

'Not with that move. Air Master just found that this morning. We have your back and are here to help. You are doing fine,' said Rorien on their bite.

Elentari watched as the Bitch stood, dusted herself off and moved back into position. She found her spot on the field where she could see Rorien. An hori had passed since the battle began fighting with air, and Elentari wondered if the Bitch could yield any other power.

"Shall we yield water now?" said the Bitch with a wide grin.

"As you wish," Elentari replied, hiding her look of surprise.

Again, Elentari took the defensive and allowed the Bitch to reveal her abilities and weaknesses. This battle was a walk in the park after being tortured with frozen water and dunking for mesiks. The hailstones and water whips the Bitch threw at her were nothing compared to what Elentari had to endure during her torture. Little did the Bitch realise, the Torturer had helped Elentari to tolerate this.

'See, we found out, guessing she may yield all four elements. How are the sight yielders going?' asked Elentari on their bite.

The plan was for Elentari to keep playing the defensive and occasional hit the Bitch, while waiting for all beings to be searched. Once movement yielders removed those with light hearts from the field, the fun would begin.

Water, ice and hail was flurry throughout the field, coming from all directions and speeds. A snowstorm, tornado and thunderstorm all mixed, creating havoc across the area. It became hard to see and at one stage, Elentari couldn't see her hand in front of her. With all the wind, it became hard for Elentari to stay upright, and even the Bitch fell.

'Getting there. We have removed some, and they have returned to fight with us,' said Rorien on their bite.

'They do know they do not need to, and they are free now?' asked Elentari on their bite.

'Yes, and they choose to bear arms for you,' replied Rorien on their bite.

The battle with water continued. Elentari put the Bitch into defensive mode a few times, just to let her know she was not weak but not showing the Bitch her full ability. Elentari knew she was more potent than the Bitch in water yielding and enjoyed showing the Bitch she was not afraid. Her real knowledge was hidden and waiting for the right moment to present itself.

'*Hoofington is here with back up,*' said Rorien on their bite.

'*Have Jasper fill him in and let every being know they are with us. This is getting interesting,*' said Elentari on their bite.

Elentari yielded and put the Bitch down and glanced to Hoofington, nodding her approval before turning her focus on the battle. Another hori passed as they fought with water, and Elentari was thirsty. She yielded a ball of water and sipped to wet her mouth and satisfy her thirst, careful not to drink too much.

"You managed a few good moves. Let's try earth," said the Bitch, and yielded swiftly.

Elentari's reflexes responded quickly, blocking the Bitch's attack. Thankful, Elentari had trained to hone her reactions and gave her the advantage. Elentari continued on the defensive and occasionally attacked the Bitch waiting for the right moment to reveal her ace.

'*We are almost finished the first search and have begun a second scan,*' said Rorien on their bite.

'*Excellent. I shall enjoy revealing our little secret,*' said Elentari on their bite.

'*Wait for my signal,*' said Rorien on their bite.

'*I shall,*' replied Elentari on their bite. Elentari continued to fight, waiting for the first search to finish. She was starting to feel sore and had healed the big wounds herself as needed, making sure she didn't extend too much energy. The Bitch hit Elentari hard, crashing through her defence and putting her down hard onto the ground. Elentari screamed as she felt her ankle bone break. Quickly, Elentari focused her energy on her ankle while attempting to stand but unable. She yielded a defence wall of earth, as Lannis had shown her. Elentari knew the Bitch would continue to hit her while she was down. As Elentari composed and healed herself, the defence walls around her shook violently as the Bitch's yielding rammed against them.

'*The first wave is complete,*' said Rorien on their bite.

'*Excellent. Here comes our ace Bitch,*' said Elentari on their bite.

Elentari dropped the earth defence wall and yielded, using the dome to create a whirlwind of debris, sending earth, stones and rocks around the dome, like a funnel, before slamming it down hard onto the Bitch and burying the Bitch. During training, yielders had discovered the dome's benefit and used it to help increase the power and force. It worked well. The Bitch was down and not moving, giving Elentari time to complete the mend, catch her breath and take another drink.

'*That worked well, the Masters approved,*' said Rorien on their bite.

The earth pile exploded, and the Bitch emerged, angry and fiery, her face contorted and her breathing heavy. Dirt and stones fell from the Bitch's hair as she shook her head and dust clouds circled her as she brushed down her clothes.

'*Good. I like her new look,*' giggled Elentari on their bite. '*The bitch look.*'

'*Concentrate. We've come too far to fail now,*' said Rorien on their bite.

Elentari stifled a giggle and wiped the smile from her face as she composed herself.

"Don't think you won!" The Bitch spat, yielding fire at her.

"I haven't," replied Elentari blocking the yield. Fire yielding was Elentari's best yielding, and she would gladly fight with it. Again, Elentari allowed the Bitch to better her, knowing the end would soon be here. The war council designed a sequence of yields to defeat the Bitch using every element yield. It was a bold and straightforward sequence which she likened to a yoga class. Elentari had practised this sequence over and over to ensure it was perfect. Once the second wave was complete, Elentari would begin.

'*Interesting. My dragon spirit is keeping me from being burnt,*' said Elentari on their bite.

'*What do you mean?*' asked Rorien on their bite.

'Every time I am hit with fire, my skin changes to dragon scales and absorbs the fire. I can't be burnt!' replied Elentari on their bite.

'That changes everything, and the Masters will enjoy this new information,' said Rorien on their bite.

'*Yes, it does. There is no need for me to shield or even worry about being hit. Let it come. Wonder why it never showed during training?'* asked Elentari on their bite.

'Who knows. Maybe it knew it was training, and you wouldn't be hurt?' replied Rorien on their bite.

'Oh Rorien, there is movement in the trees. What is happening?' Elentari asked on their bite. She kept her focus, waiting for a response.

'*It is Vosco. I have sent Jasper to inform him and word to all he is with us. It looks like our new friend is going to be handy after all,'* said Rorien on their bite.

'We must have made a good impression as they never go to war,' said Elentari on their bite.

'That or he is here to take you down.' Rorien replied on their bite with laughter in his voice.

'Don't change my focus,' said Elentari on their bite. Elentari focused her energy to fire yielding and using the dome, enjoying this hori and her favourite power. Elentari had the Bitch beat when the Bitch decided to change powers and yielded water to stop her advance. The Bitch changed the battle lines, and she released all powers. The battle quickened and intensified with more energy thrown into their yields. It was becoming draining, and Elentari hoped the second wave would end soon. She did not need to use a shield when fire came for her; her dragon kept her safe and saved her energy.

'Hurry, I am losing energy. I have been fighting for four horis while you lot have been standing around,' said Elentari on their bite.

'Get ready. We are almost done. Cormac has shown his face,' said Rorien on their bite.

'Have fun taking him down,' Elentari growled, and her angry showed in her yield.

"STOP" shouted the Bitch.

Elentari paused, taking a battle stance, ready to spring into action if needed. She did not trust the Bitch and waited for the attack. The royal army had taken down those who cheated the rules and had attempted to attack Elentari. The shield dome stopped the enemies yield, and her army removed any being who yielded against Elentari.

"We are matched almost equally in our yielding. Shall we try swords?" the Bitch asked with a smile.

"As you wish. Have your Torturer bring in a sword, a normal sword with no added extras and one found in normal wars. I shall have my guard bring me my sword," answered Elentari.

'Have Seneca bring me my sword,' said Elentari on their bite. Elentari stood facing the Bitch, watching her as they waited for their swords to be delivered.

"Will it work?" Elentari asked as Seneca approached. Her eyes facing forward and fixed on the Bitch. Seneca stood beside her facing the Bitch, watching to make sure the sword brought to the Bitch was normal and not adjusted.

"We have practised it many times, and you have succeeded during training to master it. It will work. How are you feeling?" asked Seneca.

"Not as tired. My body is healing fast," replied Elentari.

"Good. The Heal Master stepped inside the wall with me to heal you," said Seneca.

"But I see the Water Master standing there?" asked Elentari puzzled.

"They swapped robes," replied Seneca.

"Good plan," said Elentari.

"Take this. It is a concentrated elixir to replenish you. The apprentices have been working on it, found the formula last night," said Seneca.

"Great. Here's to it working," Elentari said as she drank the elixir.

"You will succeed, fight well, Princess," answered Seneca. He bowed, and the two sword carriers left the field.

Elentari and the Bitch faced each other, their swords swishing through the air as they warmed up. Elentari hobbled on her ankle and watched as the Bitch grinned before advancing towards her. She limped towards the Bitch, waiting for the right moment to hatch her plan, the move Elentari had been painstakingly practising until it became second nature. The distance closed between them, the Bitch began to run, and Elentari followed suit, revealing her ankle as healed as the distance shortened between them. Just a few more canis and their swords would clash. Elentari dropped her double-edged light-weighted longsword from her left hand and held her short sword in her right hand, continuing directly towards her opponent. A surprised look flashed across the Bitch's face.

At the last moment, Elentari stepped to her right and leapt high into the air, her left hand grabbing the Bitch's shoulder as Elentari bounded over the Bitch while her right plunged the blade deep into the Bitch's neck. Elentari felt the Bitch's sword cut across her stomach. Elentari's sword dragged down the Bitch's back as Elentari fell and hit the ground, blood running from the wound in her stomach. The shield wall dropped.

The Bitch and Elentari were unmoving on their knees. All around them, chaos broke out. The royal army was attacking and capturing those with partial hearts and placing them in chains. A rhinoceros was having fun crashing through the black hearts and tossing them high in the air with her horn. The rhinoceros' horn used to clear a path and injure as many as she could, allowing the army greater access. The giants came crashing onto the battlefield, slamming their fists onto the black hearts as if playing a game of whack-a-mole, their smiles wide in delight at their new game. Hoofington led his group, charging onto the field and fighting beside the royal army. Elentari's dream of building and mending broken bridges was visible across the battlefield as humanoids and huminals fought side by side for their future Queen, only she was not watching.

CHAPTER 17

Fendton, Jahan and Lorcan headed towards the Torturer, meeting him partway. Fendton battled against him, with Jahan and Lorcan assisting when needed. Lorcan managed to lasso him with a fire rope as Jahan lassoed him with air rope enabling Fendton to shackle his hands and feet. Fenton led him away to torture him as he wished. Jahan and Lorcan headed to Elentari as Fenton disappeared with the Torturer.

Rorien, Jasper, Sven and Lannis ran straight for Cormac. Cormac spotted them and advanced on them quickly, yielding at Rorien. Rorien was fighting hard against Cormac. Blood splat covered them and oozed from their deep cuts. Sven and Lannis assisted Rorien, while Jasper found a healer. The healer provided healing to Rorien, giving him an edge against Cormac. Jasper headed off to find another healer to assist. Cormac was fighting dirty. Rorien had Cormac in a lock and was about to give the kill shot when he slashed his pants and cut his penis off, shoving it down his throat. Cormac gagged and struggled to breathe, lashing out the remove his penis from his throat.

"Never take a female against her will or one who is not your linked," Rorien sneered as his sword sliced Cormac's throat.

Blood poured from the wound in Cormac's throat and gurgled out his mouth. Rorien let go, and Cormac slumped to the ground. His gaze shifted towards Elentari, where she knelt on the ground. Elentari had not moved, and the Heal Master was with her.

'He is gone, Elentari, Cormac is dead,' Rorien said on their bite as he raced towards her, knowing she was still alive; otherwise, her guards would be with her.

Elentari was hunched over and clinging to her belly as she raised her head to see Seneca and the Heal Master racing to her. Seneca sliced the Bitch's head off, and the Master set to work on Elentari. Elentari removed her arm, exposing the deep cut across her belly. All across the battlefield, fights were breaking out. Elentari cared not.

The Heal Master was healing Elentari, attempting to return the blood loss into her veins and stop the flow as she heard Rorien speak, 'he is gone.' Jasper came with a heal Apprentice to assist as Rorien approached.

"Prince, clean up the battlefield," Elentari said weakly before collapsing unconscious.

"Prince, we have captured those with partial hearts, and the ones with black hearts have been removed. Clean up is beginning," said a General to Rorien. His eyes were on Elentari.

"Excellent. How did the check of the camp go?" asked Rorien. He glanced up quickly to look at the general before returning his eyes to Elentari.

The Heal Master and Apprentice were busy working quickly on Elentari. Rorien noticed Sven and Lannis had disappeared. Sven and Lannis were assigned to wrap Cormac's dead body and have him transported to King Adtarian to deal with accordingly.

"Found nothing of value, no texts or information. Only general camp items," said the General.

"Allow those with light hearts to take what they want and have them transported back to their homelands. Check with them if they know the locations of the Bitch's other casas. Have those with partial hearts locked in the dungeons on the south side," said Rorien.

Elentari had not moved. Sweat was beading on the Master's forehead as he concentrated his focus on Elentari. Another Heal Apprentice had taken over to assist the Master.

"Yes, Prince," answered the General as he bowed and left.

"Prince," Rorien heard from behind him and turned to face Hoofington.

"Hoofington," said Rorien as he grabbed Hoofington's hand.

"It is an honour to serve the Princess," Hoofington said as he let go of Rorien's hand and bowed. "How is she?"

"The Master is working on healing her. Is there anything you need?" asked Rorien.

"If it ok, we would like to take the free fauns home with us and will return them to their rightful homelands when they are settled," replied Hoofington.

"Yes. If the fauns wish, they are free to do as they please. Allow them to take anything they want from the camp. When she is able, we will visit," said Rorien.

"We shall see you both soon," Hoofington said, placing a hand on Rorien's shoulder. He bowed to Elentari and left.

"Elentari, Rorien. Vosco, come help," boomed a pleased giant as Vosco came racing up to them, the ground shaking under his feet.

"Vosco, Elentari is very sick. The Master is healing her," said Rorien.

"Elentari be ok?" Vosco asked as he stopped suddenly. Sadness filled Vosco's face as he carefully made his way to sit down near Elentari and gently stroked his finger down her cheek.

"She will be ok. When she rests, and when she is better, we will visit you. She will be most happy to hear how you helped," replied Rorien.

"We did play a game. It was fun," Vosco said, grinning.

"She will love to hear about your new game. Is there anything you would like from the camp? You may take what you need," said Rorien.

"We take tents?" asked Vosco.

"Yes. If you want the tents, you may take them. Travel home safely, and we will see you soon," answered Rorien.

"Thank you, Rorien," said Vosco, and he leant over Elentari. "Get better soon, Elentari." He whispered before he joined his friends and headed off towards the enemy camp.

"Lorcan, let's get the Bitches litter to take the Princess home. Let her walk back with every being to the cuedel," said Rorien.

"On it. Jasper, come help," said Lorcan.

"Master, how is she?" Rorien turned his focus to Elentari.

"There was not much blood which we could return to her body. She has lost a significant amount of blood. We have stopped the blood flow, and the sword cut her side deep and has hit vital organs. We are working on those first," replied the Master.

"Good work. Keep going," said Rorien.

"I am concerned about how much blood she has lost. I fear the worst," said the Master. Sweat running down his face.

Two other Apprentices had joined the group. Elentari had the Master and four Apprentices working hard to keep her alive. Rorien watched on helplessly, his heart racing with anxiety.

Rorien surveyed the battlefield, watching the army placing the dead enemy in a pile in readiness for burning. Beings were collecting weapons and items of use. The free were heading towards the enemy camp to search and take what they wanted, and a stream of beings was walking back to the cuedel.

"Jahan, can you find the other Heal Apprentices, please? We need all healers here for Elentari," said Rorien.

"Yes," answered Jahan.

"Master, how long till we can move her?" asked Rorien.

"Soon, I hope," answered the Master.

Rorien surveyed the field. Hoofington had left with the fauns, and the giants had taken what they needed and left. The Movement yielders were slowly transporting the free back to the Kings in their homelands. Their King would help them return to their home. Rorien watched as the Bitch was thrown onto the cremation fire with her slaves and lit. Flames engulfed the dead.

Lorcan and Jasper had changed the Bitch's litter removing the curtains and adding a blanket to cover the fabrics. The litter was ready for Elentari and placed nearby. Rorien agitatedly moved from foot to foot, waiting for the Heal Master to stabilise Elentari enough to carry her home.

"She is stable enough to move. The Apprentices can follow and keep healing. I shall return to Thoroneath and prepare her room," said the Master.

"Thank-you," said Rorien.

Rorien and Lorcan carefully lifted Elentari and placed her on the litter. Rorien and Lorcan took the front while Seneca and Jasper were behind. Beings bowed as the Princess was carried past them towards home, offering their thanks and well wishes for her recovery. Lannis, Jahan and Sven followed behind. Fendton was nowhere to be seen.

Rorien and Sarina changed Elentari's clothes and settled her into bed. The Heal Master came to check on her and rostered the Apprentice healers to give her constant attention. The Apprentices were taking turns to heal and care for Elentari. The Heal Master came each morning and night to check her. It was Rorien's turn to care for her and help her recover. He drip-fed Elentari elixir to help her recover, building her strength and self-healing ability. The chef had meals in readiness for her for when she woke.

Within the first vika after the war, all of the Bitch's casas were found. There was no difference between the casa's, and all were built high on a mountain containing long, dark passages with dungeons, the same as where the Bitch kept Elentari. They were all designed the same with a secretive, private area set aside from the dungeons, a more homely and comfortable space with many large rooms. The casas were searched for any items of value.

Within the East casa private area, a being discovered a library filled with copies of the ancient texts. Many books filled the library and were removed to the main east library for the professors and scholars to peruse. Unusual artifacts were found in the West casa and sent to the Masters at Thoroneath for studying. All other items of value and in good condition were removed and distributed among the Unwilling. Once the casas were cleared, they were destroyed to leave no trace of the Bitch or Gornack's lineage.

During a search of an abandoned room in the East casa containing detailed etchings of Gornack's lineage, the ceiling collapsed upon King Malik. The King was scribing the details of the etchings when the cave-in happened. Earth yielders quickly set about removing the debris, but it was too late, King Malik was gone, and Prince Baldrick was severely injured.

During the second vika of recovery, Elentari awoke and had enough energy each dia to perform simple tasks. The Heal Master gave her the all-clear to attend Baldric's crowning. Sitting on the thrones across the lands were King Adtarian with Princess Elentari, in the West King Reagan and Prince Sven, in the East King Baldric and Prince Lannis, in the South King Rian and Prince Emmett and King Leopold with Prince Jahan in the North. These were the last of the royal lines.

"Masters, it is time to rebuild our link. I have won the war, the Bitch and her casas are destroyed, and the new King has been crowned. On the morrow, rebuilding our link will take place. Please ensure you are organised," said Elentari to the Masters as they returned from the East.

"Are you well enough, Princess?" asked the Air Master.

"Heal Master, am I well enough?" asked Elentari.

"Yes," answered the Heal Master.

"Yes, Princess. It shall be organised for you," said Fire Master.

"Excellent. You are dismissed," said Elentari. She turned to the King. "Papa, on the morrow after we rebuilt our link, I wish to return to Earth for a quick visit. After everything that has happened, it would be nice to spend time with Mum and Dad."

"Are you up for a trip so soon? Maybe let Rorien go and get them, and you stay home?" asked the King.

"I am well enough to transport to the East, Papa. I am well enough to portal home. Rorien will be with me," replied Elentari.

"Only for an hori, please. I would prefer if you stay in our lands until you are 100," sighed the King. "You bring me joy and grief at the same time."

"Then, I am doing my job as a child. Four horis?" smiled Elentari.

"Two, and that is all. Now prepare yourself for the morrow and your trip. Rest up, daughter," said the King.

The King watched the Princess leave, thinking how far she had come in such a short time, how she had mended the rifts between humanoids and huminals, bring many beings together as one. Elentari had pushed the Masters to extend their knowledge, with her determination to find. On the morrow, the rebuilding ceremony would fulfil her hunger for new information. The King sighed as he walked the hall, his eyes scanning the room, taking it all in before pausing by the entrance for one last scan and closing the doors for the night.

The Masters were standing with her father as Elentari and Rorien entered the royal hall on the morrow. Elentari and Rorien were both anxious and excited for the upcoming ceremony enabling them to become relinked, anxious for not knowing if it would work and excited to be whole again. Communicating on the bite was not as fulfilling as their link and feeling each other's feelings. Elentari and Rorien could feel the link connect them so much more than the bite. With the link, feelings and emotions passed between them and even each other's heartbeat.

Jasper closed the main doors, and their guards stood by, making sure no being interrupted them and there were no distractions. This ceremony was vital to them all and to the Masters, a new ceremony no Master had ever performed.

"We shall perform the rebuilding first and move onto the linking. We will not use the symbols for your linking dia. Only the ancient text is needed to complete your link," said the Fire Master as he stood in the hall.

"Is it your wish to have us all perform the rebuilding and linking, or is one Master performing both acceptable?" asked the Air Master.

"One Master will suit," answered Rorien.

"Which Master shall you choose?" asked the Fire Master.

"Master of air, you have been there for Rorien from the beginning. Please can you perform the ceremony?' said Elentari.

"I would be honoured," the Air Master replied, bowing. "The rebuilding involves stages with actions to complete. Once it is complete, you should feel your sensation again, enabling us to know it has worked. Are you ready to begin?"

"Yes, Master," said Rorien as he took Elentari's hand in his and squeezing it.

"Yes," Elentari said as tears of happiness welled in her eyes.

"Everything is ready in the King's private chamber. Come," the Air Master said, heading to the chamber.

On the table lay a bowl filled with herbs, a pestle, a teapot and cups. The Air Master plucked a hair from both their heads as he guided them to the chairs and placed the strands into the bowl. Using a knife, the Air Master began scrapping the skin on their hands to add to the bowl. The Air Master started to grind all the ingredients together, adding a strange dark green fluid to create a paste while the Fire Master heated the teapot. A strong aroma began to fill the room as the Earth Master burnt magnolia bark, valerian root, and other woods. Smoke wafted under their noses filling their nostrils.

"Please can you move your shirts to expose the top left area of your chest," said the Air Master.

Elentari partially unzipped her dress to enable her top to fall below her shoulders, holding her arm across her breasts to keep it up. Rorien removed his shirt, exposing his rippling abs.

"Take this liniment and rub onto your chest," said the Air Master holding out the bowl.

Elentari and Rorien scooped out the green liniment and rubbed into their chest as the Master began to speak the ancient text. The liniment felt rough against the skin. A warmth started to spread through their chest and changed to a tingle as the Master stopped. The Air Master picked up a knife, pierced their skin and injected a bright blue liquid into the blood-red wound as he continued to speak the ancient text. A flowing sensation began churning and swirling around their chests. The Fire Master poured a fluorescent yellow tea and handed a cup to Elentari and Rorien. Smells of cayenne, ginkgo, ginger, and turmeric filled their noses along with other scents. It tasted as bad as it smelt. The Air Master finished speaking the ancient text and closed the book. The flowing sensation and tingle fused imploding inwards before violently exploding and easing into their link sensation.

Rorien reached up to touch his chest and his link. Elentari felt his touch, and tears began to creep down her cheek. He reached his finger up to wipe away her tears.

"Our link is back, E. We have our link," said Rorien, hugging her.

"Yes, we do. Now to complete it and feel whole again," Elentari smiled at him.

The Air Master picked up another book and began to recite the ancient text, and Elentari and Rorien responded as required.

"I connect," Elentari and Rorien said, and their link began to vibrate and hum.

"I bond," Elentari and Rorien said as they felt a chain linking them.

"I combine," Elentari and Rorien, and fluid flowed along the chain between them.

"I commit," Elentari and Rorien as the chain became solid to link them strongly together again.

'*I can feel you again,*' Elentari said excitedly on their link.

'*I feel you and whole again,* ' Rorien replied on their link.

"It has worked, Master," said Rorien.

"Excellent news," answered the Air Master.

"Yes. Excellent," said the Fire Master.

"Fabulous," said the Earth Master.

"Thank you, Masters. We shall take our leave and allow you to discuss your findings," said Elentari taking Rorien's hand and entering the royal hall.

Their guards were waiting anxiously for them along with the other Masters.

"Did it work?" asked Fendton, almost screaming.

"Yes, it did, Fen. This means, for the rest of the dia you are all free to do as you please. We have completing business to take care of," Elentari said, waving them off as she transported her and Rorien to their spot.

"It was two mesiks after your 20th birth date that we stood here and completed our link. Now you are nearly 25, and again we stand here.

Will you cause the earth to move again?" Rorien smirked as his hands began to remove her dress.

"We shall find out soon enough," Elentari said as she removed his pants, her mouth finding his as he picked her up and laid her on the blankets.

Rorien's mouth explored her, kissing, sucking and biting her body as his hands travelled over her body, squeezing and caressing her. Elentari moved with pleasure under his hands, moaning at his touch. He moved between her legs and took her, thrusting his hardened malehood deep into her. They moved together, exciting each other as they approached climax. The earth beneath her began to move, but it was not her causing it. She wrapped her legs around him, and her fingers dug into him, pulling him further into her as their bodies spasmed in a climactic end.

A rapid release of power burst from them, the earth rippling out from beneath her, fire twisted with water bursting around them as air blasted with great force.

Rorien lifted off her and looked puzzled at her.

"It was not me this time. You created that," Elentari said as she moved from beneath him.

"What? How? No," Rorien said as he rolled onto his back. "I don't have other powers. It had to be you."

"Let's get back. I have a theory and need the Masters to confirm. But first, a visit to earth. I have an idea I want to try," said Elentari.

"What theory? What idea?" asked Rorien.

"A linking theory and a yielding idea. And no, I will not elaborate," answered Elentari as she smiled at him.

"You are infuriating, but I enjoy your little secrets. Do we have time for this?" Rorien asked as he lifted her on him, and she straddled him, guiding him in her.

CHAPTER 18

Elentari transported her and Rorien to their casa before opening the portal to visit her parents. It had been a while since she had been back to Earth, almost four anoks ago when they came for Donna's 21st. She, Rorien and Fendton had come for four days to help Donna celebrate. The trio, Donna, Elentari and Fendton, had raced around the block yelling and screaming it was Donna's 21st, continually spending the day letting every being know Donna was 21. For four full days, the trio hardly stopped their madness, feeding off each other and causing mayhem wherever they went. Rorien kept his distance, leaving them to their madness and being there if they needed anything. Donna's parents and Elentari's parents began to realise the twins had become triplets, and they had gained a son, Fendton. Elentari and Donna introduced Fendton to the life of Earth, showing him everything they could in a short time. Their mothers lavished Fendton, fussing over him, and Fendton lapped it up. For four full days, Elentari left her royal life and lapped up the freedom. Now, four anoks later, Elentari returned on a different quest.

"Mum, Dad. Where are you?" yelled Elentari as she walked into the kitchen.

"Lounge, Dear," answered her mum. "We always come and visit you. What brings you home?" Beth raced into the kitchen and grabbed Elentari in a big hug.

When the Masters found beings can transport between worlds many times without issues, Elentari's parents began to visit her every mesik for a few dias. Twice an anok they would spend a week with her.

"I've had a few rough months and just needed to see you both," said Elentari, wrapping her arms tight around her mother.

"Rorien, have a seat. Footy's on," said Francis, not moving from the lounge.

"I will put the kettle on, and you can explain," said Beth.

"I didn't come home to relive it. I just wanted to see you both, get away from everything to where no being can find me. We have two hours," replied Elentari.

"I know you went missing. The King sent us a message," said her mother as she turned on the kettle.

The Masters had found a way to open a small, one-way portal large enough to send letters and small boxes, about 30x30x30cm, giving them the ability to communicate whenever they wanted. It was thrilling to arrive home to find a message or a small gift, tea, biscuits, and even a bottle of gin had found its way through, gifts for her, gifts for Rorien and even gifts for Fendton arrived. Finding little things to send home was exciting. Not only did Elentari sent clothes, jewellery and even a jiwebola ball, Fendton sent gifts too.

"Of course, he did," Elentari said as she collapsed on the chair.

"He also sent message you were found and were going to battle," said Beth quietly, her head falling forward.

"Do you truly want to know what happened? It is quite horrifying," said Elentari. Her fingers rubbed against the table edge as her heart began to race at having to relive the torture.

"As was not knowing what was happening. Please tell me," begged Beth, her eyes pleading as she placed the tea on the table.

Elentari took the pot and poured a cup before she recapped. Elentari explained being transported to the Bitch's dungeons, finding out who she was, the Torturer and his tortures. She vaguely touched on being tortured and suffering, keeping many of the graphic details from her mother. Elentari continued to explain how they found a way to communicate with Rorien, the Masters' search, restoring yielding and their escape. She finished her story with details on organising the war, the battle and rebuilding their link. Beth sat quietly, listening to her recap. Tears streamed down Beth's cheeks as the understanding of what her daughter endured filled her with such distress, and the possibility of them completely losing her tugged at her heart.

Elentari stood and held her mother. Beth's grief surfaced, and she broke down. Elentari held her and let the tears flow, holding her and letting her know she was there. After a while, Beth began to calm and take control of herself.

"Thank you for telling me. It has been a burden on my heart, not knowing. Now I know," said Beth. "The King's letters explained what was happening and gave some detail but not the same as hearing from you."

"It's ok, Mum. There are no more bad beings to hurt me. Is there any more tea?" Elentari asked, rubbing her mother's arms.

"Coming up," said Beth. Beth made more tea and sat silently, lost in her thoughts, occasionally wiping away the stray tear.

Elentari sat watching and waiting, ready to answer any questions. She finished her tea, cleared the table and began to massage her mother's shoulders. "How does that feel?" Elentari asked.

"Your hands are hot, warmer than usual," said Beth, a little puzzled. "I didn't think you could use yielding here."

"I wasn't sure, and lately, I had been playing with the gems, wondering if I could store energy. Now I know I can," Elentari grinned as she continued to rub her shoulders.

"Is it just fire you can yield?" asked Beth.

"Shall I find out? It is good to know it works, but I am unsure of how much I have or how long it will last," said Elentari.

"Not to worry, Dear, it is enough for now. Try water," said Beth. Elentari moved her hands to form a water ball.

"Make it snow," said Beth. Elentari exploded the ball into snowflakes, watching it fall to the floor before yielding and cleaning it up.

"Two work. Guess all will. Let's see who's winning the footy," Elentari said, heading to the lounge, sitting down beside Rorien and taking his hand.

"What!?" Rorien looked at her, surprised.

Elentari smiled.

"You know how I've been playing with my gems while yielding, well I wasn't sure it would work, but I can store energy in them," Elentari said.

"How much energy can you store?" asked Rorien.

"Don't know, this was a trial. I wanted to see if I could use powers outside our lands and have only played a bit. You try and see if it works for you," said Elentari.

Rorien looked at her quizzically.

"You know you wear a linking ring, and I have been playing with the quartz and storing energy in it too. Now try," said Elentari.

Rorien looked at his ring and back to her. Elentari nodded, and he yielded a gentle breeze.

"Excellent. It works for you too. This could be useful," said Elentari.

"When would it be useful? I don't see us getting into trouble and needing it like you keep doing back home," replied Rorien.

"It has been useful for warming Mums shoulders while a gave her a massage, so there," said Elentari, sticking out her tongue. "Plus, you never know what may happen. Better to be prepared."

"What gave you the idea to store energy?" asked Francis.

"Well, it is said stones can store energy and decided to see if it would work. Plus, the healer was wearing a citrine ring when she healed me and didn't have it on when we took her. I wondered if it how she was able to yield," replied Elentari.

"Another new thing to inform the Masters. Will they ever find something before you?" smiled Rorien shaking his head.

"Hopefully. Remind me to try it when we get back home. I'll have the Masters create a room without yielding, the Bitch room, and try it," said Elentari.

"When will you leave?" asked Francis.

"Soon, Dad. We only came for a few hours. I wanted to see you both after everything that happened. I just wanted quiet. You always helped me through everything and gave me the peace I needed. This was the biggest thing I had been through and just needed you both," said Elentari.

"Rorien told me what happened. Glad your safe, and you know the door is always open," Francis said before screaming at the TV.

"What happened?" asked Rorien as he leant towards her.

"Umpire gave away a free-kick to the other side. It was probably justified, but in Dad's eyes, it was wrong. Then again, it is the Cats, and they are useless," Elentari grinned, waiting for the bite.

"He hardly touched him," yelled her Dad, his hand pointing to the TV as he glanced at her. "There was nothing in it."

"Yes, Dad," Elentari answered, nudging Rorien.

"Stop teasing your father. You know he hates to see them lose or them winning," said Beth

"Beth!" yelled Francis.

"Portals here, we have to go," Elentari quickly hugged her Dad and Mum. "Love you both," she said as she stepped into the portal and her casa and summoned her guards.

"What gives? You said we had the dia to ourselves," said Lorcan as he entered first.

"I'll explain when every being is here, call Awnrie and Nea," Elentari replied as Seneca entered.

"Jasper, call Sarina," said Rorien as Jasper and Fendton entered.

"What's up?" asked Fendton.

"When the females arrive, I will explain, and then we will meet with the Masters," Elentari said

"More discoveries," said Rorien as Awnrie and Sarina entered.

"Just waiting for, never mind,' Elentari said as Nea entered. "Thanks for coming. I need your help to prove a theory I have about yielding. Don't need you, Fen but wanted you to be part of this as well."

"Way to make me feel welcome, E," Fendton said, grumbling as he slumped on the couch.

"When we first had our linking dia, I lost all control over my powers and…" said Elentari.

"The whole country knew about it," replied Lorcan smirking as he cut her off.

"Moving on, this time…" said Elentari

"We all felt it again," said Jasper grinning as he cut her off.

"Only it wasn't me. It was Rorien," replied Elentari.

"How? He only yields air?" asked Lorcan, surprised.

"That is my theory. When you linked, it felt like fluid was moving between you both, flowing and connecting you, and once complete, you felt each other's heart beating within you?" asked Elentari.

"Yeah," replied Lorcan.

"Yes," replied Jasper.

"Been a while, but yes," said Seneca.

"Females?" The females nodded their agreement.

"What does it have to do with yielding?" asked Sarina.

"I think yielding passes between you and your linked. Jasper, can you show both Rorien and Sarina how to yield water? If my theory is right, Sarina, you take on the power of water, Jasper's power," said Elentari.

"Just because we can feel each other doesn't mean we take on their powers," replied Lorcan

"How else do you explain Rorien's newfound powers?" asked Elentari.

Lorcan shrugged.

"Humour me and try. We have nothing to lose," said Elentari.

Elentari could see Jasper and Sarina conversing on their link by how their faces changed as if they were talking. Sarina looked at her.

"Ok, we shall try and see. Guess doing it here is better than failing in front of the Masters," said Sarina.

"Thanks, Sarina. Jasper?" asked Elentari.

Jasper moved his hands in the basic move of producing a water ball. Both Rorien and Sarina were hesitant to try. Jasper yielded again, and this time Rorien copied. A ball of water appeared in front of Rorien. The room gasped. The shocked look on Sarina's face faded, and she turned to Jasper, nodding as she moved her hands, and a water ball appeared.

"It worked!" Sarina said as she exhaled.

"Lorcan, can you show Awnrie and Rorien please," said Elentari.

This time Rorien copied Lorcan without reluctance while Awnrie hesitated, waiting to see Rorien's result. Once flames appeared, Awnrie yielded, causing little flames to dance above her hand.

"Cool. I have an element power," said Awnrie.

"I am guessing I can move,'" said Lorcan.

"And I, to heal," said Jasper.

"Rorien, can you show me air yielding?" asked Nea.

"Yep, just move your hands like this," Rorien replied, causing a gentle breeze to blow past her.

Nea copied, and a breeze caressed Elentari's face.

"Excellent! My theory is right. Are you ready to meet the Masters and show them?" asked Elentari.

"Should we try spirit powers first?" asked Fendton.

"Why not. Awnrie, please show Lorcan and Rorien how to yield movement. Just to your casa and back," said Elentari.

Awnrie obliged, and Lorcan and Rorien disappeared before returning.

"Sarina, healing, please. Oh, and Rorien, I will give you the same support as you gave me when I was first tested," Elentari said smirking and grabbing the knife from Seneca's belt.

Elentari cut her arm and watched as shock flooded Rorien's face. He turned to Sarina, his eyes begging for help as he grabbed Elentari's arm and held the wound.

"It's ok. Just close your eyes and imagine the blood flowing back into her body," Sarina said as she cut herself and presented her wound to Jasper. "Imagine the wound binding together, cotton sewing it up."

Rorien closed his eyes and imagined Elentari's blood flowing back into her body. He could feel a prickling sensation in his hand, and a needle between his fingers was sewing the wound. He opened his eyes and looked at her arm. The wound was gone.

"Don't do that again," Rorien said.

"Why would I?" smirked Elentari.

"We almost have a Jiwebola team. We just need Fen's link," said Lorcan.

"Well... it's...I have..." stuttered Fendton.

"Later, Fen. You and I can discuss why you have been keeping her secret and why nothing has come about for mesiks," said Elentari.

"How did you know?" Fendton asked, his eyes wide with surprise.

"She knows you too well, Fen. She would have noticed something different about you, and you just confirmed it," replied Lorcan.

"Yes. Nea, can you show Seneca how to use sight as we walk to the royal hall?" asked Elentari.

"Do you not want to show me how?" asked Rorien.

"You know you have six of the eight powers. At least let the Masters have something new," Elentari replied as she looked at him sideways.

"Fine. I will let them have something. One of us has too," Rorien said, nudging her as they walked to the royal hall. "Why not just move us there instead? Or shall I," he grinned.

"No need when we are already here," Elentari said, pointing to the doors and walking in.

"Papa, we have something to inform the Masters about, something new with the link and powers. Are they here?" asked Elentari.

"No, they are not. What is it you have discovered? We all felt the earth move again; is it not that?" asked the King.

"Never living that down," Elentari sighed. "Jasper and Sarina, can you find the Masters and Scholars' for us. I would like to test my second theory before they arrive."

Jasper and Sarina bowed and left.

"Explain," said the King.

"The link allows powers to pass along. Awnrie can yield fire, and Lorcan can yield movement, Jasper heals, Sarina water, you get the point. The earth moving this time was Rorien. He has six of the eight powers. Haven't tried the last two, though we should give the Masters something," grinned Elentari.

"When it comes to you, the Masters know they get the scraps. What is your other theory?" asked the King.

"The Bitch yielded all the element powers, and we don't know if she yielded the spirit powers. We assume she could use movement, and as she was in line for the throne, it got me thinking. If my theory is right, you should be able to yield all too," said Elentari.

"Your theory is, if you are to sit on the throne, you can yield all?" asked the King.

"Yes. It would explain why I yield all and why the Bitch could yield elements," said Elentari.

"Mmm. Interesting. I should be able to yield water by the link, as that was your mother's power. I shall try. Show me how," said the King.

Elentari moved her hands to form a ball, and her father followed. Two water balls appeared. She moved her hand, and the balls vanished.

"Would you like to try the others before the Masters arrive?" asked Rorien.

"We shall let the Masters complete my testing, give them something," the King said.

"Papa, it surprises me that you haven't recognised you had more than one power. After all, you should be able to see the air and the water currents. Why is it you never realised?" asked Elentari.

"We were always told we could only yield one power. I never thought any different," answered the King.

"You can see the wind?" asked Elentari.

"Yes, but I always thought every being could," answered the King.

"I love watching the wind, watching the air currents as they move, flowing up and down and twisting around. My favourite is the way it swirls around objects, meandering around the object before finding its path again," a wistfully Elentari said.

"I prefer the water currents, watching the ebb and flow," said the King.

"Did you not have visions or hear thoughts?" asked Rorien.

"When I came into my awakening, I heard voices but closed them out. Never thought to open my senses and hear them again. I could yield fire, not sight. I always thought, what I heard was what I imagined the being would say," said the King.

"What about visions?" asked Rorien.

"My dreams I took as dreams and not visions," said the King as one Master walked in. Elentari took her seat beside her father and waited for the other Masters and Scholars to drift in.

"Now, you are all here. The Princess has a discovery she wishes to present to you. Princess," said the King.

"Masters, I have discovered yielding will pass along the link. The earth movement this time was not my doing. It was Rorien. I have tested six powers, and he yields all six. Jasper and Sarina both share powers, as do Lorcan and Awnrie and Seneca and Nea. That is the first discovery. The second discovery is for you to complete. I believe if you are to sit on the throne, you can yield all. The Bitch we know yielded all the elements, and I yield all eight. Please can you test the King to see if my theory is correct," said Elentari.

"As you wish, Princess," replied the Fire Master.

The Masters began to speak amongst themselves, searching for any information they may have found to confirm her theories before the Fire Master got them in order and tested the King. The King passed all tests, yielding all eight powers.

"Is this for all kings who sit on the throne?" asked the Earth Master.

"During the janual, we shall find out. Until then, we can confirm those who are to sit on this throne will yield all eight. This will mean any children the Princess has will be required to perform all yielding tests," replied the King.

'Kids, I don't want to talk about us having kids. We're too young,' said Elentari on their link.

'Lucky we aren't fertile until we hit 200,' replied Rorien on their link, smiling at her.

"Complete testing on powers passing through the link and confirm the link theory," said the King. "We shall confirm sitting on the throne theory during the janual."

"We shall confirm the theory for you, my King. Is there anything else?" asked the Fire Master?

"Yes. I have stored power in the gemstone I wear, and I have used this to yield on Earth. After the ceremony, Rorien and I headed home to Mum and Dad, and using the power within the gems, we both were able to yield. Please continue to investigate the ability to store energy and use it where yielding is not forthcoming," said the Princess.

"You have two theories to confirm and study. How are the studies on the Bitch's unusual objects coming?" asked the King.

"Not quickly, my King," answered the Air Master.

"Are the objects in the ancient library?" asked the Princess.

"Yes. Why?" asked the Air Master.

"Can we find another area for them, please? Even if we have to build a special area for them. It concerns me they were hidden in a back room and would prefer the ancient library to be safe and only filled with books. I haven't seen them and know nothing about them but what I do know is, the Bitch was only for herself. Who knows why the casa collapsed on the King?" said the Princess.

"Mmm. You could be right. Earth Master, please construct a room for the object away from everything. Let us be safe. I do not trust her, and she certainly was not nice. They could be anything," said the King.

"As you wish, my King," answered the Earth Master.

"That is all. Masters and Scholars, you are dismissed," said the King waving his hand to dismiss them.

CHAPTER 19

It was the 38th of Mente after Elentari's 25th birth date, and the Kings and Princes were arriving for Januel, along with their linked. Elentari was sitting with her father in the royal hall to greet the Kings as they arrived. After her first januel, Elentari met with the Princes in her casa, all except Cormac, and the tradition began to meet after supper each night at Elentari's casa. As Elentari's casa was becoming too small to hold every being, she and Fendton had changed one of the empty casas nearby into a large lounge area for entertaining and the casa beside had been converted into a dining hall to fit 40 comfortably. Elentari met with the princes, princesses, and guards to throw off their façade, act like themselves, and meet as friends.

"Are you ready for Januel this anok, daughter?" asked the King.

"Not really, father. It has been a long few mesiks with being tortured and the battle and discovering transfer of power. I am not interested in sitting listening to the boring stuff. Not interested in what is happening, what has happened or what is to happen," said Elentari.

"You have been through a lot this anok, and this januel is only the current kings and the future crowns. There can be no variation to the future. I do not believe there has ever been a januel where there could be no variation," said the King as he rubbed his chin in thought.

"Guess it has been my fault for changing the chairs. 'The returned princess who shook the crowns'," Elentari grinned.

"You certainly have shaken the foundations in a lot of areas, my child. No being can say you have been silent and non-committal," said the King.

"Yes. Oh, here comes Rian and Emmett," said Elentari.

"My King. Princess," King Rian and Prince Emmett said as they bowed.

"King. Prince." answered the King.

"My Lord. Prince. I hope your trip was smooth," said Elentari.

"Yes. The movement Professor transported us here instead of sailing. Much easier on the stomach," answered Emmett, grinning.

"Princess Twyla did not come?" asked Elentari.

"She will be here for supper. There was an issue amongst the females that she is sorting," replied Emmett.

"Wonderful. Have you settled into your rooms?" asked Elentari?

"Yes, Princess. We settled in before greeting you and shall take our leave to visit Thoroneath," said King Rian.

"We shall see you for supper," said the King.

"Enjoy," said Elentari.

It wasn't long after King Reagan arrived with Prince Sven and Princess Anya and settled in. King Baldric with Prince Lannis and Princess Jobie was next to make an appearance before King Leopold, Prince Jahan and Princess Torvi. Each had chosen to travel via movement instead of sailing, causing Elentari to wonder what was to come. It was most unusual as using movement was for urgent matters.

What reason would you give for all the Kings arriving via movement?' asked Elentari on their link.

'No idea. It is unusual,' replied Rorien on their link.

'Mmm, maybe something is up?' questioned Elentari on their link.

'What is the question,' said Rorien on their link.

'Answers, not questions. I want answers,' said Elentari on their link.

'Be patient,' replied Rorien on their link.

'Shut up. Jasper and I are on our way home. What are you and Lorcan up to?' said Elentari on their link.

'Us and Fen are in the training area. Playing with some moves,' said Rorien on their link.

'Ok. See you at supper. Love you,' said Elentari on their link.

'And I you. Until supper,' replied Rorien on their link.

"Any being have the answer to why you all came via movement and not sailed?" asked Elentari to the princes and princesses as they sat in the lounge after supper.

"I thought it was strange but dismissed it. Dad didn't want to lose me, too, so movement was the safest way. It seemed logical until now," replied Emmett.

"That would make sense. After all, we are the last of the line," said Sven.

"Protective fathers. Great, just what we need," Lannis shook his head as he spoke.

"Guess exploring dangerous areas is going to be banned, snowy mountains and caves," said Rorien.

"Keep us all chained to the royal areas, maybe," said Sven.

"Nope. Not being chained, thank-you. I have had enough chains to last all our lifetimes," replied Elentari angrily.

"Sorry, E. It wasn't meant to hurt you," said Sven.

"It's ok. I know it wasn't meant like that," said Elentari.

"What other reason could they have?" asked Emmett.

"Who would know," answered Lannis.

"Hopefully, it is not to keep us out of harm's way. Surely, we can defend ourselves. I think I proved I could," said Elentari

"We all proved we could fight together and work together during the war. It was great to feel part of something significant," said Jahan.

"Yeah, we did," said Rorien.

"Mmm. Have you all heard about yielding being able to be transferred through the link?" asked Elentari

"East is having a field dia playing with their newfound powers," said Lannis. "Not that keen on healing power. Earth is way more fun."

"I can shift. What good is that?" said Emmett.

"It would have come in handy during the battle. You could have been there with us," answered Elentari

"Suppose," said Emmett.

"I find it easier to get around now I can yield movement. Torvi is not sure about air, though," said Jahan.

"Fire and water, a great combination," said Sven, peevish.

"You know you can do this," said Elentari as she yielded a water ball in one hand and flames in the other, Rorien also yielding both.

Rorien and Elentari threw the balls into the middle of the room, where they twisted and twirled around each other before exploding into fireworks and snowflakes.

"And what is that going to get me?" grumbled Sven.

"Fun and frivolity in the parestala for one," answered Rorien as he exploded another water ball into snowflakes as Elentari exploded fireworks around the room.

"E, can you put music on?" asked Fendton, bored with the conversation.

"You know how to. You can choose, Fen. Guessing you want to get this party started?" said Elentari.

Music filled the room, and the fun began, the night going late as usual, with the princes and princesses leaving their cares behind and enjoying themselves. Ales, gins, snacks, dancing and competitions all part of the fun and frivolities of the night before the januel began on the morrow.

"Good morning Kings, Princes and Princess. Januel will be slightly different this time. I have an announcement to make before we commence." The King paused as he looked around the room. His eyes lingered upon King Baldric before continuing around the group and lingering upon King Reagan before settling on Elentari.

"I have decided to abdicate and hand over my throne to Princess Elentari," said the King, sitting straight with his hands holding on the arms of his seat.

"I, too, am abdicating and handing the crown to Prince Lannis," replied King Baldric with his face straight.

"I abdicate and hand the throne to Sven," stated King Reagan, leaning back in his chair.

"I abdicate and hand the crown to Jahan," stated King Leopold as he placed his hand on Jahan's shoulder.

"And I, too, am abdicating and giving the crown to Emmett," stated King Rian patting Emmett's back.

"You can't!" yelled Elentari standing up with her hands on the table. "I won't accept!" she said as she slumped down into her chair, her face in a scowl.

"I'm not taking the throne!" said Jahan as shock took hold of him. "I am not ready!"

"Neither am I. It was only a few mesiks ago that I became next in line. I do not want this," said Emmett quietly.

"I will sit if Elentari does first," said Lannis, staring at Elentari

"Agreed," stated Sven, nodding.

"Agreed," stated Jahan and Emmett turning to each other.

"Guess none of you can abdicate as I am not accepting the crown," said Elentari, her hands folded tightly across her chest. "I am not ready and do not want this responsibility yet."

"You have shown great leadership in the few anoks you have been here. You were able to withstand and fight for your freedom. You showed you could organise and lead in battle. You have brought peace to the different kinds, and you have helped Jahan and Emmett become ready to be kings," said Leopold, his face soft as he watched her.

"You are more than ready, Elentari. You have fallen into your princess role without an issue, and every being across the lands are willing to follow your leadership and guidance," said Rian, smiling at her.

"You all may think I am ready, but I am not. It was hard enough finding everything I knew was false. I was ripped away from everything and everyone I knew and thrown into a world I knew nothing about or even existed. To discover I was a princess and thrown into a role I knew nothing about and now this! No. I am not accepting," Elentari said, leaning forward with her hands on the table.

"You have encouraged the Masters, Apprentices and Professors to search for answers beyond what they know. You have found new ways and means for yielding. You are ready," said Reagan, nodding.

"You have brought joy to every being, finding new ways to yield and encouraging them to strengthen their link. We have not been able to accomplish what you have. You are ready," said Baldric, leaning back in his chair.

"If this is to happen, it is on my terms. Agreed?" Elentari said, her lips tight.

"What are your terms first?" asked King Adtarian, looking at her sideways, knowing she would have thought of something to rattle them but very unsure of what.

"No. If you truly want us to sit, then the terms will not be an issue. Agree, or we do not sit," Elentari said, a slight smile on the side of her mouth.

'*What are you planning?*' thought Emmett as Elentari used her sight yielding.

The King sat pondering, rubbing his chin, searching her face looking for any answer to what she was planning.

'*Linking. Rorien is already organising,*' said Elentari via sight to Emmett.

The other Kings began to shift in their chairs, not sure they were liking where she was heading, searching their sons, hoping for an answer.

'*Linking?*' thought Emmett.

"I will agree. You should be on the throne and not me. It is you every being looks to and adores," said the King.

"Thank you, King Adtarian. Kings, do you also agree?" Elentari asked as her eyes moved around the room.

'*Yep, wait and see,*' said Elentari via sight to Emmett.

"Your terms concern me, not stating before requesting. As the King accepts, so shall I," said Rian, a little uneasy.

"What you have in mind cannot be that bad. I agree," said Baldric.

"Agree," stated Reagan.

"I will go with the flow and agree too. Tell us the terms," said Leopold sighing.

"Excellent. Terms are, firstly your abdication will be on the last dia of the anok, and we shall be crown on the 1st of the new anok. New anok, new Queen and Kings. Any objections?" said Elentari as she scanned the room.

The Kings shook their heads.

"Secondly, this is for Adtarian and Rian. As we have found a way to build the link, you will both find a new female to relink. Messages have already been sent to the town criers and placed on notice boards in each parestala. You both are to complete your link before the end of the anok. If you do not complete your link, the deal is off," said Elentari, with a smug look on her face.

"You cannot expect us to relink! I'm afraid I have to disagree!" answered Adtarian angrily, slamming his fist on the table.

'*Great idea, E. Dad needs a female,*' thought Emmett.

"Then, we shall not accept. Notes have been distributed on notice boards, and females will be coming to meet with you. You cannot stop them coming," said Elentari.

"What if there is no being who is right for me?" asked Adtarian.

'*Yes. They both need company. Plus, this may be our way out of taking the throne, Em,*' said Elentari via sight to Emmett.

"We will broaden the search. Messages have only been sent to cuedels and villades within two horis of Thoroneath and Seatheas. If no female takes your fancy, we can extend the invitations further afield," said Elentari. She folded her arms across her chest and sat back with a smug look.

"I do not like this. It has been too long since I have been with my link," said Rian, a concerned look on his face.

"This is a good idea, Elentari. It is not right for you both to be alone for so long. You still have 500 anoks before you move on," said Baldric.

"Think of the fun we shall have together. We will have no duties, no expectations, no parents to stop us from doing as we want. New members of our group to get to know," said Reagan.

"No. Not liking this idea at all," said Rian, shaking his head.

"Too late, it is done. Messages are up, and females will be coming knocking. If you don't relink before the end of the anok, the deal is off, and I won't be taking the throne," said Emmett, sitting back grinning with satisfaction.

"To confirm, Rian and I are to relink before the end of the anok, and you all will take the throne on the first?" asked Adtarian.

"Yes. That is the terms for me to take the throne and to keep this quiet until you abdicate," replied Elentari.

"And only when Elentari is crowned queen will we become kings," said Jahan.

"Deal," stated Baldrick, reaching his hand towards Elentari to seal the deal. Elentari grabbed his hand before her father could object.

"Now, as you have handed us this information which has caused us angst, we shall take our leave to digest," said Elentari, standing, nodding to the Princes and heading out. The Princes followed.

"Call your links and have them meet us in the lounge," said Elentari to the Princes. "Jasper, can you let the chef know we will be having lunch at our dining area instead and meet us with Sarina." Elentari hurried out of the hall with the Princes following and summoned her guards.

'*Rorien, how can he do this?*' Elentari said on their link. She knew the Princes would be speaking to their linked as she was.

'*He knows you will be a great Queen and are who every being wants. Lorcan and Fen are at the lounge. Awnrie is on her way,*' said Rorien on their link.

'*Thanks. This is big, and I don't like it,*' Elentari said on their link as she entered the lounge, making a beeline for Rorien and grabbing him tightly, wanting to feel safe and supported.

Rorien wrapped his arms around her, rubbing her back.

"Ok," said Elentari releasing Rorien. "Every being is here. The Kings are planning to abdicate and hand over the thrones to us. We have put them off till the end of the anok. But, if the King Adtarian and King Rian do not find another to relink with, we won't accept the throne." Elentari began pacing the floor. "I do not want to sit until I am well into my 200's and beyond."

"Well, we have 122 dias until it becomes a reality or a reason for them not to abdicate," said Lannis lost in thought. "Which means we have 122 dias to get used to becoming King."

"And us to get used to being Queen," replied Jobie.

"Rorien doesn't unless that has changed?" asked Sven.

"Nope," answered Rorien.

"What I had planned has now changed, thanks to the battle," said Elentari. She turned to Emmett. "Emmett, my choice was for you to sit with me and govern from the South. Meaning, Cormac would not be able to do anything without your and my approval. Never did like or trust him. No offence."

"None taken. I never liked him either," said Emmett.

"Guess I was right not to trust him," said Elentari sighing. "You two weren't the close twin type."

"Nope. Never have been, even when we were babes. Apparently, he kept pushing me away to get all the attention," said Emmett.

"As he is no longer, you will be King. Therefore, my choice for who sits with me has changed, and it is still not Rorien. We have another who will assist me," said Elentari as she began to pace the floor again.

"Not saying who?" asked Sven.

"Nope. We are not," answered Rorien forcefully.

"If you end up sitting, how will you do it?" asked Fendton.

Elentari stopped and turned towards Fendton, her face questioning him. "What do you mean, Fen?" Elentari asked.

"Well, who will be crowned first and do we have to travel to each of the lands to crown every King?" asked Fendton.

"That would be too long and tedious. How about we all be crowned here?" asked Lannis.

"Good idea. We can be crowned one after the other. Elentari can be crowned first and then crown us," answered Emmett.

"That would work. I do like the idea of crowning my Kings, who will sit with me," said Elentari, rubbing her lips with a finger. "When we are beyond our 200's, that is."

"Ok. Who is crowned next after Elentari?" asked Lannis.

"Why can I not crown you all at once? Allocate two of the Masters to each of you. One Master can speak, and one can hand you the items. To crown you, my guards can place your crowns on your heads while I announce you all. Would that work?" asked Elentari.

"It would. I have no problems with it," said Emmett.

"Yep. Let's do it," said Sven. "In the far future."

"All agreed?" asked Elentari as she watched the Princes all nodding their agreement. "Ok. We are all agreed we will be crown together. Hopefully, on the first of the new anok, we shall not be crowned. We still have Papa and Rian to be linked before they can abdicate. So, for the next 120 dias, we come up with a solution to why we should not be crowned. Oh, and this is kept quiet. Everything said here tonight is not to be discussed."

"We have januel to attend on the morrow," said Jahan.

"Nope. I am going to request it be postponed until the new anok. There is nothing of grave importance. Janual can wait. This is way more important, working out how not to be crowned," said Elentari, grinning. "That is business completed, so let's enjoy the next few dias. Get our heads around what has happened and how we can stop it."

"I think you should take the crown in 122 dias, E," said Fendton quietly.

"Why, Fen? So, you have a new pick-up line? The Queen's guard," answered Elentari sneeringly.

"Leave him alone. At least he is enjoying himself," said Lannis.

"No, because I think you would make an excellent Queen," said Fendton. Annoyance played on his voice at her dig at him.

"We haven't checked the other theory," said Rorien changing the topic quickly.

"Oh yes, the sitting on the throne theory," said Elentari.

"What sitting on the throne theory?" asked Emmett, a little concerned.

"Papa holds all eight powers, as do I, and the Bitch held four that we know. The theory was if you sit on the throne, you hold all eight," answered Elentari.

"You think that we all should hold all eight powers too?" asked Jahan.

"Yeah. That is the theory. Wanna try?" said Rorien.

"Ok. I'm in," replied Lannis.

"Yeah, me too," said Sven.

"Ok. Let's do this and find out if sitting on the throne gives you all powers. We will start with air, water, fire, earth and then onto sight, heal, shift and movement. My guards will guide you in the moves. Princesses, want to try?" asked Elentari. The princesses nodded.

"Ready?" asked Elentari.

Seneca showed them air. Jasper showed them water, Lorcan created fire for them, and Fendton moved a stone. The Princes and Princess' followed the actions. Sven and Anya already had fire and water, and no other powers could they yield. Lannis and Jobie held earth and gained water. Emmett and Twyla gained earth and air powers, and Jahan and Torvi added fire to their air power.

"It seems minor kings only hold two of the four-element powers. Let's try spirit powers. My guess is you will hold two of them as well," said Elentari.

Seneca began with sight, Jasper helped them heal, Rorien showed them shifting, and Lorcan showed them movement. Sven and Anya added shift and movement to their powers while Lannis and Jobie gained sight to their healing power. Emmett and Twyla had healing and shift and no other spirit powers, while Jahan and Torvi added sight power to their movement.

"Sensational," said Anya, delighted in her new abilities.

"You were right, E. We hold two spirit powers as well," said Emmett.

"So, what does it mean?" asked Jahan.

"If you are next in line to sit on the throne, you will hold at least two element powers and two spirit powers. One way to know for sure you are eligible to sit on the throne," replied Elentari.

"Of course, holding all eight is the big throne," said Lannis.

"Guessing the next few mesiks will be busy for you, Princes, as you train in your new powers. I shall sit back and relax before we are all chained to the throne, enjoying my freedom," said Elentari, sighing as she stretched out on the lounge looking all relaxed and comfortable.

"Really!? You are going to relax while we work hard. Ha, good one. Like you can relax," said Jahan.

"She is right. We are going to be busy learning our new powers," said Sven as he tried to search her mind.

"I don't give away my secrets, Sven. I keep my mind closed. The future Queen cannot have every being knowing about her and what she has planned. You will find nothing unless I want you too." Elentari said, grinning as she probed his mind.

"This will mean we will have training too," said Anya excitedly.

"Yes. Guess you future queens are going to be busy too. How exciting, new powers and possibly a new position. This is shaping out to be ok after all," said Elentari as her mind wandered off in thought.

"It is," said Lannis as he gazed into the future and became lost in thought.

All the princes and princesses became lost in thought, thinking of what was to come in 122 dias, a new life with new powers and possibilities.

CHAPTER 20

At Elentari's request, the King postponed the januel, and the minor Kings returned home while the Princes stayed another dia to spend time discussing what was coming and what changes they would like. The Princes and Princess agreed to meet each mesik on the tenth. Each mesik being in a different land, spreading themselves around and showing every being their land was as important as any other land. In 10 dias, they would meet together in the West.

"So, the Princes have left, yesterdia was our anniversary, what do you have scheduled for todia?" asked Rorien as he leaned against the door watching Elentari shower.

"First up, Fen and I have a trip to make and once I am back, preparing for the ball tonight. There is a lot to organise," Elentari said, enjoying the feel of water droplets hit her skin and running down her body. This was one sensation she thoroughly enjoyed and always stayed there until the water ran dry. She stepped out, and Rorien yielded water to refill it.

"Still not used to you being able to yield all. And to think, if you hadn't come to your senses, you would still be a boring air yielder," Elentari said, smiling.

"Yeah, yeah, yeah, whatever," Rorien said, rolling his eyes and stepping into the steaming hot water.

"Hopefully, Fen and I won't take long. Hoping for a meet and greet and come back. Fen is unwilling to let me know who she is or discuss her, which has me intrigued. It makes me even more eager to meet her. I do wonder who she is? Also, wonder why he kept insisting he hadn't found her." Elentari paused as she dressed, staring off into space, lost in her thoughts.

"You will know soon enough. Fen has his reasons for not wanting to discuss this. Let him be, and don't be forceful on him," said Rorien as he lathered his body in soap. "How long have you known?"

"I will not force him to do anything. As if I would," Elentari snapped at him and continued dressing. "I've known for near on an anok."

"Yes, you would if it suited your needs. Now behave," said Rorien.

"Whatever. I'm outta here. Catch you later," said Elentari. She kissed Rorien and disappeared to Fendton's casa.

"Morning Fen. Ready?" Elentari asked as she appeared in Fendton's kitchen.

"Morning E," replied Fendton. "Wish you wouldn't just pop in like that. It scares me every time."

"When you are linked, it won't happen. I shall use the door like every other being," said Elentari.

"Why are you doing this?" asked Fendton, a pained look on his face.

"If you had explained to me you had an answer from your link and were meeting her, would I be here pushing? It was nearly an anok ago she answered you, and you have not said a word. Even when we were locked up, nothing. That makes me very curious as to why my bestie is not sharing."

"You won't like her, and I'm not completing the link, so why bother?" Fendton shrugged a shoulder.

"That is for me to find out. How could you know I won't like her? And do not get me started on the specialness of the link," Elentari tilted her head, looking at him out the top of her eyes.

"Is there any way I can stop this? A slight chance you could change your mind?" asked Fendton.

"Let's go," Elentari said, grabbing Fendton's arm and transporting them to the north cuedel. "Not a chance I am changing my mind, we are here."

Fendton and Elentari stood in the parestala. A slight chill on the breeze sent a shiver through Elentari. Many beings were bustling about, chatter filled the air, and the smell of freshly baked bread wafted by them. Fendton's stomach growled.

"You haven't eaten? Another ploy to stop the inedible. Grab something, and let's do this. It is going to happen," said Elentari.

"Fine," grumbled Fendton as he grabbed some food. "She's this way," he said between mouthfuls, heading away from the parestala.

Fendton and Elentari wandered through the streets and alleyways, seeming to be meandering around and not going in any specific direction. Elentari stopped.

"Fen, stop delaying and take us to her," Elentari said, anger in her voice and on her face as her hands held onto her hips.

"Hoped you wouldn't notice," said Fendton.

"Really? Me not notice. You have known me long enough to know this would not work. Now let's go, directly," said Elentari forcefully.

"Fine," Fendton said, turning around and heading down an alley, turning into a street and stopping. "She is in there." He pointed to the blacksmith shop.

"Are you going to give me any other details, or am I finding out myself?" asked Elentari.

"What do you want to know? She is in there, and this is where she works," Fendton said, shifting his gaze from her, avoiding contact with her.

"Ok. She works in a blacksmith shop, nothing wrong with that. Shall we?" Elentari held her arm out to take his. Fendton begrudgingly held his arm out for her to take and led her in.

"Harlian, it is good to see you," said Fendton sarcastically. "May I introduce…"

"Princess Elentari. Harlian, it is lovely to meet you," said Elentari, cutting off Fendton.

"Fendton, I said I wasn't interested," said Harlian as she turned her back and continued her work.

"Princess, what an honour," said a blacksmith bowing to her. "What can we help you with?"

"We have come to visit Harlian. Fendton is her link," Elentari answered. "What is it you are creating?" she asked, glancing over at the metal in the fire.

Fendton moved away to the door and leaned on it. He folded his arms across his chest and turned his head away. His eyes stared at the floor, avoiding any contact.

"I am making a sickle for harvesting wheat. Over there, he is making a bucket, and he is making knives for the butcher," said the blacksmith, pointing to each male.

"You use a fire. You do not yield fire as the others do?" asked Elentari.

"No, my great, great grandfather owned this blacksmith shop and yielded fire. He passed his knowledge down through the generations, but no being yielded fire. Hence this fire. I enjoyed watching him as a boy and began to help him. The others moved on when they could, but I continued to learn. It has been over 600 anoks I have been blacksmithing," said the blacksmith.

"It is good to follow your passion and keep your grandfather's shop open. Please continue," said Elentari. Elentari watched the blacksmiths working, watching the different ways they heated the metal before hammering it into shape and heating it again. Sweat poured off the blacksmith using the fire while the other blacksmiths who yielded heat were fresh-looking, without a drop of sweat. She turned her gaze to Harlian and noticed Harlian did not yield but used the fire as well.

"You do not yield fire, Harlian?" asked Elentari.

"No," answered Harlian, not bothering to turn around.

"What intrigued you to begin blacksmithing if you do not yield fire?" asked Elentari.

"A job to annoy my mother," answered Harlian.

"Do you enjoy it?" asked Elentari.

"Get out both of you and leave me alone. I have no interest," snarled Harlian dropping the metal into the fire and staring at them.

"Harlianna! That is no way to speak to the future Queen. Learn your manners. My shop does not treat customers that way and certainly not the future Queen," the blacksmith said, anger in his words. "Forgive her, Princess. She does not speak for my shop," he said as he turned to her.

"It is alright. I know Harlian speaks for herself and does need to learn some manners. It is ok, thank-you," said Elentari.

"Yes, I enjoy it," Harlian replied with sarcasm, rolling her eyes and pulling a face.

Fendton rolled his eyes and kicked the dirt.

"We are about to find somewhere for tea. Would you like to join us, Harlian?" asked Elentari.

"Not really," Harlian said, turning away from them.

"Harlianna! The Princess has asked you to tea, now go," growled the blacksmith.

"I shall rephrase. Harlian, you are coming to tea with us. Please pack up now," said Elentari.

"Do I even have a choice?" Harlian asked as she turned to face Elentari.

"You do have a choice. I suggest you choose wisely," answered Elentari, standing straight her shoulders back and her stance letting Harlian know she would not back down.

Fendton smirked and straighten up. He was enjoying Elentari making Harlian uncomfortable and demanding her to attend to tea.

"Fine, tea it is," Harlian said as she shoved her way past them and headed up the alley.

Fendton turned to Elentari and went to speak.

"No need, Fen. Let's go," Elentari said as she followed Harlian. Fendton fell into step beside Elentari, his shoulders hunched forward with his hands in his pockets. Harlian stopped at a café and flopped onto a chair.

"Here's a tea shop," Harlian said, turning away from them.

"I will get us something, E," said Fendton.

"Thank you, Fen," Elentari replied as she sat down across the table from Harlian. "You are not interested. Why?"

"You've seen him. He is nothing, a dweeb, a skinny, weak male," replied Harlian.

"A skinny, weak male would not be part of the King's army nor the guard to the future Queen. Fendton is much more than you see and far from boring. Please get to know him, and you find out who he is. Looks are not everything," said Elentari.

"Whatever. He is not who should be linked with me," said Harlian.

"And whom is it you should be with?" asked Elentari.

"Some strong, strapping male who is built solid. Some being with thick muscular arms and large, broad shoulders," replied Harlian.

"Mmm. Why is that?" asked Elentari.

"Look at me and look at Fendton. We are not physically matched in any way," said Harlian.

Harlian was a large, tall female standing 6 foot. Her body was not feminine, with her strength showing in her arms and chest and sizeable strong thigh muscles. Even her dark brown hair was cut short, almost shaven and looked more male than female.

"Whether you are physically matched or not, he is your link," said Elentari.

"I do not need a male. I am as capable as any male," said Harlian.

"Guess you haven't heard the rumours," said Elentari under her breath.

"What?" snapped Harlian.

"Spend some time with us and see what comes," said Elentari.

"Not interested," Harlian said as Fendton returned with tea.

"The blacksmith calls you Harlianna, is that your full name?" asked Elentari.

"Yeah. But I hate it, so don't call me that or I'll punch the crap out of you," said Harlian angrily.

"Would it be ok to know why?' asked Elentari softly.

"Mum named me after some being she knew who was the perfect female. She wanted a perfect daughter. So, I rebelled. The blacksmith knew my mother and is the only non-family member who gets away with calling me that," said Harlian.

"Tell us about Estelaur," said Elentari to Harlian, changing the subject.

Harlian spent the rest of their time together explaining all about Estelaur, all the exciting things to do and places to see. She spoke about her childhood and growing up in Estelaur and how she became a black-smith. Soon they had finished tea and said goodbye before Elentari and Fendton returned home.

"She is insufferable, difficult and genuine pain. No wonder Fen kept her from me," said Elentari, pacing in her lounge, her mind spinning with ways to bring Harlian here.

"It went that good," said Rorien as he reclined on the couch, picking at a piece of cake.

"He is her link, and the two of them need time together. Maybe that will change their minds," said Elentari. "Guess Fen's reputation has not hit Estelaur." Elentari was smirking.

"Reputation? What are you talking about?" asked Rorien.

"The delinked females talk highly of Fen and his bed warming skills. Of course, I agree with them on how enlarged he is. That is true, very true," said Elentari, raising an eyebrow.

"Ease up. Way to put me down. And yeah, he does get around the delinked a bit," said Rorien.

"A bit? Really? Come on. You know it is more than a bit!" said Elentari, stopping to look at Rorien. "Lucky he isn't fertile, or there would be hundreds of little Fen's running around."

"Ok. Yes, he spends a lot of time around the delinked," said Rorien. "They are lonely and do want company, you know."

"Yes. It must be hard to lose your linked at a young age and not be able to link again," said Elentari, a touch of compassion in her voice. "Of course, that has changed, thanks to us." She smiled before pacing again.

"Suppose there will be more relink ceremonies to come, especially if the King relinks," said Rorien.

"Yes," said Elentari, still pacing with her mind racing. "Oh, I have a plan." Elentari stopped pacing, turned to Rorien and smiled.

"Interfering is going to get you in trouble," said Rorien.

"No, it won't," said Elentari with her hands on her hips. "I know the blacksmith in the stables wants a scene change." Elentari dropped her hands to her side.

"I know where you are going, and it may not work. Just because she is here does not mean they will change their minds," said Rorien.

"Then I will have to work out ways to make them change their minds," said Elentari.

"Don't get disappointed if it doesn't work." Rorien sighed. "Let me organise the blacksmith. When will they swap?" asked Rorien.

"On the morrow," said Elentari, sitting beside him on the couch.

"For?" asked Rorien.

"However long HE wants. Harlian can take over here for as long as our blacksmith wants to stay there. Go and find him and let him know he needs to pack for a scene change. I will organise everything else. The morrow is going to be challenging, and hopeful I shall succeed," said Elentari.

"You will. You always end up getting your way," said Rorien.

"Usually, I am not up against some stubborn female," said Elentari.

"Welcome to my world," said Rorien under his breath.

"Careful I heard that," said Elentari waving her fist at him.

"I know you did, and you will succeed," said Rorien. He glanced at her and smirked. "Two stubborn females up against each other. Maybe I should go with you on the morrow."

"Not a chance. You only want to come to watch the showdown. I can see you now, sitting there throwing a line in here and there to stir the pot. Forget it. You are staying here," said Elentari.

"As you wish," said Rorien. He kissed her and headed off to find the blacksmith and put her plan into action.

CHAPTER 21

"Todia is the last dia of the anok, and along with the minor Kings, my crown is being removed. It is a happy dia for me," said the King as Elentari entered the hall, his face full of happiness.

"Maybe for you, Papa, but it means on the morrow, I will be chained to the crown. I still have time to change your mind," Elentari said as she slumped on her chair and folded her arms across her chest.

"You all agreed to take the crown if both Rian and I relinked. We both have, and now it is time for us to live our lives again. It will be nice to explore again with Baldric and Reagan. We did have some great times together," said the King as his eyes stared off into the distance heading down memory lane.

"It would be nice to live a little before this chain's wrapped around me. Come on, Papa, there must be something we can do or say to change all your minds?" asked Elentari.

The last time the Princes and Elentari were together, they planned how the crowning would flow and which Masters would speak and which would hand the crowning items, just in case.

"No. You made the deal, and we have met all requests. The Kings will be arriving soon with the Princes, and our abdication will take place. On the morrow, you will be taking your rightful place as Queen. Every being wants to see you on the throne. Why can you not be excited?" said the King.

"Because...oh, good, here is King Reagan and Prince Sven. I've been saved from this conversation," said Elentari.

The Kings and Princes began to arrive with pleasantries exchanged, and the topic of abdication and crowning avoided. Instead, talk of how the weather was, how the season was fairing and general non-business. The Kings congregated together, whispering to themselves while watching the Princes and Princess, discussing how to encourage them to accept their destiny and wondering if it was right to abdicate. Elentari smiled inwardly to herself and glanced at Jahan and Sven, both nodding to her. They, too, were listening to the Kings, using their sight to listen.

"My King, when you are ready. We can begin," said the Fire Master as he and the other Masters entered the hall.

"Kings, are you ready?" the King asked the minor Kings.

"I am," replied King Reagan.

"As am I," replied King Leopold.

"Do you think I relinked for the hell of it? No, I relinked to prove I was serious. I am ready," said King Rian.

"Ready. Looking forward to adventures again and watching my son rule," said King Baldric.

"I'm not," mumbled Elentari.

"Same," mumbled Emmett.

"Masters, we are ready," said the King, glaring at Elentari.

"If you are all agreed, I shall receive all abdications," said the Fire Master.

The Kings nodded.

"Please take your place on the pomp. These chairs will act as your thrones," said the Fire Master.

The Kings stepped onto the pomp and sat on their chairs. King Adtarian's throne was in the centre, slightly in front of the chairs, with King Reagan and King Rian to his right and King Leopold and King Baldric to his left.

"Do you abdicate your throne?" asked the Fire Master.

"Yes," the Kings answered.

"Are there any objections?" asked the Fire Master.

The room went silent. The Kings shifted their gaze to their child, holding their breath, waiting for the objection. Elentari smiled at her Papa and shook her head. She knew it was the right thing to do, and every being was waiting for her to sit on the throne. Still, she was hesitant.

"Do you relinquish governing and maintaining this land?" continued the Fire Master.

"Yes," answered all Kings.

"Do you renounce your judgement on these lands?" asked the Fire Master.

"Yes," all Kings answered.

"Do you surrender your crown?" asked the Fire Master.

"Yes," all Kings answered, removing their crowns and holding them out in front of them. The Masters took the crowns from the Kings and placed them in a padded, velvet box, and closed the lid.

"I accept your abdication on behalf of the Masters, Professors, Scholars and all beings living in these lands. You will no longer be called Kings and will take on your Prince name once more. On the morrow, the crowning of the new Queen and Kings will take place," said the Fire Master.

The Masters bowed to the past Kings, turned to the Princess and Princes and bowed.

"Princess, the Kings have handed over their crowns. On the morrow, we shall crown you all. Is there any objections?" asked the Fire Master.

"No, Master. We are ready," said Elentari.

"Until he morrow, Princess," said the Fire Master. The Masters bowed to the Princess and Princes and left. The past Kings watched the Masters go, a slightly puzzled look on all their faces.

"No objections?" asked Adtarian, a little relieved and slightly confused.

"There never was going to be. Still very hesitant about the morrow," said Elentari.

"We wanted you to believe we were not ready, and some of us are concerned," said Emmett.

"You threw this on us all, and we wanted you all to sweat over your decision," said Sven.

"Well, you managed that," replied Leopold.

"On the morrow, you are to be crowned. It shall be marvellous to see my son crowned," said Baldric.

"We have things to discuss and organise for the morrow," said Elentari as she moved to the pomp. "Your crowns will be sent home to be packed with your throne and crowning items. We shall leave you past Kings to enjoy your new-found freedom. Do not be late on the morrow." Elentari waved them off.

"Starting early, are you? You are not Queen yet, my child. You cannot just wave us off," said Adtarian as he stood with a smile on his face.

"I may not be Queen, and you are not King. As I am next to sit, I shall wave you off if I please," Elentari replied, grinning, before kissing his cheek.

"We shall take our leave, Princess. There is much celebration to be had, the end of the anok and the end of our reign. Until the morrow," said Leopold waving and heading for the door. The past Kings bowed to the Princess and Princes and took their leave.

"The Masters have everything ready for the morrow. They shall organise the room with our thrones and crowning objects, and all that is left is for us to arrive. The rest of the dia is yours to enjoy as you wish. Supper in the princess parestala," said Elentari as she began to remove the chairs.

"Wow. Our last dia as Prince. Did not ever think I would be under 100 when this dia arrived," said Lannis, the oldest of the princes at 78.

"Speak for yourself. I haven't even reached 40!" said Emmett, the youngest of the princes at 36 anoks, stepping up to help Elentari.

"All of us, other than Sven, have had this thrust on us in a short time. It was five anoks ago I arrived to find I was a Princess and next to sit on the throne, in the same anok, Jahan stepped through the ranks from third to next. This anok, Emmett became next in line after the battle, and so did Lannis. Sven, you have been next to sit since you were born," said Elentari, picking up the last chair to remove.

"It has been a massive five anoks for us all. On the morrow, we each begin a new journey together. One I am happy to take with you all," said Jahan.

"Hear, hear," replied Lannis. "Let's celebrate." He fist-pumped the air as he did a little hop.

"Good idea. I need a drink," said Sven.

"So do I. Still nervous about the morrow," said Emmett.

"Let's get out of here and enjoy our last dia of freedom," said Lannis grabbing Emmett.

Lannis boulted out the door with the other Princes following. Elentari watched them go before she walked into the private chamber and heard footsteps enter the hall, listening to them head towards her. She scanned the room, noticing Papa's had removed his things and all that he left was royal items. Elentari felt a hand wrap around her waist and pull her backwards. Grasping his hand, she leaned against Rorien and sighed. Elentari felt so safe in his arms and thought she could do anything with Rorien by her side.

"On the morrow, this is yours. How are you feeling?" asked Rorien.

"Ok. This is a huge job, but I know I have support around me. At least Papa will still be here to help me. The only thing playing on my mind is the following dia when I announce my King to govern with me," replied Elentari.

"That is going to be very interesting. You have been through different scenarios with me and have the answers to any issues. It will be ok. It will work," said Rorien.

"I hope so. It is massively different and is going to cause controversy," said Elentari.

"Different and controversial go hand in hand with you," Rorien said, grinning and kissing her head.

"Thanks," said Elentari. She turned to face him and wrapped her arms around Rorien's neck.

"It will show who you are and your plans, looking forward to this. Jasper is outside with Lorcan. Shall we go?" asked Rorien, kissing her.

"Yes. All this can wait. Let's go celebrate the last dia of the anok and my last dia of freedom," Elentari said with a smile on her face.

"Celebrate the last dia of the anok and the beginning of your new adventure," Rorien said, kissing her.

"Yes. Our new adventure together starts on the morrow," Elentari said, kissing him.

"Come on. Every being is waiting for you to arrive, including Rewa. Mum and Dad arrived before with Donna's Mum and Dad. Both mothers are fussing over Fendton and grilling Harlian. I thought you were bad," Rorien said, taking her hand and leading her out.

"Poor Harlian. Both Mums' will be a big challenge. Did Fendton save her? Hi Jasper," said Elentari, strolling towards the parestala. Jasper nodded before he and Lorcan fell into step behind them.

"Yeah. Harlian was thankful for that. She is starting to open up to Fen," said Rorien.

"Told you she would. I had better distract the mums' away from Harlian. Jasper and Lorcan, can you make sure Sarina and Awnrie keep the mums' away from Harlian, please," said Elentari, glancing over her shoulder.

"On it," replied Lorcan.

"Rewa is growing up fast," said Elentari.

"Yeah. A big, almost nine anoks painful little sister," said Rorien grinning.

"She is excelling in lessons beyond what the teachers can give her. Maybe she should come here to learn?" asked Elentari.

"What!? Live with us?" asked Rorien.

"That or I transport her here each morning. She only has to stay for lessons," said Elentari. "She is bright and should be extended."

"Yeah," said Rorien.

"Guess she got the brains in the family," said Elentari. Both Jasper and Lorcan stifled a laugh.

"Whatever," said Rorien.

"If she works with the Scholars, she will excel, and her future will be bright," said Elentari

"You've seen something," said Rorien.

"Yes. I also had another plan, and she fits it perfectly," said Elentari.

"Plan?" asked Rorien.

"Yes. When the Masters choose the next Apprentice, I will reveal," said Elentari.

"Ok, I know where you are going. So, Rewa transports daily, not stay," said Rorien.

"Yes, transport," said Elentari. "Give us time to get used to a child around. Maybe in the future, she can stay. Not ready for that type of responsibility."

"That will work. I'll chat with Havid. Look, every being is here, including Hoofington and the fauns. Vosco and the giants are down on the field," said Rorien as he stopped to point to the parestala.

CHAPTER 22

Elentari wore her traditional robe with her necklace representing all the powers and matching earrings. She stood alone facing the closed doors to the royal hall, staring into space, waiting. She could hear the rise and fall of the voices inside the hall. The past Kings would be seated at the front with their linked, the future Kings and their linked. Her guards were inside with Rorien at the front, where she would be able to see them. The Masters would be standing on the other side of the door in front of her. Elentari was waiting for the door to open to announce her crowning to begin. Her stomach was tense and anxious, and her heart was racing with excitement.

The Master of fire opened the door as a colourful carpet rolled down the aisle, and the hall became still and quiet. Elentari straightened up, chin up, chest out and shoulders back as she stepped into the hall and onto the carpet. All eyes were on her as she slowly walked the full length of the hall towards the pomp. Here, Elentari stood facing her throne with the Element Masters standing to the left and the Spirit Masters on the right.

Elentari looked at her throne. It was made of fine mahogany and carved with dragons slinking down each leg with their faces staring out from the feet, their eyes a different power gemstone. Delicate strands of silver lace entwined the high back, the elegant filigree interlacing around eight large gems all cut differently to represent the eight powers. At the height of the chair was carved a large elegant E. The arms and seat padded in a velvety fabric to match her traditional robe.

The Air Master stepped forward with the Sight Master. The Sight Master held the varita in his hand, a full-length delicately carved staff laid with all the power gemstones and a silver royal crown set on top. The Masters read the ancient text.

"I shall govern according to the ancient text," said Elentari as the Sight Master placed the varita in her left hand.

The Masters bowed and returned to their place. The earth and shift Masters approached with the vorbola sitting in the Shift Masters hand, a smooth opal orb with four silver bands circling it, crisscrossing over each other and etched with power symbols. The Masters read the ancient text.

"I shall, to my utmost power, maintain this land," Elentari said as the Shift Master placed the vorbola in her right hand.

The Masters bowed and returned to their place. The water and heal Masters stepped in front of her with the vasokop in the Heal Masters hand, a mother of pearl handleless cup etched with the power symbols surrounding an E. The Masters read the ancient text.

"I shall use compassion in all my judgements," Elentari said as the Heal Master put the cup to her lips to drink before placing it in the cup holder on the throne.

The Masters bowed and took their place with the other Masters. The fire and movement Masters approached with the velo in the Movement Master's hand, a moonlight topaz cylinder with a large graceful E etched on it and a candle in the centre. The Masters read the ancient text.

"I shall uphold the ancient text and honour the minor Kings of each land," Elentari said, shifting the varita against her side to light the candle.

The Movement Master placed the candle on the colourful pedestal beside the throne. Elentari stepped up the pomp's four steps, reading the two virtues written on each step, judgment and mercy, honour and respect, prudence and courage, truth and selflessness. She turned and faced the hall running her eyes around the crowd before settling on her guards and Rorien, smiling at them before taking her seat.

The Fire Master stepped in front of her, holding her new crown high above her head, a delicate silver halo with eight tall spikes, jewelled in

888 sparkling gems with a large asscher cut mystic topaz as the centre-piece.

"I claim you Queen Elentari, Queen of all the lands," said the Fire Master placing the crown on her forehead, the crown encircling her head. The Fire Master stepped off the pomp, bowing.

"Hail Queen Elentari," said the Fire Master.

The hall erupted in accolades of 'hail Queen Elentari' as every being bowed to her. Her eyes meet her Papa's. His smile was wide, and tears of joy forming in his eyes. She smiled and nodded to him, turning her gaze to her parents and Donna's parents, who were beaming their faces showing such pride for their daughter, before finding Rorien.

'*Hail my Queen,*' Rorien said on their link, a grin over his face.

'*Remember your place now, Prince,*' Elentari giggled, teasing him on their link.

'*Oh, I will. My place is your link and lover,*' Rorien smiled, winking at her.

Elentari began her slow walk back down the carpet to her litter. Her four guards lifted her high in the air and paraded her around the cuedel before returning to the royal hall, a quick procession before the next crownings. As they came to the royal hall, the doors were closed and the Princes stood outside. Her guards lowered her litter and headed inside the hall. Elentari stood behind the Princes.

The Masters stood inside the royal doors while the Princes stood with Queen Elentari outside. The four Princes were nervously shifting, waiting for the doors to open. The Masters opened the door, and four Princes stood straight and tall, ready for their coronation. All eyes turned to them as the Princes followed the Masters down the hall. Elentari followed behind them, watching those in the hall and her future Kings. Four thrones were added to the pomp, two on either side of Elentari's throne and set slightly behind hers.

The Masters took their spots in front of the Princes. Standing across the front, from left to right, was Sven with Masters of fire and water, Emmett with Masters of sight and shift, Jahan with Masters of air and movement and Lannis with Masters of earth and heal.

In the hands of the Spirit Masters was the varita. Sven's varita was red, Lannis's was blue, Emmett's green and Jahan's yellow. The Masters read the ancient text.

"I shall govern according to the ancient text," said the Princes as the Masters placed the varita in their left hands.

The Spirit Masters held the vorbola in their hands. Sven's vorbola blue, Lannis's green, Emmett's yellow and Jahan's Red. The Masters read the ancient text.

"I shall, to my utmost power, maintain my land," said the Princes as the Masters' place the vorbola in their right hand.

The Spirit Masters grasped the vasokop. Sven had a purple vasokop, Lannis's vasokop was white, Emmett's orange and Jahan's black. The Masters read the ancient text.

"I shall use compassion in all my judgements," said the Princes as the Masters put the cup to their lips to drink.

The Masters placed the vasokop in the cup holder on the thrones. The Spirit Masters held the velo. Sven's velo was black, Lannis's had an orange velo, Emmett's was purple and Jahan's white. The Masters read the ancient text.

"I shall uphold the ancient text and honour the Queen of all the lands," said the Princes as they glanced in the Queen's direction, shifting the varita against their sides to light the candle.

The Masters placed the candle on the pedestal beside each throne. The Princes stepped up the pomp and took their seat as Elentari's guards stepped in front of the new Kings. Lorcan in front of Sven and Jasper in front of Emmett. Seneca stood in front of Jahan and Fendton in front of Lannis. Each guard was holding the new crown high above the King's head. Elentari looked at her Kings, the youngest ever rulers, and breathed in deeply. Respect, compassion, honour and admiration filled her.

"I claim you King Sven of the West lands, King Emmett of the South lands, King Jahan of the North lands and King Lannis of the East lands, minor Kings of my lands. I shall sit with you and govern our lands together," Elentari said as her guards placed the crowns on the King's head.

"Hail King Sven. Hail King Emmett. Hail King Jahan. Hail King Lannis," Elentari said, bowing as the hall erupted in hails and tributes.

The Kings stood and scanned the crowd to find their loved ones and exchange a private moment before walking through the hall to be congratulated. As they exited the hall, the movement professors transported them to their land to parade through their cuedel and join in celebrations. The Movement Apprentices transported their thrones and crowning items to their throne rooms and their loved one home. The new Queen's throne and crowning items were the only items on the pomp.

Elentari began a slow parade through her cuedel to adequately greet those who came to see her crowned. As she walked, many came to place symbols made of stone, wood, metal and fabric, tied to ribbons on her arm, symbols of virtues, prosperity and wisdom, symbols to help her as Queen. Some symbols were placed on bracelets and necklaces for her to wear. Her arms became full and heavy with so many ribbons, and Rorien found a basket to put them in, carrying it for her. Her heart was bursting with such love and admiration for her subjects. Love for all the beings living within her lands, both humanoid and huminal.

"Dear, you were marvellous todia. You made us so proud," said her Mum as Elentari entered the princess parestala.

"Thanks, Mum. I was a little uneasy, concerned I might not do the right thing," said Elentari as she hugged her mother.

"You were fantastic. So strong and in control," said Donna's mum.

"Thanks, Mum. I am glad you came too. Having both my earth parents here made my dia," Elentari said as she hugged them both.

"Well done, girly," said her Dad as he hugged her.

"Thanks, Dad. I am glad you all were here to support me on the biggest dia of my life. On the morrow will be an even bigger challenge and afterwards I shall be able to spend quality time with you all. For now, I must go. Love you all," Elentari said as she kissed them and continued to meet with every being.

By the end of the evening, Elentari felt quite drained, her jaw sore from smiling and talking so much, and her feet hurt from being on them all dia. Sitting on her couch, wrapped in Rorien's arms, was the perfect end to a dia, quiet time with Rorien before the morrow and her massive, controversial announcement.

After breakfast, Elentari and Rorien walked into the private royal chamber. Their guards and their guards linked were in the hall to greet every being. News of Elentari not choosing Rorien had spread, and beings were filing in to find who would rule with her, who would be the Queen's King. An area had been sectioned off at the front for the Kings, Masters, Scholars', and Generals. Throughout the hall beings, both huminals and humanoids were cramming in to hear the new King.

"You will be fine," said Rorien as Elentari paced the private chamber.

"I hope so. Still, I am anxious," Elentari replied as she leant her head on Rorien's chest, taking a long, big breath in before slowly releasing it.

"Nothing revealed by sight? Haven't seen the future?" asked Rorien.

"No. Nothing to give me any indication on if this was successful," said Elentari.

"Ready?" Rorien asked as his hands rubbed her back.

"Yes, but no," Elentari said, looking up at him.

"Come on. Let's get it over with," Rorien said as he led her into the hall and to her throne where her guards stood, Lorcan and Fendton on the left and Jasper and Seneca on the right. Her new Kings, the past Kings, Masters, Scholars, Professors, Apprentices and other beings filled the hall. Fauns and Dwarfs were mingling with humanoids, all joining together without angst. Elentari took her seat on the throne and scanned the crowd, waiting for every being to quiet down.

"My Kings, Masters, Scholars', Professors', past Kings, males and females. Todia, I announce my King, the Queen's King, to sit with me, and as you may have heard, Rorien is not my choice. You see beside me a chair which is not a throne. It is not a throne because what I have to request is controversial and may not be agreeable. I have chosen another to sit with me and help me continue to bridge the rifts within the lands, another who will help me understand every being and use compassion in all my judgments for every being. Every being throughout all lands needs to be represented, represented by one who is approachable and they feel safe in their request," Elentari said.

Elentari paused and scanned the room. All eyes were fixed on her and waiting for her announcement. The anticipation in the hall was growing. She straightened up.

"My choice is one I have discussed at great length with Prince Rorien, and we have both agreed, the best choice would be…Hoofington," said Elentari.

The angry voices erupted through the hall, coming in waves, ebbing and flowing around the room, fists and hands flying about as beings showed their disagreement while others stood still. The new Kings stood quietly, their faces portraying their decision. Arguments began to break out around the room as beings put forth their views to those around them. Elentari stood and raised her hand, calling for silence.

"You all have your opinion on my decision and will have a chance to voice it. My Kings, please voice your concerns first, King Lannis?" asked Elentari.

"No King or Queen has ever given the crown to another who is not their link. It is not usual," replied Lannis.

"I have not lived my full life in these lands. My testing found I held all the powers, most unusual. It was unusual to mend the rift between kinds. I found a way to relink without the Masters, unusual to seek knowledge outside of the Masters. I am not usual, and to choose the normal would not be me," said Elentari, her eyes focused on Lannis.

"King Sven?" asked Elentari, turning her focus to him.

"No huminal has EVER sat on a throne. It is not right," replied Sven.

"Masters. Please can you read the text which states whom the King or Queen may choose," said Elentari.

"The King or Queen who resides on the throne may choose any being to sit on their left side and govern with them as their confidant. The secondary ruler may be chosen from any being living within all lands," said the Air Master.

"Scholars'. Please define being?" said Elentari.

"Any individual who exists or lives and has certain capacities or attributes such as reason, morality, consciousness and is a part of an established form of social relations," said Cornel.

"Any individual who exists or lives. This includes both humanoids and huminals?" asked Elentari.

"Yes, my Queen. It includes both humanoids and huminals," replied Cornel.

"Based on the ancient text, which my Kings and I swore to govern and uphold, I may choose any being who lives and exists within any of my lands?" asked Elentari, staring directly at Sven.

"Yes, my Queen," said Cornel.

"King Jahan?" asked Elentari.

"Hoofington is a bold choice. He is frightening and unapproachable," said Jahan.

"Meeting the Master for the first time is also frightening, and every Master seems unapproachable until you get to know them. Fauns and Dwarfs have no issues with approaching him and feel safe with him. Do the fauns and dwarfs feel they can approach you, King Jahan?" asked Elentari.

"They do not need to," said Jahan.

"Can you speak for every faun, and do you know if they have needed to seek council with the King?" asked Elentari.

"No, my Queen," answered Jahan.

"In your lands, fauns have required the King for an issue. Hoofington's correspondents in the North have dealt with it and brought peace to their community. Do you know about the incident within the East of your lands?" asked Elentari.

"No, my Queen," replied Jahan.

"King Emmett?" asked Elentari.

"He can't use compassion in his judgements for us. He knows us not," replied Emmett.

"Are you able to use compassion in your judgements when it comes to the huminals?" asked Elentari.

"I would like to think I could, but am not sure," said Emmett.

"When it comes to being compassionate, you need the ability to understand any beings situation and the desire to take action to improve their lives. Hoofington has compassion for huminals and has proved himself, keeping the woods safe for them," said Elentari, watching Emmett.

"You have heard the Kings speak and my answers. I shall give you time to discuss between yourself what you have heard before deciding," Elentari said.

'You're doing great,' said Rorien on their link.

'Thanks. It is not over yet,' said Elentari on their link. Elentari sat back on her throne and watched the room, listening to the conversations and reading body language. The past Kings and her Kings stood silently, listening to the conversations around them.

"It is time to voice your decision. Those who agree with my naming Hoofington to sit with me, please bend a knee," said Elentari. Elentari watched the room as some took the knee straight away while others stood tall, not moving, and others shifted on their feet, unsure which way to vote.

"It seems we are in a tie. Two of my Kings agree, four of the Masters agree, two of the Scholars' agree. We are in a deadlock. I have another proposal," said Elentari as she waited till every eye was on her.

"Instead of Hoofington being the Queen's King and sitting with me, what if he became a minor King of the huminals and governed alongside my minor Kings. Does any being have an objection to Hoofington becoming a minor King?" asked Elentari.

Beings began to discuss the proposal amongst themselves. The Kings stood quietly.

"Please bend a knee if you agree to Hoofington becoming the fifth minor King," said Elentari as she scanned the room, and only a handful of beings were standing.

"Of those who are still standing, are there any issues which will cause you not to accept the appointment of a new minor King? I understand you disagree with Hoofington. I ask, can you accept it?" asked Elentari and watched as they shuffled on their feet before slowly bending.

"It has been decided. Masters and Hoofington, once we finish here, please stay behind to discuss the new appointment," said Elentari.

Jasper removed the chair as Lorcan and Seneca placed a smaller throne beside hers.

"This leaves my King to sit with me open. As my first choice is now becoming a minor King, I choose Rorien to sit with me and govern the lands with me. Any objections?" asked Elentari.

'You planned it this way to get your way, didn't you?' said Papa by sight power.

'They would not have agreed to have a huminal king, having them think he was going to rule with me and giving them a safer choice, I knew I would get my way,' said Elentari by sight.

'What if they all agreed?' asked Papa by sight.

'We had a backup plan. Rorien was always going to sit with me.' Elentari said and turned to Papa and smiled.

"As there are no objections, Masters, please can you swear in Rorien as King," said Elentari.

Rorien stepped up to the pomp, standing before the throne and the Air Master read the ancient text.

"I shall govern, beside the Queen, according to the ancient text," replied Rorien.

The Air Master read the ancient text.

"I shall, to my utmost power, assist the Queen to maintain this land," replied Rorien.

The Air Master continued to read the ancient text.

"I shall use compassion in all my judgements to support the Queen," replied Rorien.

The Air Master finished the ancient text.

"I shall uphold the ancient text and honour the Queen of all the lands," replied Rorien as he looked towards Elentari meeting her gaze and smiled.

Their plan had worked. Rorien walked the steps and took his seat beside Elentari. Elentari stepped in front of Rorien, holding his new crown high above his head. She looked into his eyes, and admiration filled her.

"I claim you King Rorien, the Queen's King, the King to sit at my right and govern our lands together," Elentari placed the crown on Rorien's head and took her seat as the hall erupted in cheers of 'Hail Queen Elentari and King Rorien.'

Rorien took Elentari's hand in his, squeezing it to let her know he was here for her. He led her through the hall and outside to proceed through the cuedel, greeting every being. They finished at the main north parestala.

Elentari surveyed the parestala and to the field beyond. She saw humanoids and huminals celebrating together, humanoids including the giants, dwarfs and earthlings, huminals including the fauns and minotaurs, all sitting together. All beings were chatting and laughing together as one big happy family, her family. Her dream to bring every being together was happening. Across the royal lands, beings could see the mending of bridges between kinds. Her eyes found her Kings and watched them as they chatted with the fauns and Hoofington, drinking together and laughing. Her heart was full, and all the cares of the morrow gone.

Beside her was the only being she needed, Rorien. Their lives forever combined, entwined together always.

Glossary

Hori	Hour
Dia	Day, 28 hori
Vika	Week, 8 dias
Mesik	Month, 5 vikas
Anok	Year, 8 mesiks
Vekulo	1,000 anoks
Vari	Centimetre
Cani	Meter, 100 vari
Stadi	Kilometre, 1,000 cani
Casa	Home
Cuedel	City
Villade	Village, Town
Parestala	Park, Village Square
Januel	Yearly meeting
Link	Person you are to marry
Linked	Wife/Husband
Mesmoon	Honeymoon
1st month	Luftaer
2nd month	Augavesi
3rd month	Lume
4th month	Erde
5th month	Mente
6th month	Curar
7th month	Wegung
8th month	Canvio

ABOUT THE AUTHOR

Whilst some may say Dee Verhagen's major accomplishment would be raising her children, others might say it is her National Service Medal. Dee would probably argue that publishing her first novel, A Distant Land Beyond, is fairly awesome considering she just passed Year 12 English!

Originally from rural NSW, and spending the bulk of her life in Victoria, the now Tasmanian mother of two has drawn on her world travels and love of sci-fi novels and movies to complete this intriguing tale.

Connect with the Author:

Instagram - deev_author
Facebook - Dee V - Author